centrepiece

NEW WRITING AND ART FROM NORTHEAST INDIA

Edited by Parismita Singh

zubaan

ZUBAAN
128B Shahpur Jat, 1st Floor
New Delhi 110 049
Email: *contact@zubaanbooks.com*
Website: *www.zubaanbooks.com*

First published by Zubaan Publishers Pvt. Ltd 2017

With support from the Heinrich Böll Foundation and the Sasakawa Peace Foundation

ISBN 978-93-85932-41-0

Design: Pooja Saxena
Printed at Replika Press Pvt. Ltd, India

Zubaan is an independent, feminist publishing house based in New Delhi with a strong academic and general list. It was set up as an imprint of India's first feminist publishing house, Kali for Women, and carries forward Kali's tradition of publishing world quality books to high editorial and production standards. Zubaan means tongue, voice, language, speech in Hindustani. Zubaan publishes in the areas of the humanities and social sciences, as well as in fiction, general non-fiction and books for children and young adults under its Young Zubaan imprint.

acknowledgements

The invaluable support of the Heinrich Böll Foundation and the Sasakawa Peace Foundation made this book possible.

I would like to thank the Zubaan team: Meghna Singh, Ishani Butalia, Satish Sharma and Urvashi Butalia for their support through the making of this book. Thank you!

There were many others who helped with contacts and conversation, editing and polishing the text. Much gratitude to Amit Baishya, Anahita Lee, Iris Odyou, Korou Khundrakpam, Hemant Katoch, Shruti Debi, Xonzoi Barbora and Yengkhom Jilangamba.

And of course, a big thank you to all the contributors, for their patience and persistence in seeing this book through.

— **Parismita Singh**

contents

publisher's note

THE ZUBAAN TEAM

Several years ago, Zubaan began publishing writers from the Northeastern states of India. As feminist publishers, it is our mandate to address different kinds of marginalizations — whether of language, or region, or religion, or caste or indeed of peoples and geographical areas. We thought we would begin with what are generally seen as the 'peripheries' and in doing so, we would question how these very terms are created and legitimized. One of our early books, a compilation of writings by writers from the different states of the region was, accordingly, called *The Peripheral Centre*. Over the years, it's been our privilege to make writing from this region central to our feminist publishing enterprise. It is for this reason that we are today delighted and privileged to be publishing Parismita Singh's wonderful edited collection of writing and visual art that showcases a stunning group of writers and artists, all women, from Northeastern India (and one or two of its neighbours).

Despite being set an impossible deadline, Parismita agreed enthusiastically to be part of this enterprise and throughout its making, she has been cheerful and proactive and, as we were told by one of the writers, the kind of editor writers dream about. Thank you Parismita.

A logical offshoot of Zubaan's Northeastern list, is the Cultures of Peace festival of the Northeast, which we have been running for many years now. Writing in the Northeastern states, as elsewhere, is never only about writing; somewhere music, art, theatre, song, performance too enter the picture. It was to reflect this symbiotic relationship that we began our Cultures of Peace festival, many years ago, and with the support of our longterm friends, the Heinrich Böll Foundation, who have come back year after year to work with us on it. Two years ago, another partner, the Sasakawa

Peace Foundation, entered the picture and both organizations have generously also supported the research for this book. We are more than grateful to them.

As publishers we love and are proud of every book we publish. *Centrepiece* is no different, and it's easy to fall in love with this book. It's rich with stories and images, it's experimental, it's varied, it is of the earth and the sky, of the drudgery of work and of women's resilience and their enjoyment of it too, it's funny, and it's serious. We have found, over the years, that our publishing practice has, almost organically, moved beyond words to take in the visual in different ways. It began for us with a six year project that involved collecting posters of the women's movement in India as a way of mapping a visual history of the movement. Our collection of over 1500 posters, put together as an archive called Poster Women, led us to other visual histories and soon, our list included artworks by Radhaben Garva (*Picture This*), a Dalit woman from Kutch who works with the Kutch Mahila Vikas Sangathan; a collection of stories by Indian and Australian writers and artists called *Eat the Sky, Drink the Ocean*; books showcasing our poster collection which could also be used as teaching tools (*Our Pictures Our Words*); graphic stories on violence against women (*Drawing the Line*) and a second collection, *The Elephant in the Room*. We're proud now to have *Centrepiece* join this canon as we move towards understanding how the visual and the written, words and pictures, are so inextricably intertwined. Thank you to our authors and artists and designers for teaching us to look differently at books. Thank you to everyone who's made them possible.

editor's introduction

PARISMITA SINGH

It was a little over a year ago that Zubaan's Urvashi Butalia and I began discussing the possibility of an anthology from the Northeast. At the onset, the project seemed to me a little bit mad, with a tilt of the windmills about it and a near impossible timeline. But plunge we did, with an ambition that was almost reckless, as we set about planning a book with works of art, poetry, photography, essays, fiction, textiles, around the theme of 'work'. Zubaan had more at stake than I did, but backed the project to the hilt, with a belief in the impossible that only seasoned feminists could carry off with such ease.

First, the Northeast. Northeast of what? Of whom? Indeed, what to make of this 'unfortunate directional category'[1] as a friend chooses to describe it? Technically, the Northeast is used to refer to the Indian states east of the chicken neck bordering Myanmar and Bangladesh: Assam, Manipur, Mizoram, Tripura, Nagaland, Sikkim (not very east of the chicken neck), Meghalaya, Arunachal Pradesh. These are diverse states with many different communities, religious practices, languages, histories; the term Northeast having originated as a sort of shorthand for grouping together a diverse region for administrative and military purposes. This colonial legacy of exceptionalism and racial apartness has continued post Indian independence, with insurgencies and draconian laws an integral part of the recent history of this region. And one might ask, is it wise to categorise art and writing by region? Especially through a construct predicated on the idea of a hostile, exotic, racialised entity?

Indeed, like many other terms with a controversial past, some contain within themselves a potential for their reclaiming by the people they describe. Perhaps what

1. Sanjay Barbora. 2008. *Under the Invisibility Cloak — Reimagining the "Northeast"*, Biblio: Review of Books, 13 (5&6), May-June.

unites this region is this shared history, yoked together in a shared destiny through the experience of insurgencies, uprisings, wars as well as the weight of counterinsurgency and violence by both state and non state actors. Migrants from this region to other parts of India, who went to study or work, often developed solidarities beyond their own ethnic or political identities, identifying as "Northeastern" when forced into cheap housing with others from this region in urban ghettos or while mobilizing for protests and rights. This is one of the ways in which the term Northeast is used by its own people; a flexible, fluid identity that creates a potential for sharing and mobilization, going beyond borders or defined limits. This volume aspires to such a 'Northeastern-ness in spirit'.

Of course, there have been many anthologies and exhibitions devoted to the Northeast, of prose, poetry, writing, academics and art. The Robin Ngangom and Nongkynrih edited *Dancing Earth: An Anthology of Poetry from North-East India* made a particularly interesting contribution to the debate by dwelling on poetry's relationship to nature, roots and the home, as well as calling out the spectre of violence that compels the poet from this region to 'master the art of witness.'[2] This volume, I hope continues the debate on the many ideas of a Northeast aesthetic.

The representation of work and women is an integral part of the folklore and oral repertoire/culture of the many communities of this region. The image of the woman at work has also had a presence in colonial photography, and is now a part of the stock imagery of tourism campaigns and the imagining of indigenous lives: women with baskets of wood walking along hilly paths, bending over the rice fields in the valley, fishing by lotus decked lakes and rivers, and so on. These images of the indigenous or rural woman at work are an integral part of the 'ethnographic' section of museums. Dioramas show the woman in her ethnic costume, working on traditional implements like the weaving loom or the field alongside her male partner, an image of diligence, duty and tradition frozen in time. Then there is the figure of the dancing woman in traditional costume, celebrated in tourism campaigns and festivals as well as internalized by the community as reservoir and reproducer of tradition and culture. This has been supplemented by newer icons: the image of the woman boxer, air-hostess or spa masseuse with 'Northeastern features' on hoardings. Most of these images or 'world –picture(s) implanted in our minds' tend to put forward a view of the woman as one in harmony with nature and tradition of her community,

2. Robin S. Ngangom and Kynpham Singh Nongkynrih, eds. 2009 *Dancing Earth: An Anthology of Poetry from North-East India*, New Delhi: Penguin India.

engaging dutifully, cheerfully in her (gendered) tasks, without a deeper understanding or investigation of the nature of work and her position in society. These images also ignore the vast array of work and responsibilities that exist in the quotidian, the everyday experience of life. The varied, often imperfect and transgressive women of folklore and song are much more adventurous. Then there is the depiction of work in art and literature, from the motifs of Tangkhul weaving to characters in Arupa Patangia and Rita Chowdhury's novels or the Lotha woodwork depicting women's objects of work. Tracing a path through these stories, we stopped to ask: How do women artists and writers, journalists, poets, academics, designers from the Northeast choose to interpret work? Could we begin a conversation along these lines?

The act of preparing the book itself held up a mirror to several other debates around work in all forms. Most of the writers and artists I approached with our ambitious commissions and impossible deadlines were often themselves mired in the very circumstances that the book would eventually come to speak of and reflect on. Many of the initial exchanges were indeed about taking time out from academic commitments and child care routines, managing art careers with toddlers, school holidays when writing flagged, looking for a job that will pay the bills while balancing interviews in the field, and a range of other concerns. Questions revolved around work in the domestic realm, of caring and looking after the elderly and children, the family and community, the question of tradition and work, day jobs and their challenges and of course, the quest for the devalued labour of art and writing. Many of us extended the conversation to the misogyny and patriarchal structures embedded in the home, the workspace, family and finally and most distressingly, ourselves. Keeping that room of one's own continues to remain hard work. Preparing the book went beyond the mere transaction of commissioning a piece and receiving it; there were debates on the ethics of representation, responses to political exigencies, the politics of appropriation, along with the day to day challenges of writing and creating art. Debates and concerns that I hope will be reflected in the work going out to the reader. It was a far cry from the image of the self contained writer/artist in her ivory tower or tree house; much as we tried, it was impossible to keep life out of this book. It became in a sense, what the poet June Jordan called a 'spirit task,[3] as much a project of solidarity and support for each other, as an artistic endeavour. 'Life is not personal'[4], this oft quoted, charming

3. Quoted from an interview with Alternative Radio in *https://www.poetryfoundation.org/poets/june-jordan*

4. Gilles Deleuze & Claire Parnet. *Dialogues*. 2007. tr. Hugh Tomlinson & Barbara Habberjam Deleuze, New York: Columbia University Press.

and brutal line from Delueze comes to mind. It is tempting to give it a new (mis) interpretation that reflects on the making of the book and speaks, perhaps, of the book itself: Life is not personal. But art is.

Keeping in mind, the burden and weight of representation, historical and current mentioned before, the book would have to work towards what Christopher Pinney said of non-eurocentric photography, that it must 'reconfigure a powerful set of expectations'[5] in order for it to challenge the tyranny of the canon. This set of expectations then can be stretched to include not just content and theme, ways of looking and representation, but to the idea of genre and form as well. What are the many, many ways of telling a story? What if we were to attempt this telling of a story through a variety of means: through poetry and portraits and essays, older traditions like textile art and appliqué and new, home cooked genres like hashtag poetry tapped into a smart phone? Where would it take us, what would the world look like? Is there a chance here of reclaiming the construct of the Northeast, infusing it with potential for disruption, shaping it into a *mis en scene* of writing and thought and art? The photo essay by our 'guest' contributor from the Chittagong Hill Tracts of Bangladesh serves as an interesting entry point into rethinking the geography of this book; if anything, it reminds us of the power of art, of its unerring ability to question ideas of borders and the nation state. Could a book give us this space, to loiter past sundown, serve as a vast gallery of work that could potentially reconfigure our idea and experiences of the Northeast and women's work? These are some of the questions that guided us through the planning of the book.

One way of giving the reader a sense of what this may entail, is to briefly speak of the works in the book. But before that, there is the question of selection. All volumes of writing, of art, must of necessity be marked by exclusion: who to choose to delineate and include, and who to leave out. This volume on work is but a sprinkling of talents from the region it attempts (or fails) to represent. And foremost of what it excludes (lack of time and resources, as always), what we leave for the next, are the writers and singers in different tongues, and the necessary and excellent exercise of translation. Like the proverbial spider web, an oft repeated metaphor in writing, the volume has pulled into its net a selection from the vast arrays of ideas, thoughts, images, currents, whispers coursing through the elements; some have made an imprint, others we have missed. Though I would also venture forth rather meekly, that this volume could

5. Christopher Pinney, 2012 *Seven Theses on Photography*, Thesis Eleven, Thousand Oaks: Sage.

be read as a step towards a different translation of sorts, a reaching out to diverse genres and forms, rarely met with between the covers of a book, though they co-exist in life. To begin, there are the urban centres of the Northeast, shaped by decades of militarization, migration and development, and essays that unravel their different narratives. Aheli Moitra's essay is part reflection on the peace process in Nagaland and part memoir charting her own journey as a journalist with a Nagaland based newspaper. What emerges is a unique portrait of Dimapur and its dynamics through the lens of the 'insider-outsider'. Meanwhile, Gertrude Lamare's piece on Shillong and its fractious relationship with development, chronicles the struggles and mobilization of women hawkers in the city. What are the relationships of work and ethics, the interplay of power, development and resistance in these urban centres? How do groups like women hawkers and reporters negotiate this complicated, fraught terrain?

The idea of the 'home' continues to be tied to identity, belonging, tradition, nostalgia, making it rich with anger and longing, as well as sympathy and understanding. What is this home? How does work shape our imagining of it or our critique? Alyen Foning uses mixed media to create a textile art narrative that traces her journey from the city as a designer back to her hometown and the hills, using the symbolism of her Lepcha heritage. Alyen's piece, like every other piece in the book, demands multiple readings, for the meaning embedded in the stunning tapestry of textiles, drawings, found pieces and embroidery. How do we narrate our life's journeys and experiences, if not through text and textiles?

The home is of course, not a simple proposition, or even a secure one, rife with contradictions and challenges, whether it is Aheli's *Naga neki?* refrain or Dolly Kikon's passionate engagement with patriarchy and resistance in her essay that analyses the movement in Nagaland against 33 per cent reservation for women in the municipal body elections. How do we engage with the idea of a tribal feminism that resists patriarchal norms while, at the same time, takes into account the history of Indian intervention and decades of militarization? How do women and other groups speak out, rage against and resist these debilitating structures – often the intimate other, the domestic hearth, one's community?

Rini Barman's essay looks at this confluence of the domestic, tradition and development, through her conversations with women from several tribal communities of Assam who brew traditional alcohol, often for use at home or sale at the local market. A piece that leaves us with larger questions of the hardship and sisterhood of women's labour, and its precarious position in the larger structures of power and economic and policy decisions. Mamang Dai's short fiction (an extract from a novel) posits itself at similar junctures of development and change; emancipation and transition seen through the metaphor of the weaving loom. The piece by the Bumbum Collective uses design and textiles, but tells a similar story. Nitoo Das's poems of fish cutting and Nabeena Das's short story engage with the realm of the domestic and the sharp underbelly of subversion layers these works. Sanatombi's brilliant short story rages against life and how it is pitted against the artist's vocation. The witty title of her story has a resonance across time: 'Women's Literature'. A theme encountered again in Soibam Haripriya's poem: 'There is a half written poem. /There is a bawling baby on the bed.' Is it so different, the nihilist rage of Sanatombi Ningombam's character or the fierce independence of Nabina Das's Chitto? The nature of creative work and the artist's struggle is a pervasive concern: How does one deal with this near paralysis of creative work, under the double yoke of motherhood, domestic pressures and a precarious, militarized environment? Writer and journalist Thingnam Anjulika produces a set of witty, scathing poems that uses this very paralysis and impossibility, to give shape to hashtag poetry; writings that emerge unfiltered, almost at the edge of consciousness, tapped away on a screen.

Sometimes, we turn to the mythopoetic, the stories and folklores passed down through the ages. Jacqueline Zote does a rendition of the unruly, transgressive female lasis, women of the skies and phungs who populate the unseen realms around us, and are often able to make the ruthless necessary choices that women sometimes cannot in this realm. There is humour and fantasy, as they bustle about in their daily chores and supernatural mischief; but what do they tell us about ourselves?

Some of the art works look at similar themes; but does art move us differently from an essay or a story? Kundo Yumnam's self portrait is a case in point: in what directions does her fierce, almost brutally honest painting take us? How do we read this painting in relation with the other works, the essay and poems in the book? There is no easy answer, but the form that one can look towards is that of the conversation. Many of these pieces were written especially for the book and in the process, conversations across genre and form and material have taken shape; of the different evocations and realities and perceptions of work and women and art. Why for instance, do the haunting, meditative paintings from Minam Apang's collection speak of war, of scales, of hurt and yet, foretell of the rising of a million stories?

The photography projects follow a range of themes, venues, positions. Aungmakhai Chak's playful staged rendition is at one level, nostalgia and remembering through an oral history (of work) going back to her grandmother and mother's memories, but at the same time, the photos also question our expectations and prejudices.

Are we as the consumers and purveyors of the photographs of indigenous women also implicated by our very (historical/conditioned) gaze? How do we engage with identity, as many projects in the book do, and yet, question borders, boundaries and polarization? Prashansa Gurung's photo project works with the documentary mode, capturing moments in the life of Josie Paris as she goes about her work as a makeup artist on film sets. Atmospheric, with a rare sensitivity in her lens; the intimacy of these moments of work leave us with many questions of form and content: can photos indeed be the telling of a life? Where does the artifice end and life begin? The lens is once again suspect with Zubeni Lotha's photos of Dimapur, looking at how women are photographed, how subject and object perceive each other in the making of the photo. Mona Zote's poem rather presciently draws out the shadows of these streets: 'What we are left with is a mirror showing our movements/Some who are mothers and some who are sailors/Some who stand under streetlights displaying their embroidered beauty/ Some who reveal a sense of daring in photographs.'

What we offer the reader is not so much a single, unifying narrative or a worldview, rather an invitation to trace a line, through a diverse, complicated and contrary universe, along the wings of an uncertain flight. Can the Northeast exist in spirit beyond the confines of geography and representation? Is it rather like the unseen parallel world of flying spirits and lasis that everyone knows exists but no one can pin down with an exactness of latitude and longitude? Can it exist as a concept in the realm of aesthetics for a brief, brief while; is that what we attempt through an anthology of the Northeast? If so, even as it is being constructed or woven together from numerous strands, it must at the same time be demolished, taken apart thread by thread; for art and writing cannot and should not be confined to categories, and must remain, restless, always moving even if in the same place. Restless and yet comforting, art and writing, if anything, gives us a sense of the possible in these unsure times, allows us an 'understanding of what it means to live as free subjects in an unfree world.' [6]

6. bell hooks, 1995. *Art on My Mind: Visual Politics*, New Press.

untitled

ZUBENI LOTHA

FROM THE SERIES "HOW DO I LOOK"

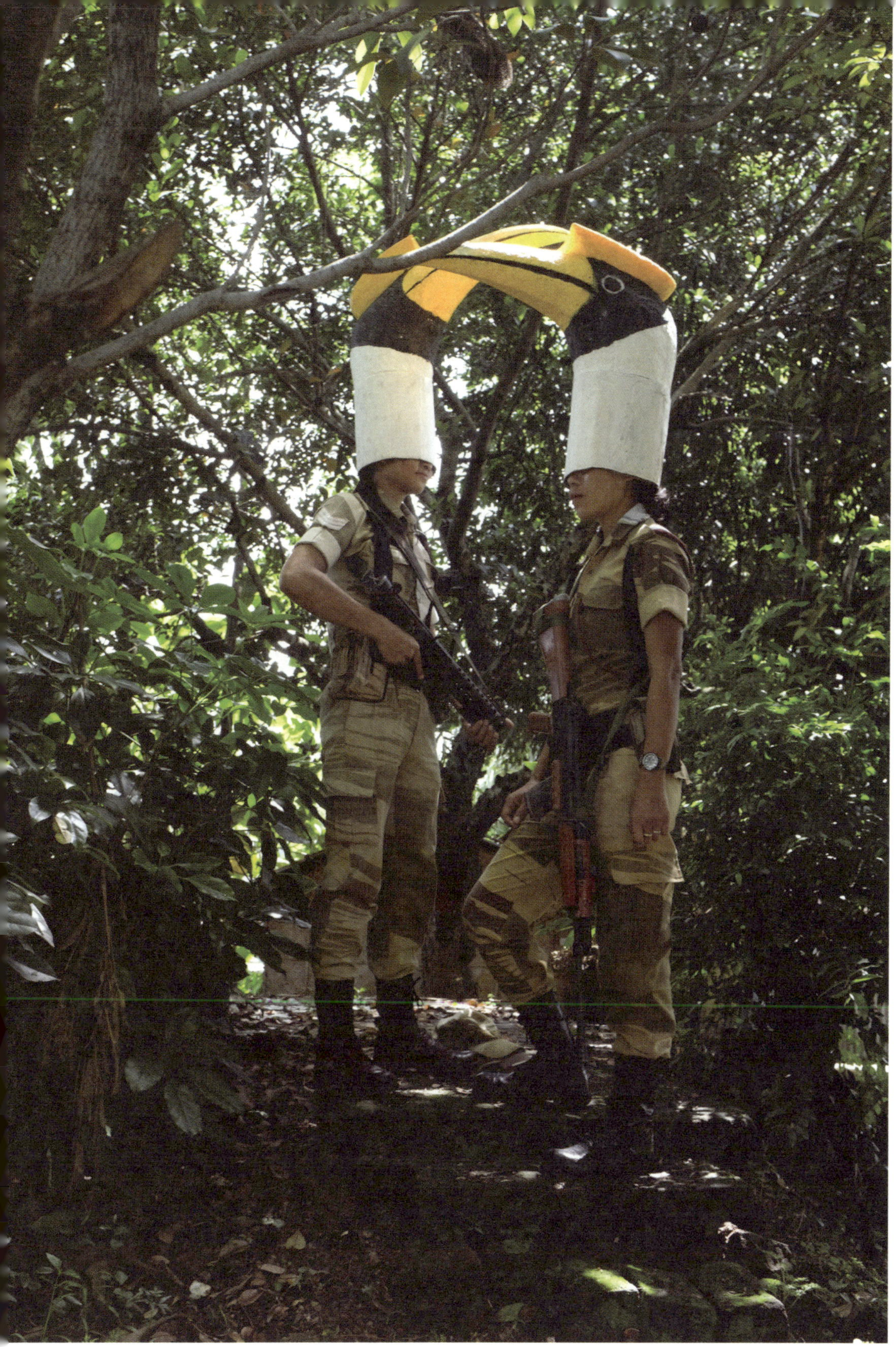

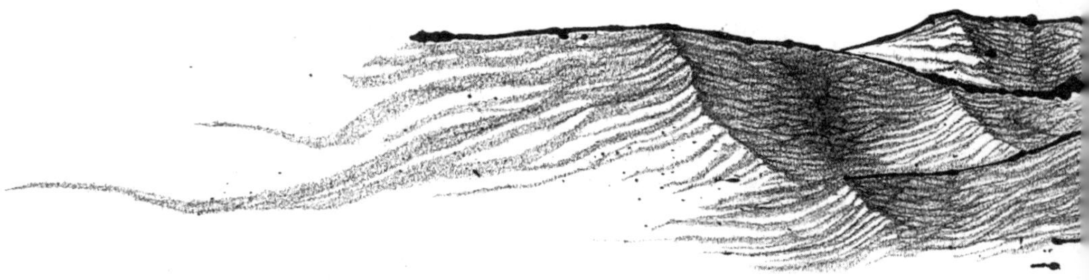

a sleeping army may stir

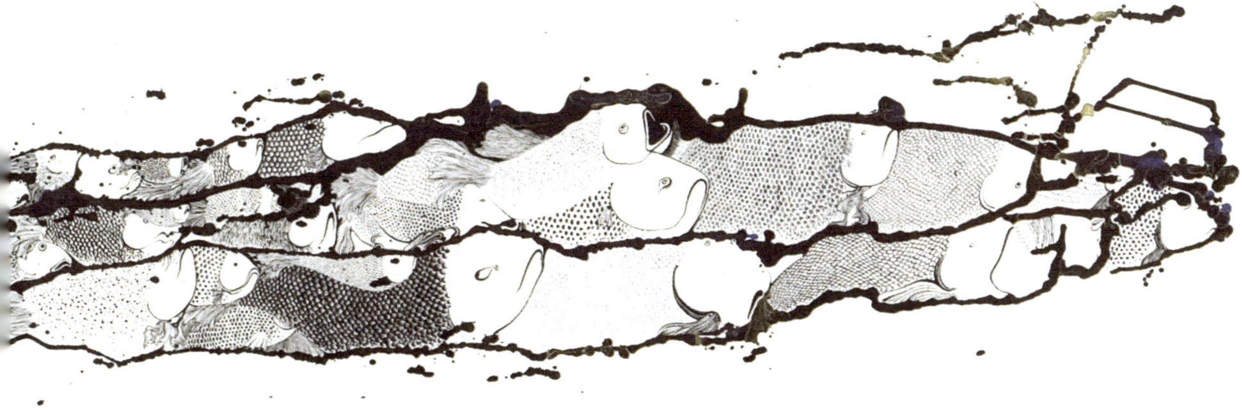

MINAM APANG
FROM THE SERIES "WAR WITH THE STARS"

COURTESY THE ARTIST AND CHATTERJEE & LAL

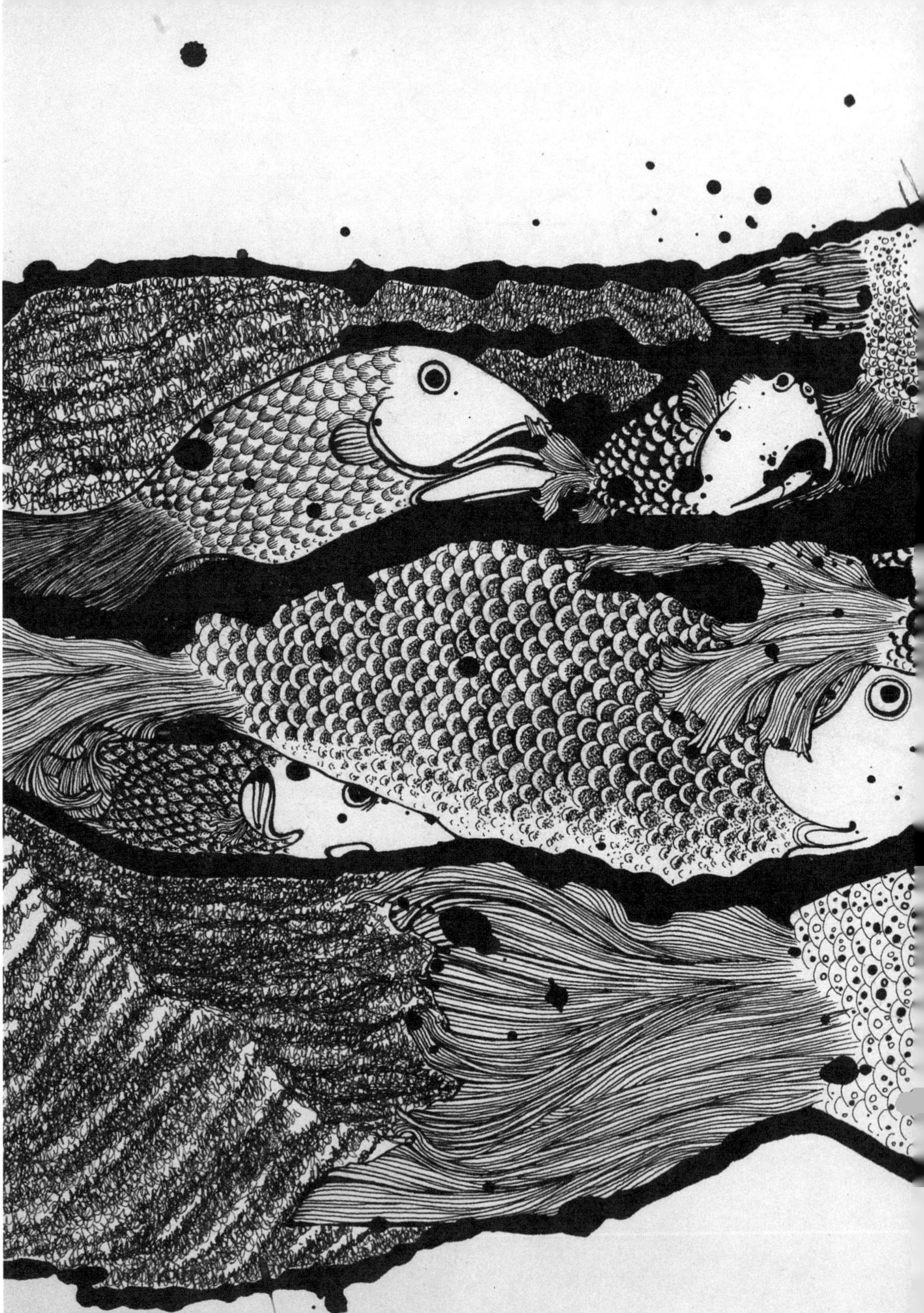

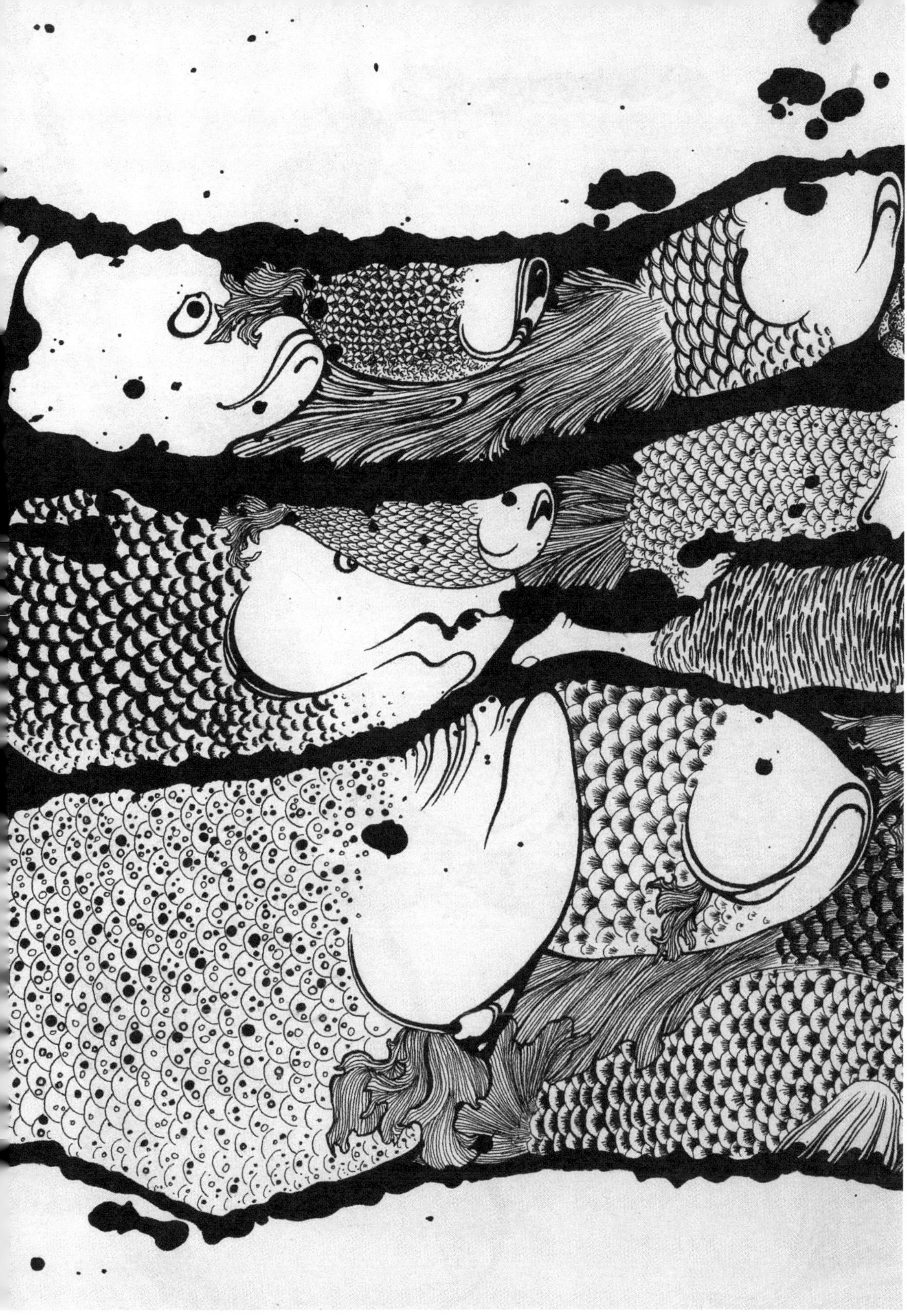

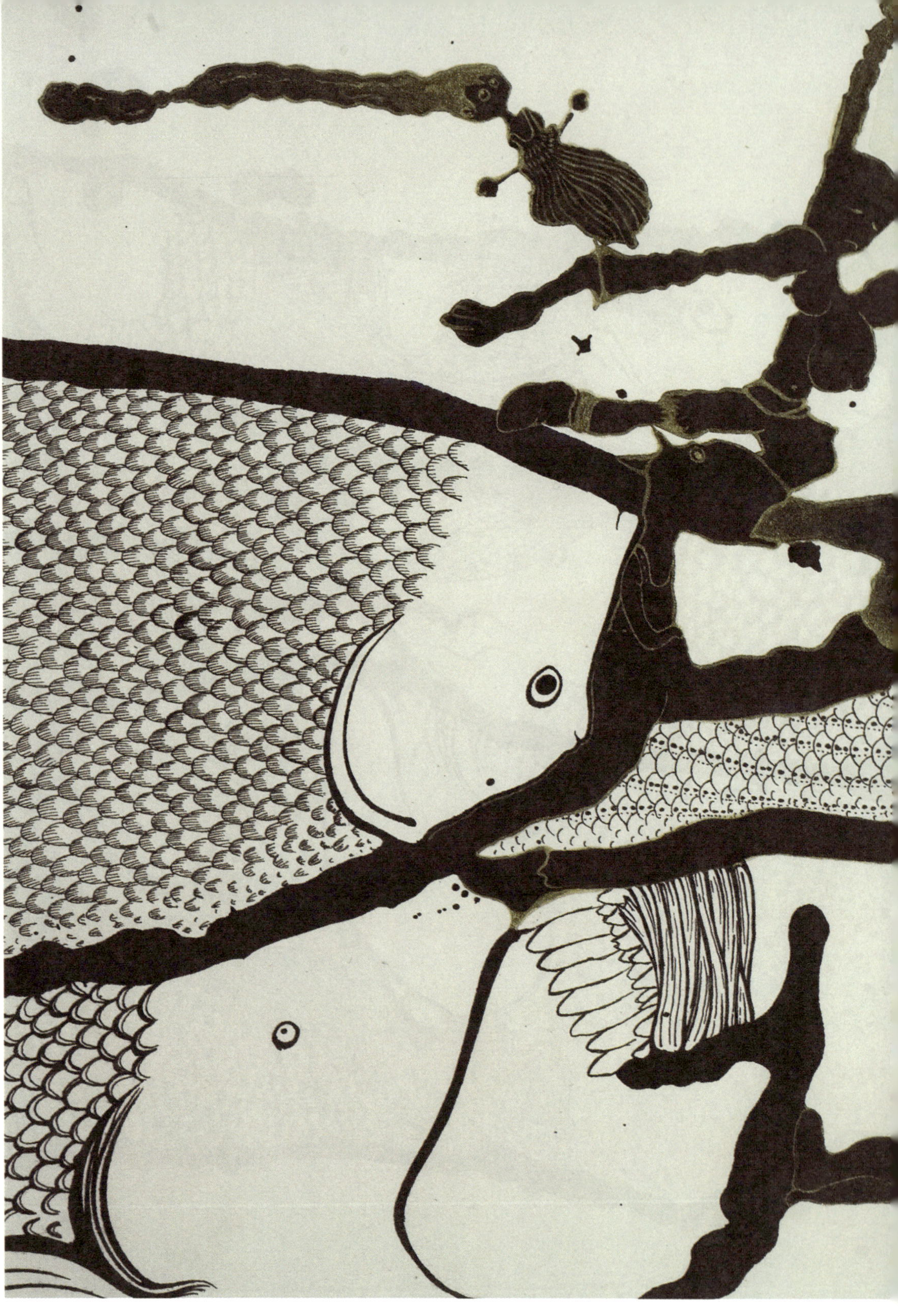

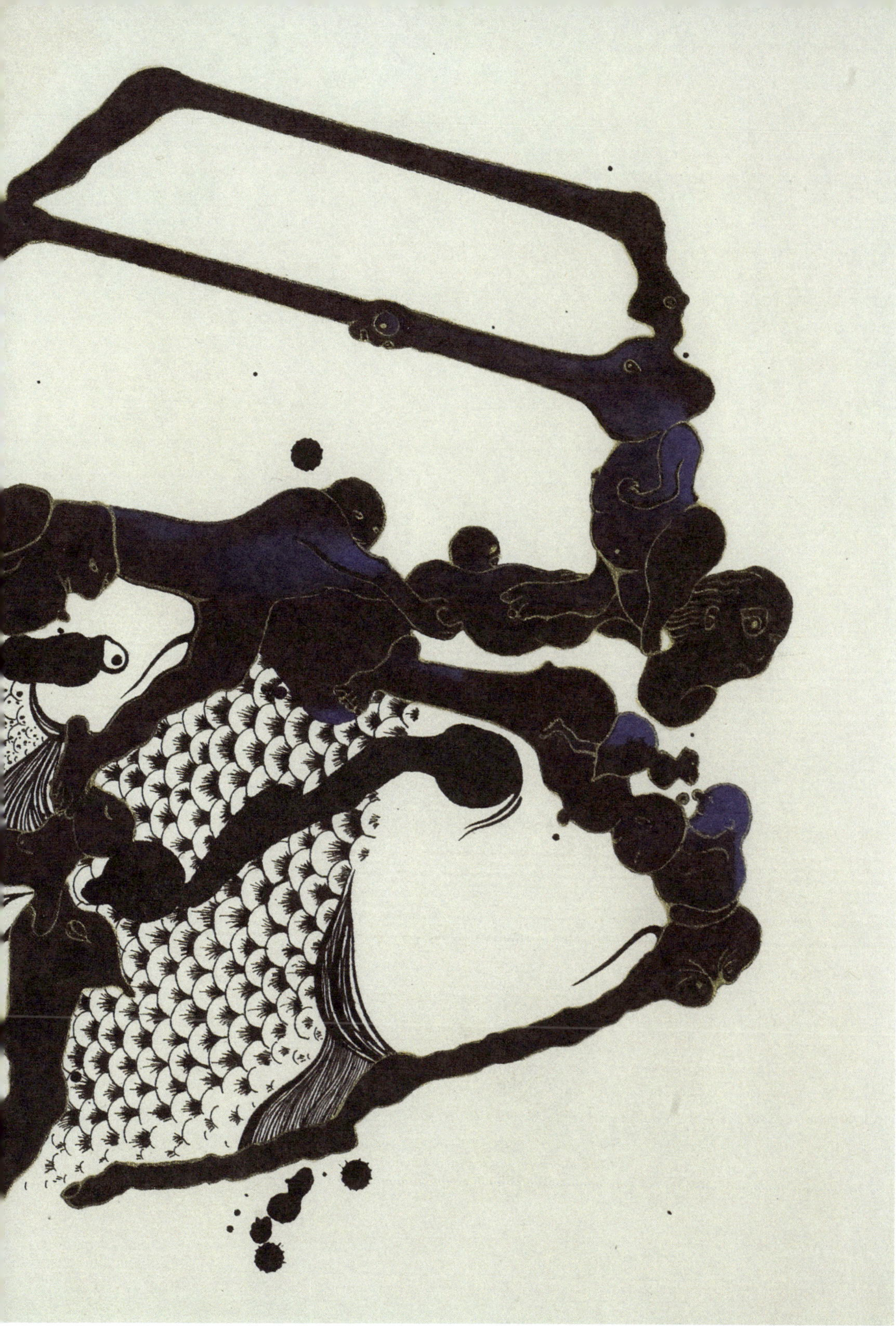

mayel lyang

STORY AND ILLUSTRATIONS BY **ALYEN LEEACHUM FONING**
INITIAL CONCEPT SKETCHES BY **ALYEN LEEACHUM FONING**

HANDIWORK
Saroja Lepcha, Norjina Foning, Sunanda Pradhan, Anmol Bhramacharimayum Sharma

WOODEN FRAMES
Prakash Tamang

LIGHTING
Tenzing Nyentsey, Taarini Singh, Kunga Tashi, Chewang Lepcha

PHOTOGRAPHY
Kunga Tashi

SPECIAL THANKS
Chhaya Vani Namchu, Legain Foning, Vania Khandijian, Kripashna Dhamala, Echo Stream, Burtuk Family

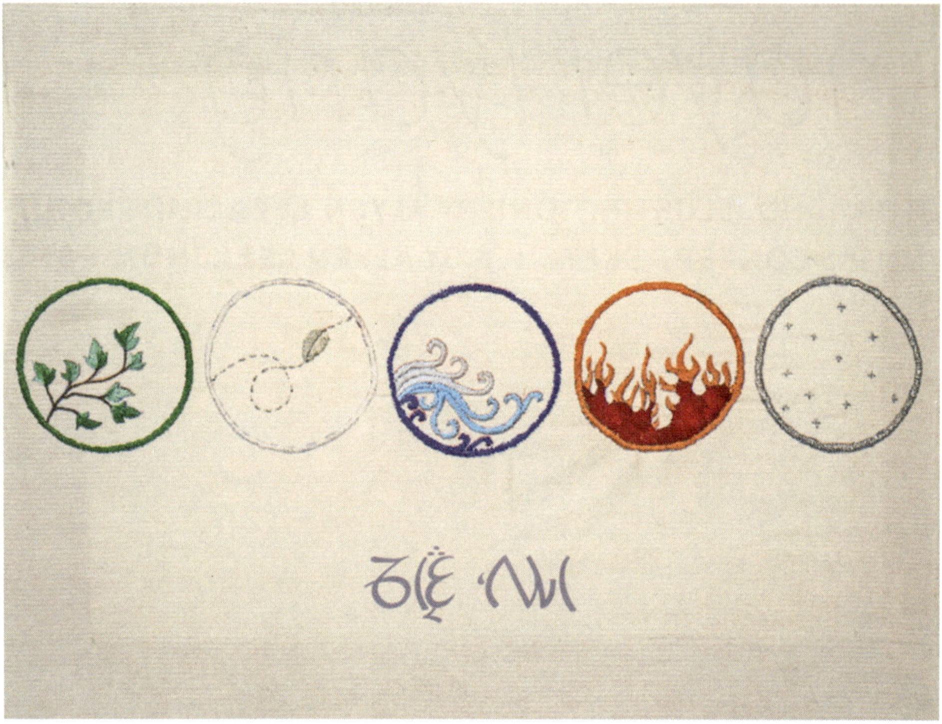

Mayel Lyang

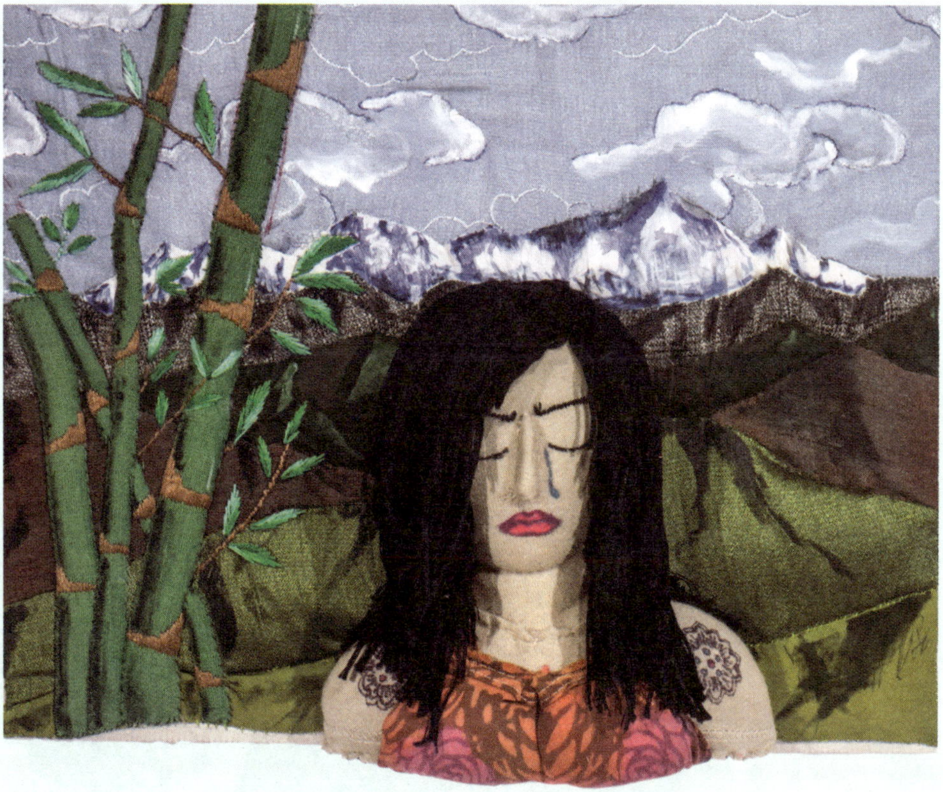

Home

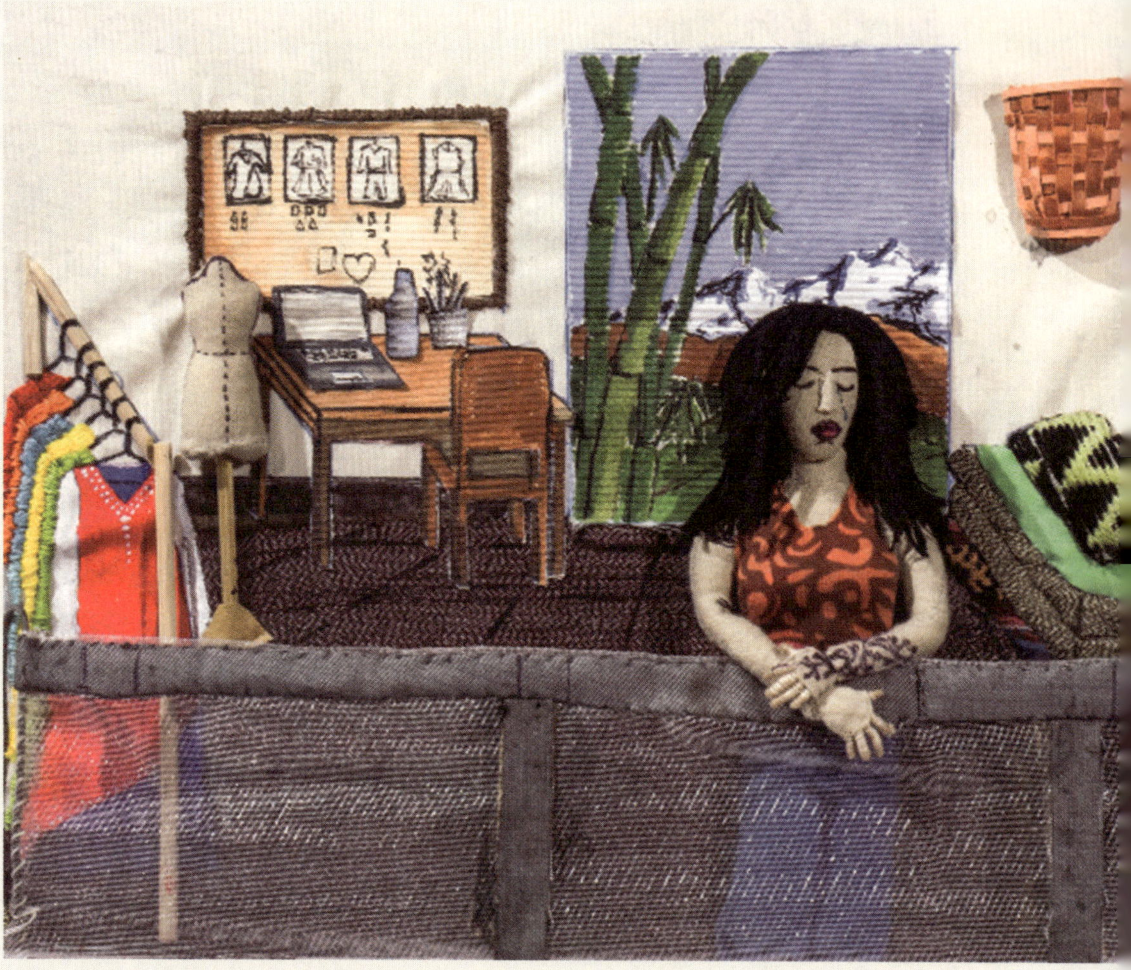

I think of home

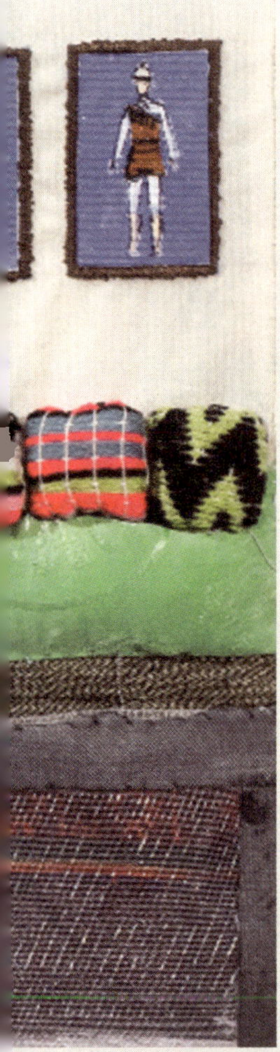

It seems like
lifetimes away

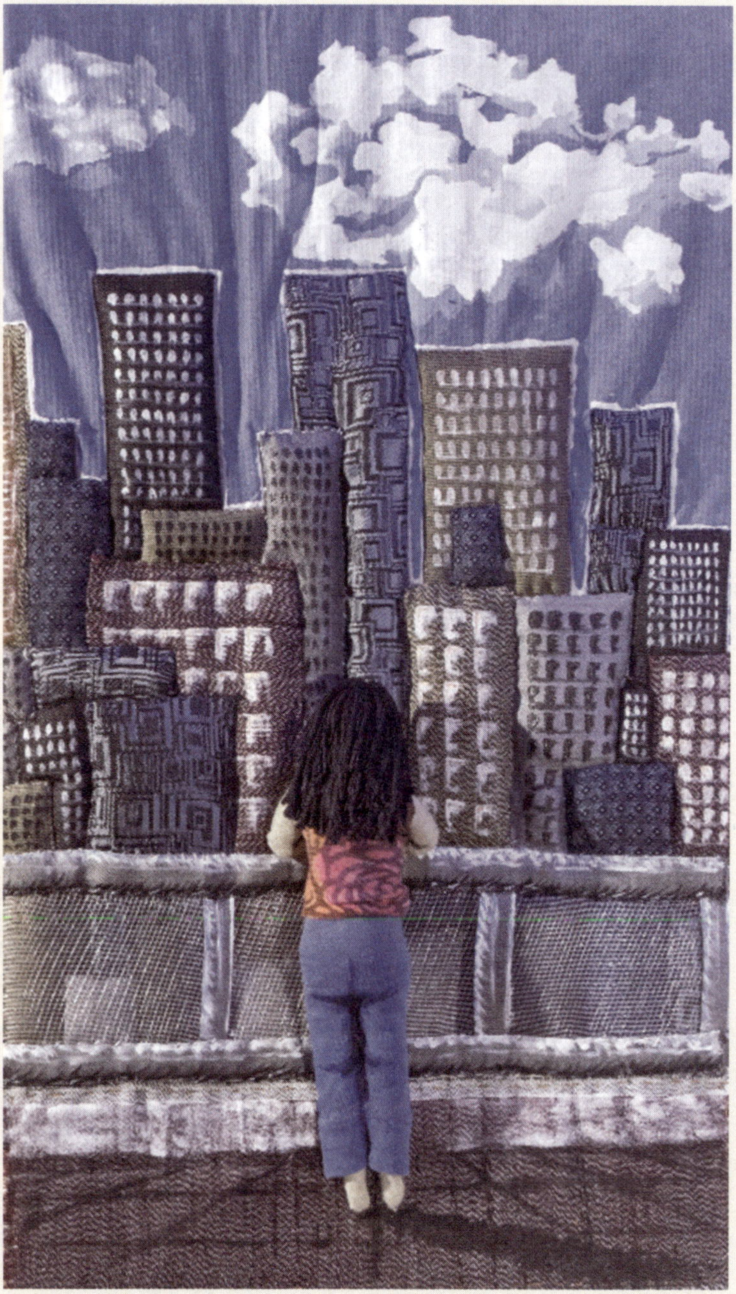

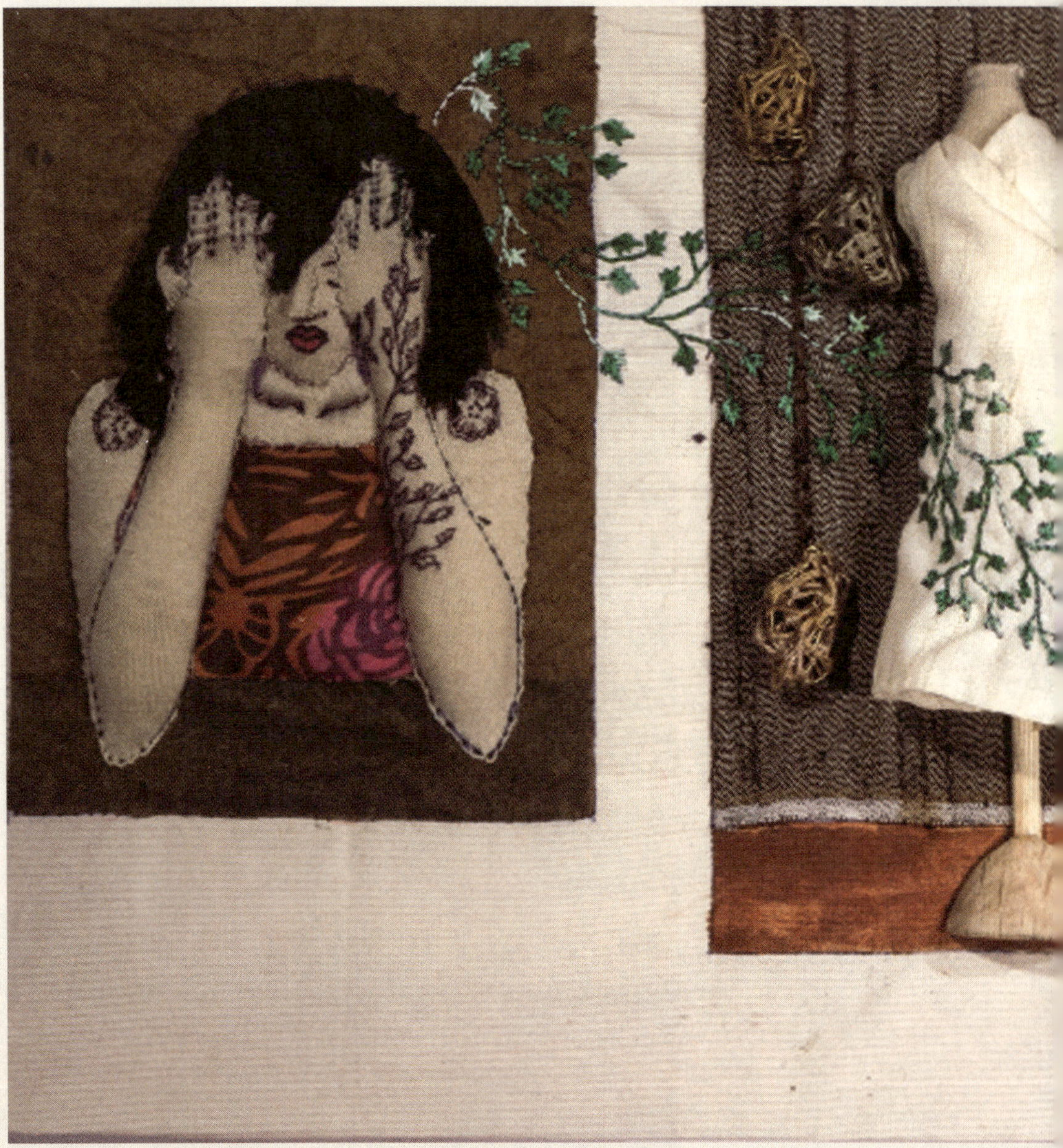

I carry memories of it on my body
Images of it projected onto my work
Constantly reminding me of something
I don't seem to remember anymore.

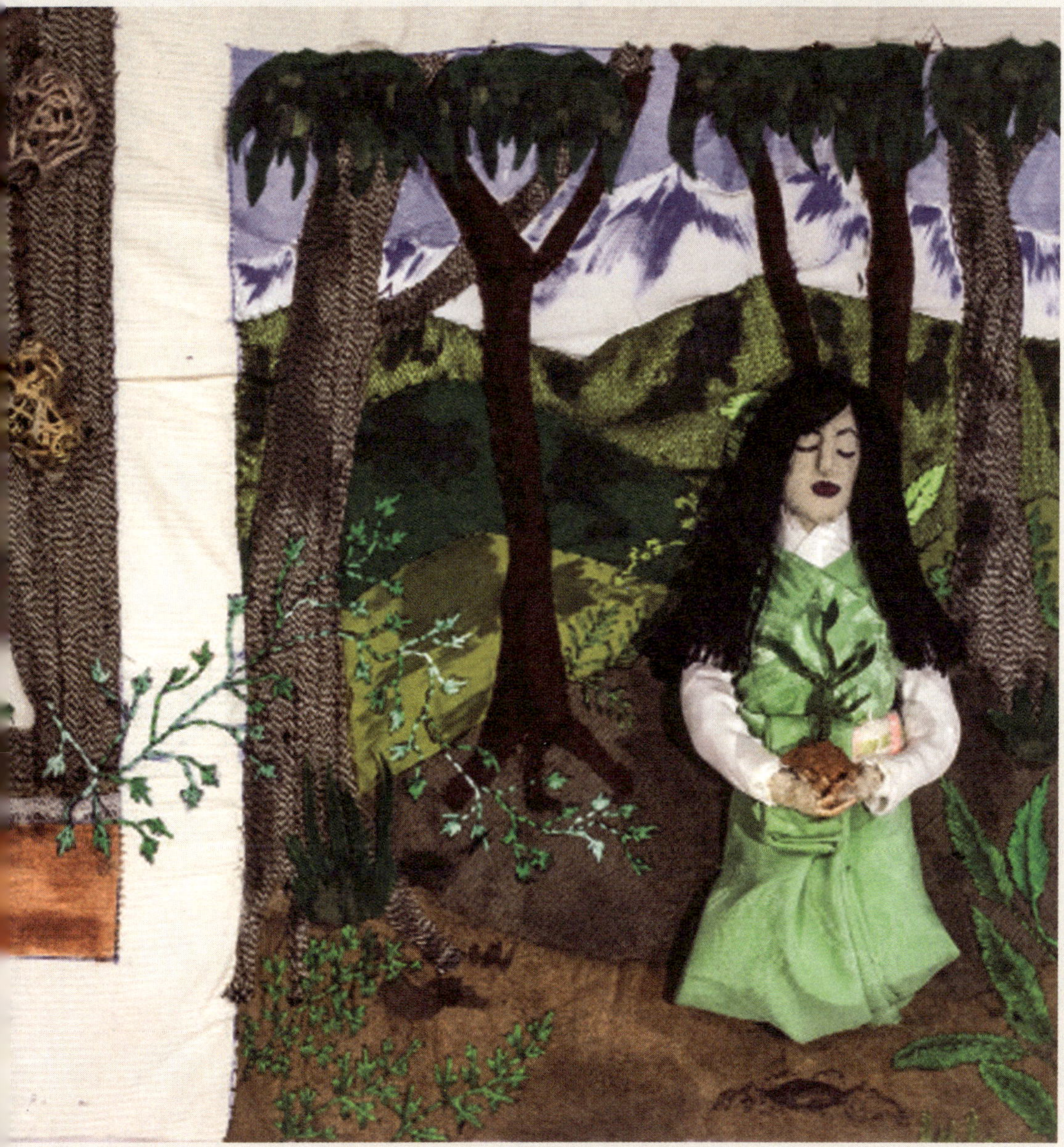

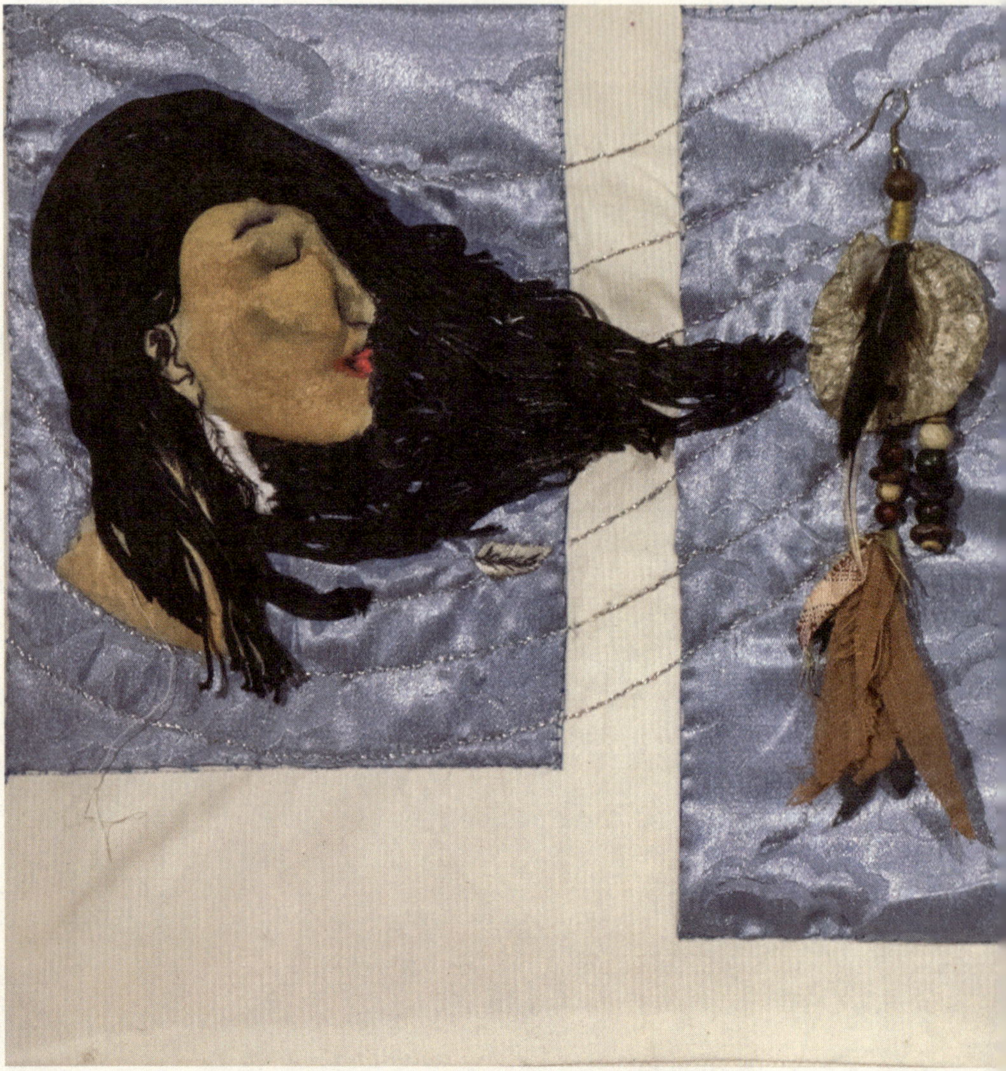

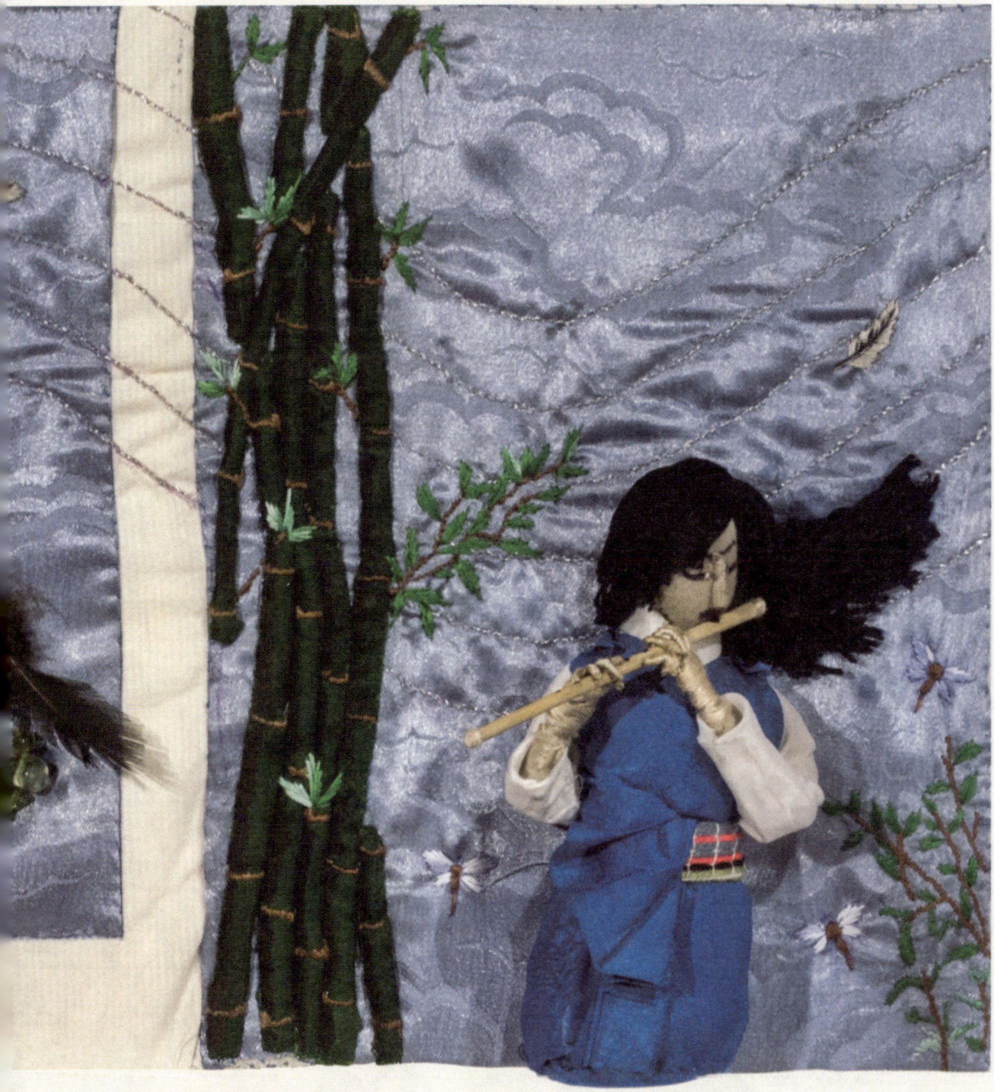

I listen to its sound,
I feel it in my soul.
Somehow I've forgotten,
Its song and the stories it told.

I travelled farther away,
Created images of it some more,
In my quest to find meaning and purpose,
I strayed from the way back home.

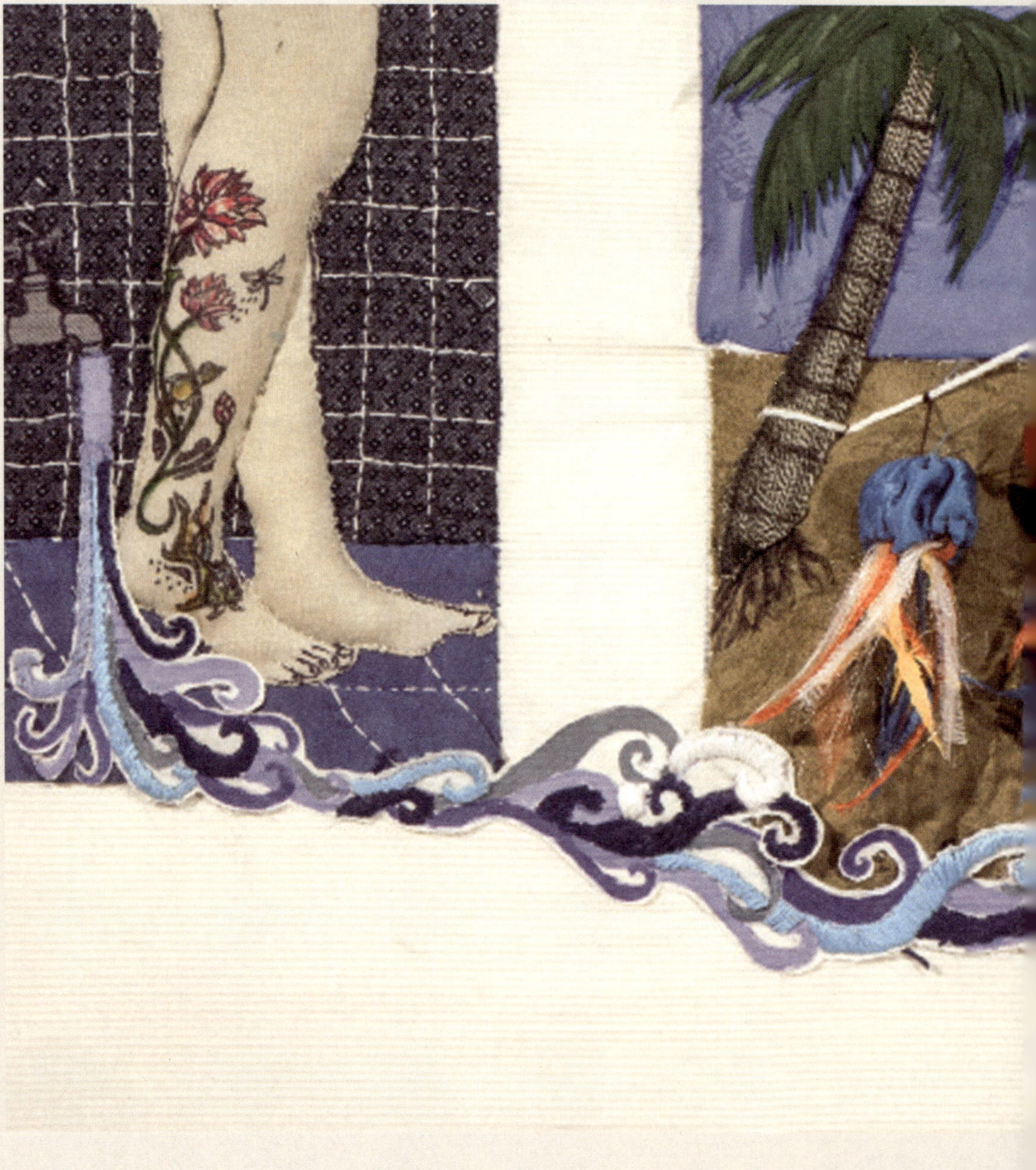

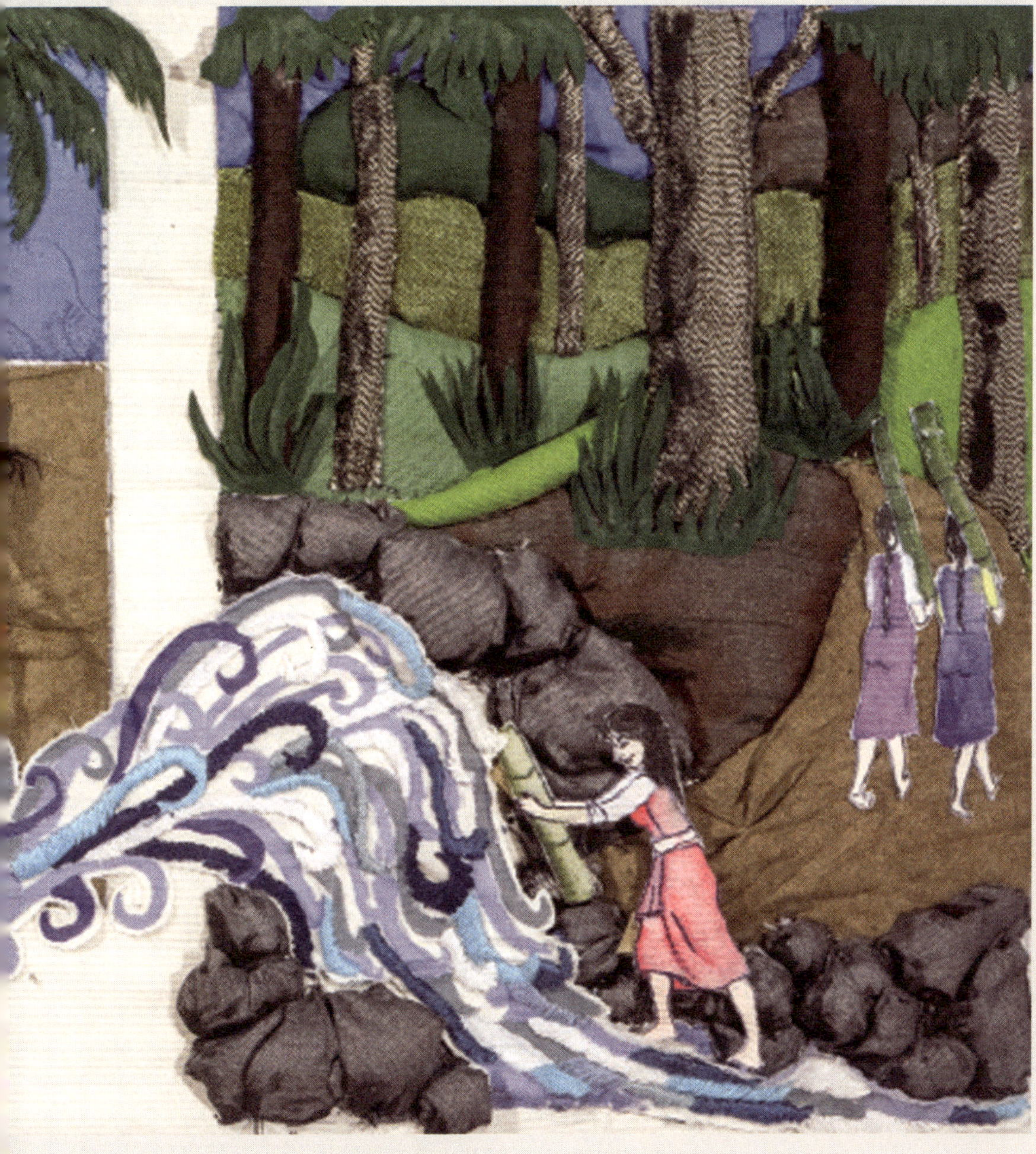

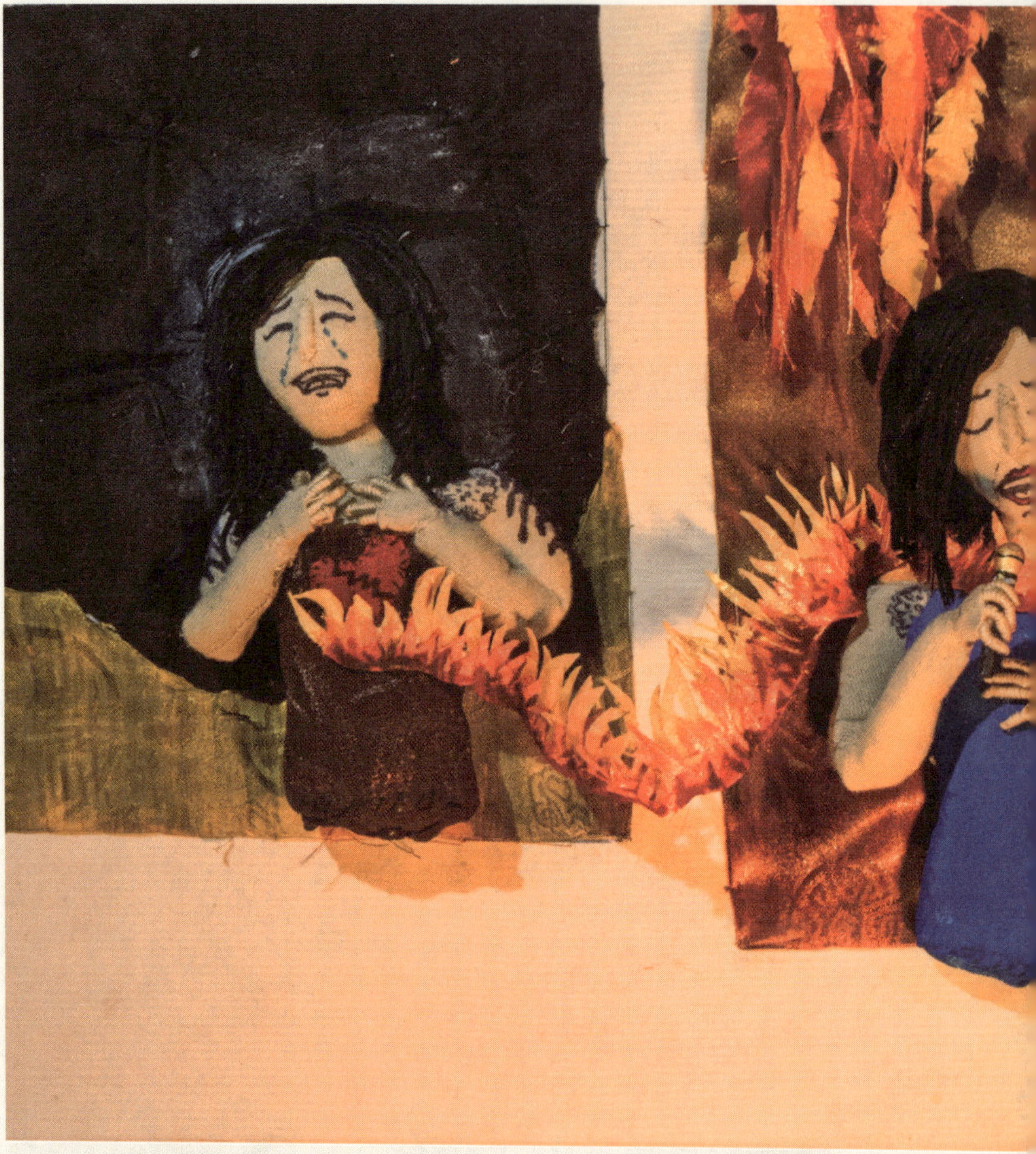

I lost myself completely,
Broke everything I've known.
I didn't remember what I was looking for, Sunk
deeper than ever before.

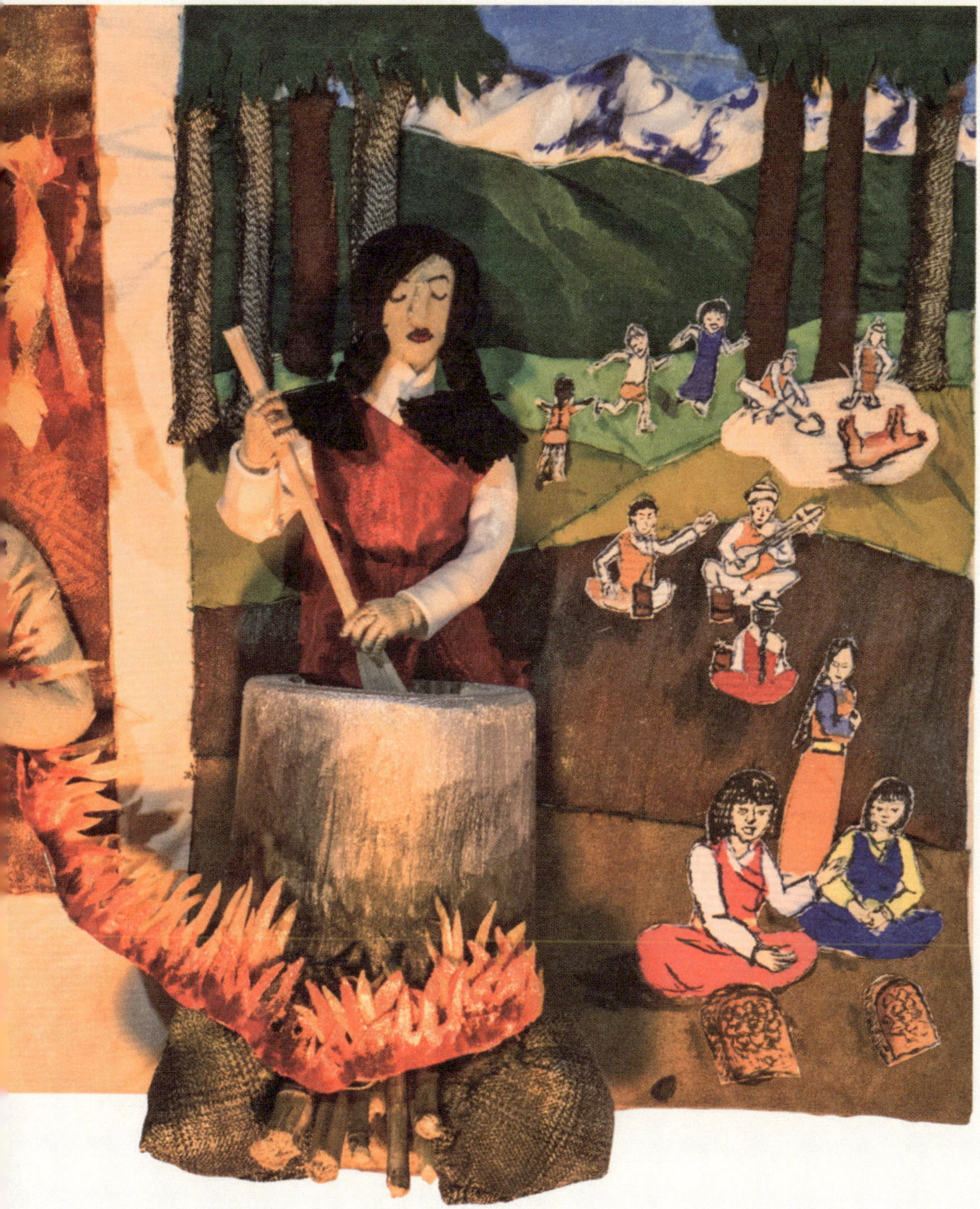

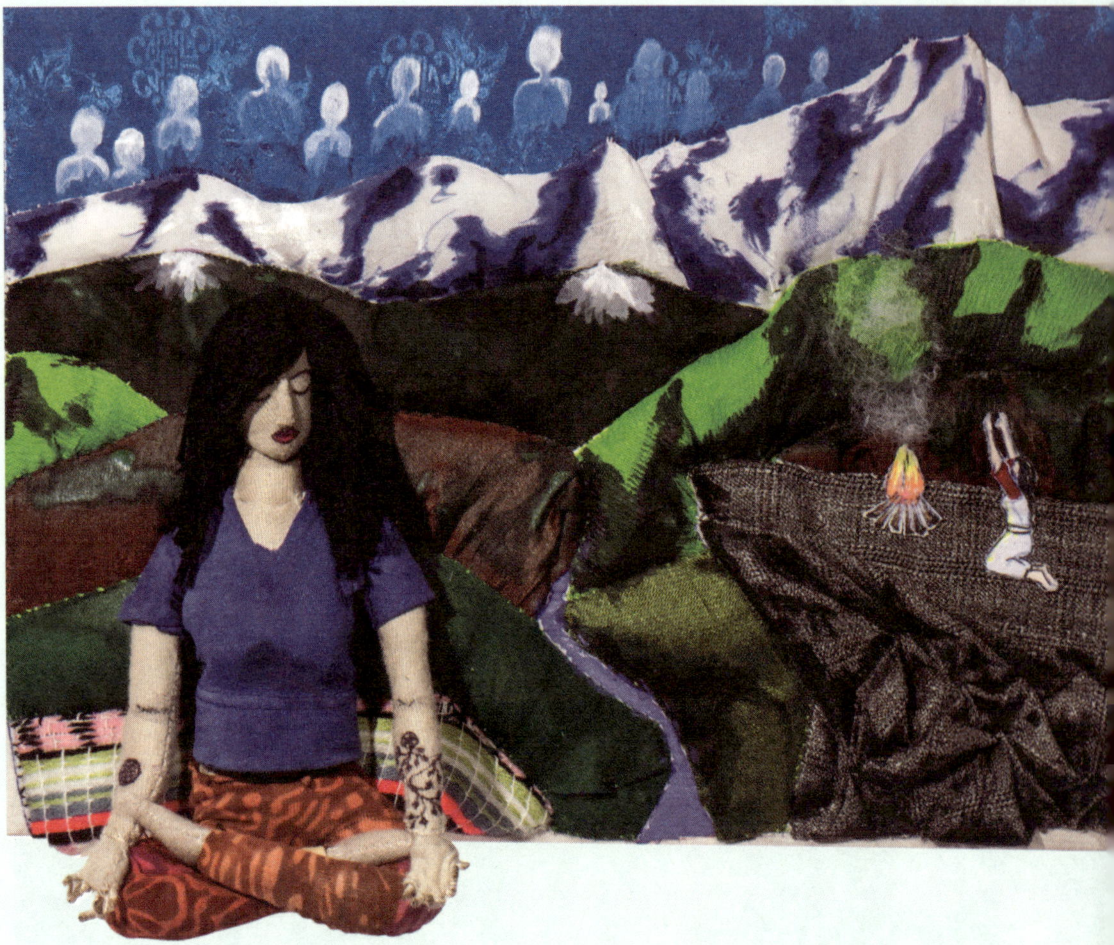

Slowly, I picked up the pieces.
Tried connecting to the source.
Searched for the wisdom of my ancestors,
Began looking with the eyes of a new born.

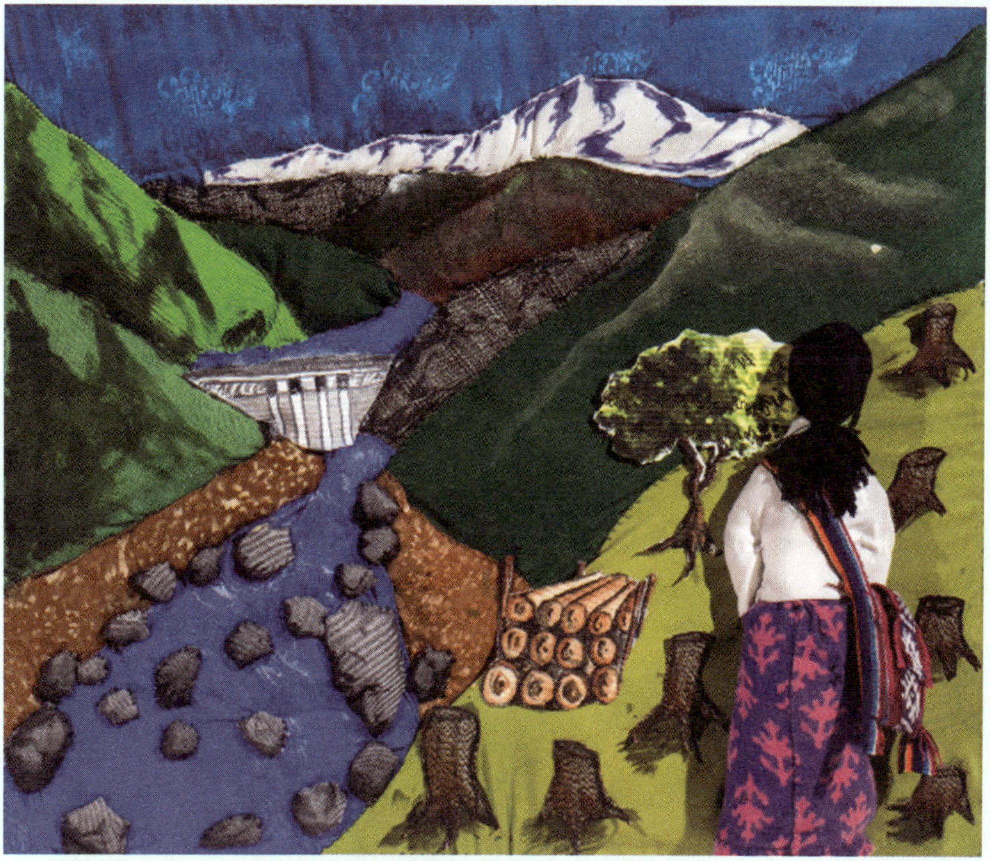

So I finally listened,
To the call of Mayel Lyang and my ancestors. To
the voice inside my soul,
Though things were not the same anymore, I
still made my way back home.

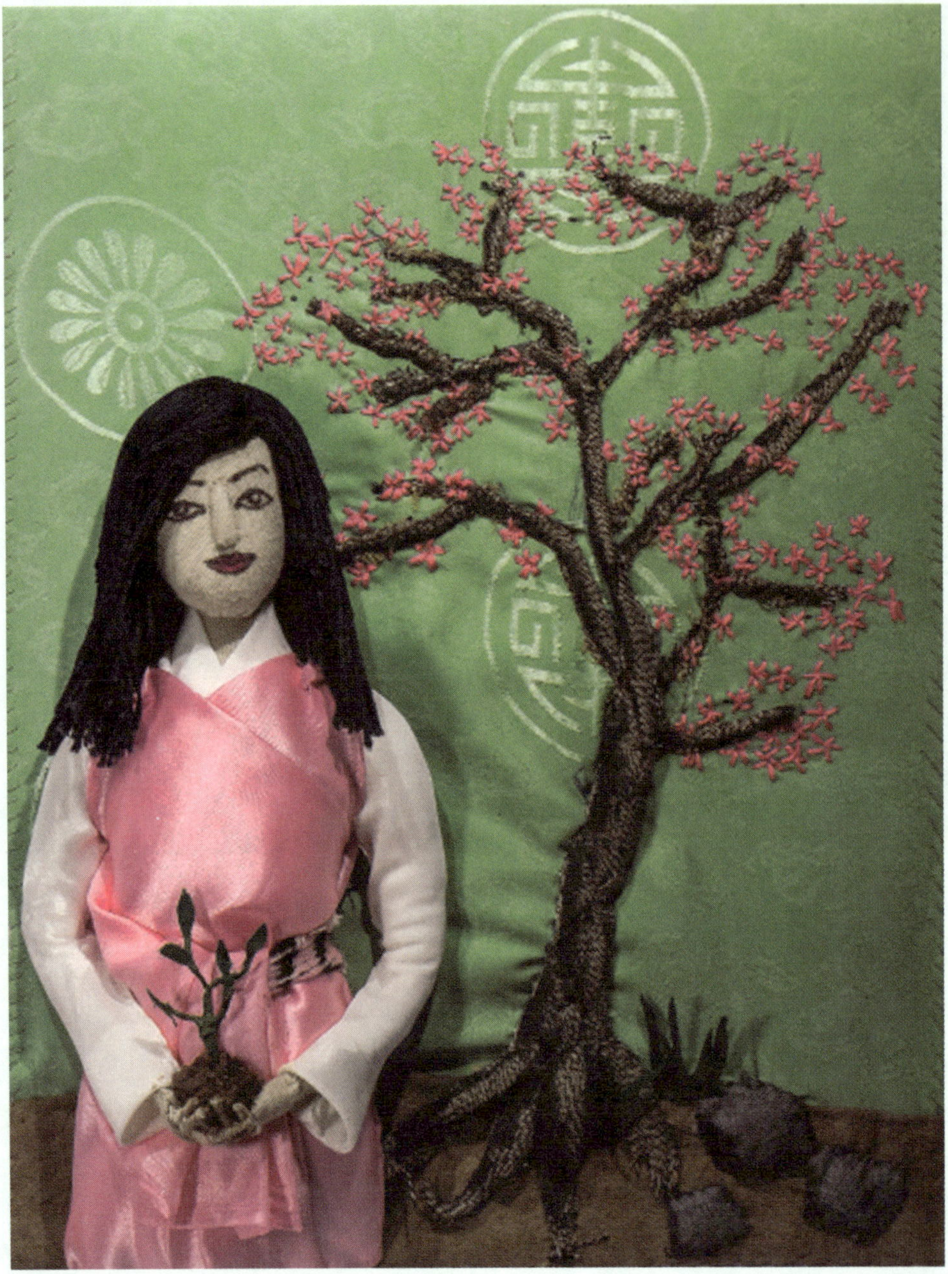

The journey has been unforgiving and long,
But, here I am now,
I pray with faith to bloom,
To finally sing my soul song,
And humbly stand in my truth.

naga naki?
travelling with a caravan on a journey of common hope

AHELI MOITRA

I arrived in Dimapur on 30 July, 2011. A Maruti Omni van with 'The Morung Express' painted on its door waited at the station. R Sharma, who had come to pick me up, just smiled when I complained of the dust and grime that defined Dimapur's summer. We were on our way to Duncan Bosti where *The Morung Express*, a newspaper produced in Nagaland, is headquartered. I was to begin a two month long collaboration with them.

It was my first time in Nagaland. As Dimapur whirled by, my mind reeled. Why was I here? It had been a year since a project on 'Understanding Impunity: Failures and Possibilities of Rights to Truth, Justice and Reparation' in the Indian Union had come to an abrupt end for some of us. The project had attempted to document how impunity operates, how reparation models could be framed, and how people who undergo human rights abuse could work in solidarity for justice. It took a different route with the death of its ambitious director, Ram Narayan Kumar, a prolific figure in India's research and advocacy battle for human rights. The project could not be completed in its entirety without his commitment, mind, drive and energy to conjoin difficult concepts at play, or indeed his ability to bring together people to share and discuss ideas.

The last research trip Kumar had planned, right before his death, had been to the 'Northeast' (of Bengal, first classified as such by the British)—a whole landmass, and its peoples, that had escaped my probashi (nonresident Bangali) upbringing. Apart from

Assam's cha bagan, a romantic idea of heaven on earth for my family, the 'Northeast' was a blur. An introduction to Xonzoi Barbora (now Dean at the Tata Institute of Social Sciences) at a human rights research capacity building workshop in Guwahati (2009) began to change much of that. I was introduced to the world of peoples' rights organizations of the 'Northeast'—political collectives that work on the fulcrum of the right to self-determination.

This framework was unclear to me at the time. It took a whole lot more to propel me to begin a study. Following the workshop, I decided to travel. It was Rongali Bihu and Guwahati station was chaotic. The train to Jorhat had been cancelled. A first time lone traveller here, fear crept in as the word 'bombing' was whispered around. As I began to panic, a familiar face surfaced in the crowd. Xonzoi Barbora. Nudging my way through the crowd, I tapped on his shoulder.

Barbora and his friend, a professor of geology, were headed to upper Assam for Bihu; since the train was cancelled they would drive there instead. I could come along! The car journey from Guwahati to Jorhat gave me fresh insight. As we drove along, the duo introduced me to Manu Chao and bits of Basque nationalism; the khat system that had enabled revenue and relations between the Nagas and Axoms; the history and paddy fields of upper Assam. Their stories had me entranced. I travelled thereon, a couple of days later, to Sibsagar (also with them) and later to Imphal, meeting more storytellers; by then, I was a 'Northeast' convert.

After two years of dreaming of coming back, Barbora introduced me to Aküm Longchari, then managing director of *The Morung Express*. Once we had figured out a way to work together, I took the train from Kolkata to Dimapur, leaving a petrified mother behind.

2

The Dimapur rail station is two platforms and a footbridge. Its simplicity ends there. A sticky web of collaborations takes shape underneath and around the bridge, finding ways into the city.

Dimapur is an urbanscape that has neither the paranoia of Guwahati nor the quiet gait of Diphu. Like both, it is a city of mixed nationalities. Home to the last railhead before the hills roll all the way through Nagaland to Manipur and Mizoram, passing unconnected valleys on the way, Dimapur is a near holy marketplace for the region.

Here, the private, state, non state, patriot, revolutionary, men, women, transpeople, local, foreign, traditional, contemporary, queer of the region north east of Bengal come together in an alliance still visible in Guwahati, slowly disappearing from Kolkata and found in small pockets of Mumbai, Delhi or Bangalore.

The Jama Masjid is set next to one of Dimapur's biggest markets, Hazi Park. Established in the city in 1906, the Masjid is simple and small, its dome adorned in an old Islamic architectural tradition of coloured tile chips. Not far from this, surrounding the crucial area around the Dimapur railway station, is the Marwari Patti dotted with old buildings. Some of these portray jali work from the Marwar region of Rajasthan and Gujarat. Jain and Hindu temples flank the area. On the other side of the railway station is a Bangali habitation, a settlement that, much like Lumding, was probably started by the North East region rail workers who were, at some point, predominantly Bangla speaking people. On the other side is the Kuda village, segregated into its neat numbered lanes, that painfully merges into National Highway 29 and the Naga hills thence.

Elsewhere, a lone flyover takes you away from the station towards what was once called Church Road, later changed to Nyamo Lotha Road, but it continues to be popular as Church Road. Hongkong market shows up in its many forms, from roadside stalls to over-pouring buildings that house top fashion gear from the east. Its backyard gives way to New Market. This is the domain of everything affordable, from dry fish and fruit to prayer paraphernalia and shoes. Run by people of varied origin and nationality from the subcontinent, its horizontal equality tapers into the second hand clothes bazaar without which many of us in Dimapur would look the living we make.

Walking away from the Dimapur railway station and the New Market, we approach the city clock tower. Surrounded by institutions like a petrol pump and KFC, the mini Eiffel Tower look-alike is both a symbol of the class aspirations of the city's many peoples as well as a site for protest. Alongside advertisements of mobile telecommunication companies, one can spot banners protesting corruption, signature campaigns and candle-light vigils at any time of year—the killing of a man by a mob on 5 March, 2015 at the site did little to take away its glamour.

Traversing this web, I arrived at the three-roomed headquarters of *The Morung Express* in Duncan Bosti - a colony for urban Naga habitation - with little knowledge of Naga people and politics. Now editor of the newspaper, Aküm Longchari, and then editor, Along Longkumer, walked me through endless hours of discussion on Naga history and the location of the people today. My first assignment seemed simple: they asked me to explore "contradictions" in Naga society.

Like any place, Naga society was full of it. Contradictions. In Dimapur, people from west or north India run entire markets—when Naga vegetable growers wanted to sell a load of cabbages one year, they had no buyers. The whole market was syndicated.

Dimapur city requires no Inner Line Permit as applicable to the rest of Nagaland state. It works in the shadow of the liquor prohibition regime that applies to the rest of the state. The former allows for a comfortable in-and-out through the city, and the latter for a tinge of rebellion when indulging in its many watering holes. The rule of law finds marginal space and traffic cops have recently appeared to control the bloating vehicular population.

Indian Army trucks, like perennial ants, ply from unknown directions towards their shrine in Rangapahar Military Station—a territory reported to be larger than Dimapur city—preparing for an unforeseen perennial winter. The Assam Rifles parade the city streets openly in jungle fatigues to produce an effect contrary to that of camouflage; they intend to be seen. Cadres of Naga national groups in their ordinary tamul-chewing, slipper-toting garb, watch them go by as taxes pass hands.

Dimapur is a city of control, physical and psychological. It is a city of controlled violence, on edge but rarely ruffled. In its flat lands and the hills around, Naga people live in a perennial state of contradiction. Here, in a family of six, one could be a village council chairperson, another a Nagaland state government bureaucrat, one in the civil set up of a Naga national/political group, one in the army, another one in the Nagaland Police and one an 'educated unemployed' person.

Conflict creates strange bedfellows. Making sense of these contradictions called for deeper engagement. For the next few years, thus, my home became a room with a family in one of Dimapur's many colonies. From here I walked every day to *The Morung Express*, becoming a cog in the city's collaborative wheel; a part of the caravan to explore the Naga journey for common hope—the Naga Reconciliation Process.

3

Are you Sümi?

Naga naki?

Naga humour is as difficult to explain as it is easy to laugh with. The overpowering stench of militarization is often bottled at its altar. Without any experience of such violence, I learned to laugh along with the loud group laughs, waiting for a better moment to clarify what the joke meant. So, when the first person asked me, '*apuni Naga naki?*,' (are you Naga?) I laughed it off as a joke I understood.

But I didn't, and a response came to be expected. Almost every Naga person I met had the question. *Naga naki?*

Turns out, at the time of birth, my parents gifted me with more than life. My name. 'Aheli' is often identified as a Sümi Naga woman's name. So, after every interview I conducted in the Naga areas, or before, the question would play on my interviewee's mind—*addha Sümi asse?* Is she half Sümi? Moitra's Bangali tilt balanced the scale.

By the time I revealed my Bombay-Bangali scheme of life, hearts had already softened. For those harder to win, there was suspicion—had I taken a new name just to fit in? *Agent nahoi na?* (You are not an agent, na?)

While such questions have a place in a society ravaged by seven decades of war, the truth was that my mother had picked a Bangla name, aspiring for little in terms of greatness from her first child. She named me 'Aheli,' which simply means 'pure.' Little did she know that in the world I came to share with the Naga people, it dissolved the lines that separate an insider from the outsider; my name became a spark for bonds and jokes tying us together in unimaginable ways.

One such incident occurred early on in my stay. Post revelry at an underground 'club' called 'Pebbles,' a journalist from *The Morung Express* and I stumbled off to another bar. Here, I saw what it meant to be a journalist in Dimapur.

On a table of four, we spotted a senior leader from a Naga political group. We approached him hoping to get an interview lest no other opportunities arise in the two months I was slated to be here. A few beers down, this seemed like a great idea.

My name did wonders. "Aheli? Sümi? Please come, come, sit." Completely ignoring our "no nos," he pulled out the additional chairs insisting we join him at the table with his friends, as a henchman guarded the door. We boozily agreed. Stories of his days 'underground,' of the violence he saw as a child pushing him to join the Naga movement, the jungle wars, later signing a ceasefire agreement with the Government of India, came flowing out. All was well.

And then, he suggested we join him for shooting practice at a private range the upcoming Saturday. My journalist friend and I looked at each other nervously. Before we could control the situation, it got worse. From a holster strapped to his waist that we had previously not noticed in the dim light, he drew a black gun of some sort and placed it on the table.

"Would you like to try it?" he asked us with a grin, as if offering the latest smoked pork on the menu.

"No, no, thank you," we said in unison. "*Lobi, try koribi!*" (Try it!) came the order.

The booze evaporated. At the cusp of the greatest interview of our lives, perhaps even an imagined award, we were faced with a firearm. My only experience with a gun of any kind in close proximity had been when an uncle in the Maharashtra Police would visit us. His first ritual on arrival was to take his gun out of a body holster and keep it in a safe. We had no interest in it.

Destiny had it otherwise. As I took this black, heavy, semi automatic revolver in my perennially sweaty palms on that night in Dimapur, the upper frame that I needed to slide to 'cock' the gun slipped out. Nothing happened. Petrified, I grinned silly and shrugged. Only then he showed me the bullet cylinder that he had emptied, and everyone (but I) had a big Naga laugh.

I was promised a real interview another day.

The day the leader and I were to meet at an 'undisclosed location,' my heart throbbed. Sweaty palms again, I was nervous. I had not informed the editor. I was in this alone. A black Scorpio picked me up from Metro Hospital. The drive was nerve-wracking. We were driving to the Hotel Tragopan, located at the busy Golaghat Road junction, an unlikely venue for a kidnapping, if I had thought about it. But having heard hostile stories of Naga 'undergrounds', and nothing diluting this perception now, there was little doubt in my mind that I was being kidnapped.

My fears were rooted in ignorance drawn from our education's dehumanization of revolutionaries, I realized when the interview took off at the Hotel Tragopan's restaurant. The leader was as human as any of us, with incurable dreams. He held memories of violence. He understood the Naga historical and political situation. He had his reasons for joining the particular group he did. He had his fears and doubts, and was admittedly part of an all-consuming corrupt web. Their group had a vision for a Naga 'solution'; in a ceasefire agreement with the Government of India, they hoped to begin negotiations for a political settlement.

This was not to be, as several 'internal' and 'external' circumstances had come to plague the Naga struggle. Too many arms meant too many had started their own factions; intractability meant ideological side streaming. The interview helped me shed much of my own romanticism as he narrated facts of daily life; confined mostly to a camp, potbellied and slow, he told me how his ideas differed from the rest and drew a sketch, perhaps to the umpteenth visiting journalist, of how the Indian Union and the Nagas could share power. But how will the Nagas share power with each other, I asked, going beyond my mandate.

"There are ways. We are in reconciliation," he said, quickly concluding the interview, hurrying me to finish my tea.

4

"We are a people who must learn to live."
– Wati Aier, Convenor, Forum for Naga Reconciliation

I left Dimapur in October 2011, only to be back in December. The two prescribed months of work with *The Morung Express* had turned into three. Emerging from a background of security studies, peace building was not something I had been educated in till I began working with the Nagas. It had fuelled a fire in me to learn more.

In the first rungs of the interviews I conducted to get a general understanding of the Naga movement, everyone asked me to look in the direction of the 'FNR.' And I did.

The Forum for Naga Reconciliation (FNR) is a collective effort of Naga civil society to bring together Naga political/national groups. Once united, the hope was for a collective pursuit of determining Naga historical and political rights, and forging a relationship of equals with the Indian Union. The Naga Reconciliation Process—*A Journey of Common Hope*—that the FNR initiated in 2008 was a people's effort, with the state (legality) playing almost no role, as was the case for such processes in post conflict societies around the world. For the Nagas, there was an added complication: they were attempting reconciliation amidst active conflict.

Reconciliation is a strong sustainer of peace, helping restore relationships broken during the course of conflict. So I learned. Here, reconciliation was attempted internally, first of all, to serve the larger arc of political negotiations, justice and peace. The Naga people who I visited in Nagaland, Assam and Manipur had opened their doors to me in the last few months, helping me understand and prepare for the reconciliation meeting I witnessed in 2012.

On 29 February, 2012, nearly 50,000 people gathered at the Agri Expo ground in Dimapur; at least the metal detectors placed at the dusty venue detected as many. The FNR had called for a public meeting of leaders of the Naga political/national groups with the Naga people. Video camera in hand, I was not going to miss this historic opportunity.

When I look back at the recordings, I am thankful for the device; little can be said about my skills with handling it. As leaders rarely seen in public, and of whom I had only read in articles and books, walked in—Isak Chishi Swu, Thuingaleng Muivah, Khole Konyak, S Singnya, Zhopra Vero, Kitovi Zhimomi—I tripped on a rock and fell. The camera lost sight of the revolutionaries. It caught only the mobile toilets placed at the back of the stage.

Thankfully, a long meeting lay ahead and I gathered plenty of footage. On one side was a small stage set up for the Oriental Theological Seminary's (OTS) choir. OTS is a premier institution of learning for Naga Baptists; music and sports are key elements of the OTS pedagogy designed meticulously by the former principal of the Seminary, Rev. Dr. Wati Aier, also the Convener of the FNR.

'We are a people who must learn to live. This is the past narrative of our songs. My quest was to bring this back to the context of our warring factions,' Dr. Wati told me in an interview years later. The songs he wrote, and which the OTS choir often sang at reconciliation meetings, were songs of forgiveness, of common belonging; songs of approaching a shared future.

A genuine sense of re-igniting lost friendships was felt at the Agri Expo on that day in February 2012.

The reconciling leaders stepped on to the mega stage as attendees waved miniature Naga national flags—the flag, a rainbow and David's star streaking up through a light blue sky, is a symbol all Naga groups agree on. The OTS choir rang out with their '*long long night is over... freedom shall be coming... praise and sing to the Lord.*' The drum beats painted an epic atmosphere.

The backdrop of the main stage was also the Naga national flag, with 'Naga Reconciliation Meeting' written across in three lines. It was being held in place with long bamboo sticks placed diagonally and equidistant, almost as a metaphor for FNR members who were working in consistent ways to hold the meeting together. A peace meet like this required that even armed groups leave their arms at home, for instance. A safe space needed to be created for the groups as well as the people. The FNR team crafted their way through many little negotiations ensuring smooth sailing through the day.

And there I was with my wobbly videography skills: swinging the camera 360 degrees sometimes, up and down the stage, running from one corner to the other, zooming in and out. I wanted to capture it all: the people who had come to see their leaders together after years of fear on the streets; the expressions on the faces of the leaders; even the leader I had interviewed earlier in my act of self-proclaimed daredevilry was there! I had to get the music of the moment.

Such were the hopes from the Naga Reconciliation Meeting that Rev. VK Nuh, while offering an invocation, said a simple prayer. "Let us sit together, pray together, talk together." The power of prayer in the Christian faith as part of the reconciliation process was not obvious to me then, emerging from a non-Christian upbringing. This aspect began to unfurl some years later when I worked on related stories with Naga scholar and lecturer in Religious Studies at the University of Edinburgh, Arkotong Longkumer.

The revolutionary poet Varavara Rao attended the programme alongside Naga people from Myanmar, Arunachal Pradesh, Assam, Manipur and Nagaland. Also present was the Committee for Release of Political Prisoners to express solidarity with the *Journey of Common Hope*. The Indian and Naga civil societies were no stranger to each other, nor were the revolutionary movements that had sprung from the soils of each. Stories from elders presented such nostalgia of the days of cooperation that young people, like me, felt a tinge of envy when we looked at the polarized world order we inherited.

At the meeting, Naga civil society leaders poured their aspirations out—some congratulated each other, others reminisced about history. Some messages rang out in their critique. Keep the process clean, outcome will be okay. Naga elder, Niketu Iralu, had repeated this basic mantra multiple times over the years. Truth and transparency—moral grounding of the soul—played a central role in his worldview. Reconciliation had to be based on these principles.

One of the reasons why transparency evaded the reconciliation process was that the "Indo-Naga peace process" remained shrouded in secrecy. The Government of India had signed a ceasefire agreement with the National Socialist Council of Nagalim (NSCN-IM) in 1997, thereafter embarking on political negotiations with them to forge a solution to the Indo-Naga conflict. Despite signing ceasefire agreements with other groups, talks with the Indian government remained confined to one group, and a solution was sought to be designed behind closed doors instead of opening up the process to the people in order to make it holistic.

The NSCN-IM considers this positions justified as it speaks the language of the masses, based on the regular consultations it organizes with the Naga civil society. For a new crop of organizations that have come up in Nagaland state though, these consultations hold little weight—the discourse here has become anchored in Article 371-A of the Indian Constitution, often described by Naga nationalists as a "sellout," which yet defines the relationship between the Nagas in Nagaland state and New Delhi.

As I stayed longer in the Naga areas, I came across more facets of this complex relationship.

For many young people in Nagaland state, who grew up in a post 1997-ceasefire world, the Indian state came without its violent deficiencies. The untoward division of Naga people into many states, the undermining of their self-determination and continued militarization were inescapable matters; the ceasefire generation wanted to take a different approach to self-determination, by developing their roads, schools and hospitals. Nagaland state was created in 1963 through a political agreement and two prominent things unfurled over the years: firstly, some political 'agreements' were slowly manoeuvred to suit the Government of India's policies and secondly, the Nagaland state government's politicians and bureaucrats siphoned off monumental amounts of money without any accountability. Nagaland's state government provided neither for all round development of infrastructure and resources nor was it able to grow under the light of Article 371-A of the Indian Constitution which provides for limited autonomy under the Indian federal governance structure.

And what about the Naga people in Assam, Manipur, Arunachal Pradesh and Myanmar?

The Morung Express, a site for education as much as the news, gave me the opportunity to travel and explore this last topic. In 2012, I travelled with Zeliangrong Naga youth for a 'pilgrimage' to sites of historic significance. If post-colonial processes had undermined indigenous peoples of the region, the Zeliangrong had faced one of its worst lashes. When borders were drawn, they were inadvertently divided into the three states of Assam, Manipur and Nagaland. Here, they remained at the peripheries of decision-making and territory. In Manipur, for instance, their lands had been auctioned off, without their consent, for hydrocarbons mining by power blocs in Imphal, but development was at its worst.

Only lightweight Maruti Gypsies could travel through the region's roads. Healthcare and education were unseen dreams. For the apex bodies, or civil society organizations, it was difficult to keep track of what happened in these far-flung, unconnected areas. During a visit to the camp of a Naga political group deep inside the hills, we were told that other Naga armed groups could attack the camp anytime. Enemies were internal, not just external.

It is here that reconciliation was needed. Violence among the Nagas had also divided civil society. To bring unity among them, and strengthen the community's capacity to stand up for rights, reconciliation was needed. A person from Tamenglong town in Manipur had volunteered to guide the process locally, drawing from the larger Naga Reconciliation Process at play.

The Reconciliation Process had created the safe space needed to start talking about the political issues that plagued the Naga people in each of the administrative setups they found themselves in.

On a rainy evening in Ukhrul town (Manipur), for instance, Tangkhul Naga elder PR Machung sat on a chair next to his fireplace sharing old stories. His family and I sat around listening to him speak of the Naga relationship with neighbours, the Kuki and Meitei. His memory had faded and he referred to handmade notes from a box of diaries, painstakingly prepared at the Central Library in Imphal when he was young. Established in 1968, the library was burned down in 2005 by Imphal-based activists demanding that Manipur's ancient script be brought back. For Uncle Machung, the loss of the library meant that his only reason left to visit Imphal no longer existed. The journey for a Naga person to Imphal was thorny—on arrival into the valley, hill vegetable vendors, for instance, being roughed up by local security forces was a common sight. Cars with an 'NL' (Nagaland) registration plates were subject to harassment. Violence had become entrenched, and Uncle did not wish to witness it. For many like him, this journey is avoidable unless necessary.

Reconciliation was necessary for Naga people, like him, to strengthen the Naga political negotiations with the Government of India. It would build the opportunity to start a new relationship with Imphal; if not in his lifetime, perhaps in his grandchild's. But he acknowledged that at least in Manipur, the Nagas are populous enough to shape a strong voice. In Assam, Naga people live in worse conditions, reduced to such a minority that they cannot even talk about becoming an equal people—a whiff of such talk could raise insecurity and conflict among the people they have come to share their lands with. In Myanmar, the Naga people live in poverty that leaves major diseases undetected—too many have died in epidemics.

Many of these people had braved harsh geography, security concerns of intelligence tapping and instigation of neighbouring peoples by state agencies to attend the Naga Reconciliation Meeting in February 2012.

But the leaders of the Naga national groups gave mixed signals at the public meeting. Some sought forgiveness from the Naga peoples, while others stressed on the need for a pragmatic approach; another spoke of an out-of-box approach and another said they do not want to be 'taken advantage of' in the name of reconciliation. They had come together on a grand stage but where was the united front? Could I not see it?

What I did see, and hear, though was a noisy deep olive green helicopter that hovered over the Agri Expo ground as Isak Chishi Swu spoke. This was not a civilian helicopter. This destructive martial tendency of the Indian state had made the Naga Reconciliation Process that much harder, as a cumulative sense of impunity and lack of accountability seeped from state power blocs to non state power blocs.

Yet, the FNR did not lose courage, optimism and consistency. From March 2008 to February 2012, it convened several small and large meetings of differing Naga groups based on common Naga historical and political positions, acknowledging every contribution to the cause. These were feats achieved in a climate of hostility, with '*guli khabo*' (just another phrase that factions used with each other on a daily basis). The

FNR stood up to the herculean task of intervening in a pervasive and violent conflict, leading to transformation of the lived space—the violence that the state could not bring down, the reconciliation process did.

5

It was not just the Naga people who benefitted from this. I did too, as did my Indian counterparts. As did media houses and journalism industries.

The news industry in Nagaland is among these. My first stint as a journalist was with *The Indian Express*, Mumbai edition, in 2003. The context in which the Lower Parel office of *The Indian Express* worked was in sharp contrast to how the Duncan Bosti office of *The Morung Express* does. They differ widely in terms of resources—human and financial—as well as scope. In a city like Mumbai, at the time, the brutal murder of an octogenarian received a middle page slot of a newspaper for 150 words if space permitted. In Nagaland, the murder of a person is a time of mourning for the whole community—it requires appropriate balance in published details. For days after, civil society organizations rally for justice. In a place where the rule of law is nullified by the law itself, the consistency of these protests often determines if justice is done. These aspects are covered in depth by a pint-sized team of journalists.

"Just Peace"—that peace is possible in the presence of justice—is the fulcrum around which *The Morung Express* operates. Established in 2005, *The Morung Express* was conceived by a group of young people who had travelled extensively through the Naga areas and heard people speak of their voices being absent from the polity. Truth was a prerogative of the state—when people's truth could not be heard or read, no political process could encompass community participation. *The Morung*[1] thus rose from the "Naga people's historical realities" and sought to be "guided by their voices and experiences."

While this is a well-grounded idea, it is no easy task to reconcile the world of objective news with people's struggles and still arrive at the 'truth' while affecting change.

Propaganda, for instance, is galore and reaches the newspaper in the form of press releases. The newspaper is often obligated to publish press releases from state agencies, like government departments or the (para)military. Not carrying propaganda, or questioning its content, could send the newspaper into the 'anti-national' file. There are few avenues to run fact checks on most of these pieces, which may include

1. A morung is a traditional Naga school located in the centre of each Naga village.

information on how an orphanage was 'helped' or a water tank constructed in an interior village. No one holds the agencies, or the newspaper, accountable for propaganda—on any day, one can find 'news' pieces on how medical camps by the military are resolving the medical needs of a village.

However, tilt the scales a bit: imagine that the same state agencies were involved in a shootout that led to the death of civilians. In an overtly violent situation, people reach out to newspapers to relay information. But carrying people's voices comes with a price for the people as well as for any newspaper that carries narratives that do not support the state narrative. Newspapers, and journalists, are scrutinized and harassed to the point that people's voices are made to disappear. To protest this, newspapers in Nagaland carried blank editorials in 2015. The press in Nagaland is subject to such policies as 'divide and rule' by the multiple security agencies that lurk around every corner of the Naga areas. This is normalization of violence on a daily basis.

In this world, *The Morung Express* attempts to keep itself from being subsumed by the state narrative. The process of reconciliation in the midst of active conflict is at the core of the newspaper's work—to strengthen the voice of the people, Naga society, spread across four states in India and across the international border in Myanmar, needs reconciliation far beyond the national/political groups. The newspaper faces the arduous task of bringing these geographically dispersed unrepresented peoples' voices together on a platform.

My work often entails writing stories from as many unrepresented spots as possible. This includes the voices of neighbouring peoples, like the Zomi or the Karbi, who find themselves in similar conditions as the Nagas. *The Morung Express* has created a platform for people of, say, Güzenlanyu village in the Naga areas of Karbi Anglong to be heard and share their experiences with the Nagas in the Somra Tract of Myanmar or in Kolkata, and vice versa. They can read and connect with each other's festivals, sorrows and fruits; discuss what it is like to be a Naga in the 21st century. Through *The Morung Express*, I explored community-building, nonviolent forms of collective action, rights, reconciliation, sowing and harvest festivals.

The whole *Morung* team works on this praxis. Here, we can be journalists, teachers, researchers and activists at once, and separately—a challenge that my former years of work as a journalist, campaigner, fundraiser, researcher or activist could hardly withstand even in their deafening singularity.

I struggled for a while to come to terms with this harmonious, interdisciplinary, world of journalism. At first, I frowned at the non-competitive, laidback culture. I was not sure why everyone shared sources and leads like free water. But this was not a world of irritable, arrogant, inaccessible seniors. The press in Nagaland helped me learn to shift focus from competition in a newsroom to building relationships, personal and professional. Reconciliation was not just preached, it was actively practised both within the newsroom as well as outside it.

The newspaper sustains itself through business but 'maximizing profit' is not at the core of its value system. *The Morung Express* is one of the few, and first, newspapers in the Northeast region to adhere to the Majithia wage board—it has never skipped on delivering a month's salary despite struggling to buy the basic necessities required to run a newspaper, like newsprint that is delivered to Dimapur from a far off 'mainland' at an exorbitant price.

The Morung Express struggles with business and marketing. We struggle with state actors and agencies taking us to the courts to settle scores. We are stretched thin between the Freedom of Speech on the one hand, and the Press Council of India's guidelines on the other. We are pulled between hundreds of narratives, all projected as the truth. We make glaring mistakes, leaving paragraphs undone and spellings floating in the air.

Yet, it is from here that we strengthen our wings of engagement with a fractured society.

6

It has been more than five years into my rickety ride with the *Morung* Caravan. The Naga hills are still difficult for me to reach and people remain confused by my name. Dimapur continues to be a maze, parts of which I inadvertently discover; sometimes after a Christmas night carnival when a jawan from the Indian Reserve Battalion is needlessly violent because s/he has a gun and a license to kill. In the hills, we are all suspects, our acts dictated by the roving eyes of bullets. The state projects an act of violence every day. I see a little bit now, of what it means to be repressed under an oppressive setup—how crushing the denial of a just life can be to the dignity of beings.

Should we silently comply with the injustice?

At our office in Duncan Bosti, I often find myself turning lights and fans off in empty rooms. Last week, I dialed *The Morung Express* office phone number twice while aiming to call home. The week before I did just the opposite, confused to find my mother's crackling voice at the other end of the line. When I mixed my Bangla up with my Nagamese as we spoke, she surprisingly said, "*Naga naki?*"

No. But the Naga lens has helped me find a vision of the self, and the determination required to get there.

details of the war

MINAM APANG

DETAIL FROM THE SERIES "WAR WITH THE STARS"

COURTESY THE ARTIST AND CHATTERJEE & LAL

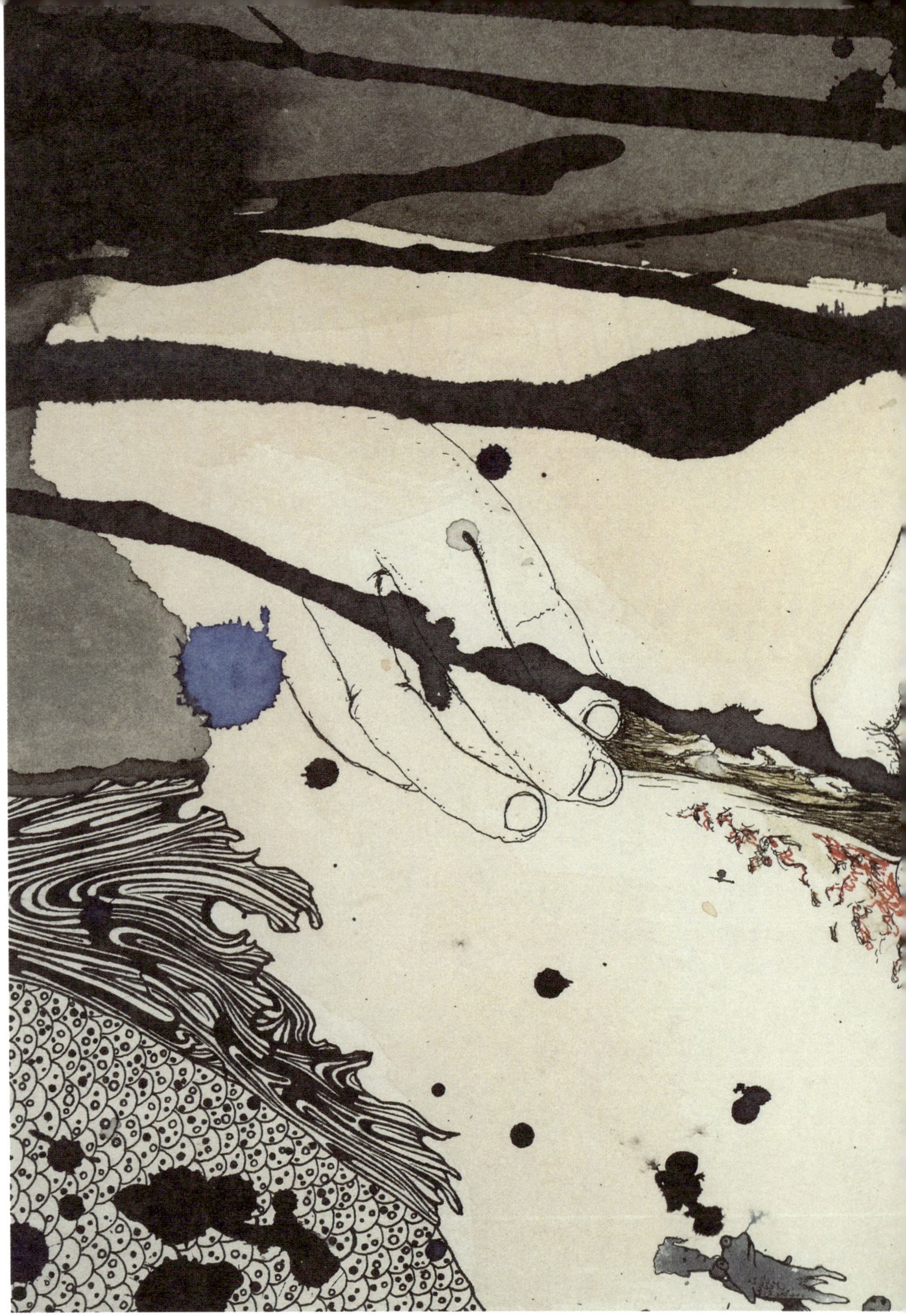

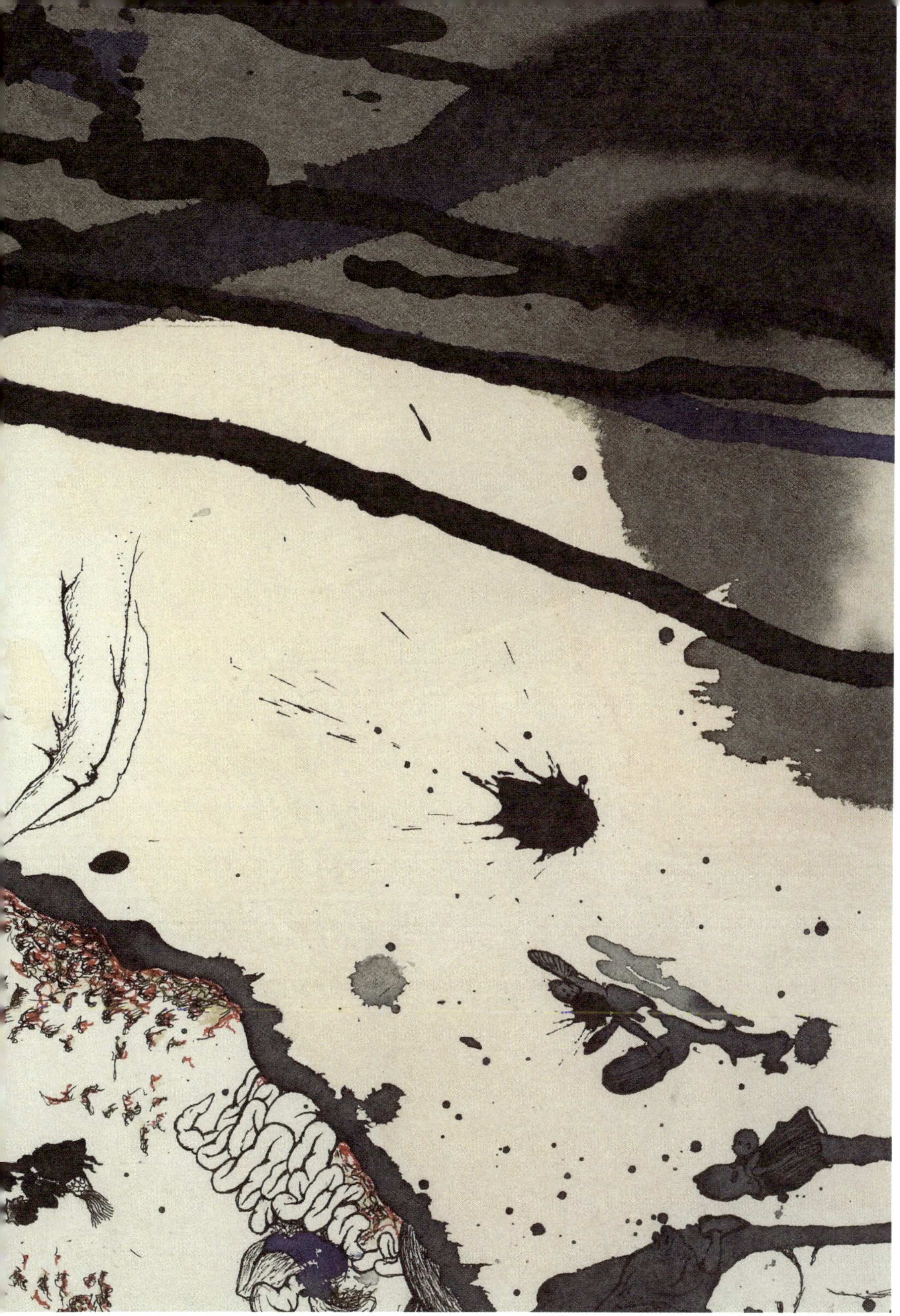

Curfew

SOIBAM HARIPRIYA

Curfew and rains,
and you are home
thinking slowly
of how life evades you.
There is a half written poem.
There is a bawling baby on the bed.
There is the rain still;
you want to watch the rain.
You want to run in the rain,
but there is no romance to it –
just the notion of motion,
an indulgence but a necessity,
an acknowledgement
you were once a person
who ran into rain showers
before you became
a pair of milch breasts.
Do you want to cut them off,
place them in cups and run away?
You are scared of such thoughts.
You are scared of the what-ifs.
What if your wishful thinking
gives you a malady
and you have to cut them off?
give up a part of yourself,
give up your flesh
because it has become your enemy?
Biology is your arch enemy.
There is on the table, a book
you began reading so long ago.
You've already forgotten the beginning.
You know that each time you have time
you'll have to begin at beginning.
There are several such books –
You know the beginnings of each
and the endings of none.

from the streets: women hawkers in shillong

GERTRUDE LAMARE

The issue of hawking has emerged as a central point of public debate in Meghalaya in recent years; this has happened as a result of legal interventions by the state and the responses of hawkers' movements to these. State intervention is not a new phenomenon. In fact, hawkers and street vendors in Shillong city and other urban centres of Meghalaya have had a historically antagonistic relationship with the Shillong Municipal Board and the police. Often, the conflict revolves around the two parties' opposing views on the idea of "public space" and the question of the rights of hawkers to this space. The confrontations faced by hawkers in Meghalaya are similar to those experienced by hawkers nationally and indeed globally. Such confrontations with authority are experienced by street businesses in third-world and first-world cities alike. However, what is unique about the hawker population in Meghalaya, more specifically in Shillong, is the huge presence of women hawkers, who constitute 68 per cent of the total number.[1] In this essay I examine this particular dimension of the hawkers in Meghalaya, documenting as well as analysing their positions and experiences as they are pitted against the patriarchal dominance of public spaces and aggressive state machinery.

1. The percentage from a recent membership drive of hawkers organised by the Meghalaya and Greater Shillong Hawkers and Street Vendors Association.

Context

Before moving on to my main argument, I shall briefly elaborate on the recent history of hawking in Meghalaya, for a clearer understanding of the current context. On the one hand, there is the Meghalaya government's implementation of the Meghalaya Street Vendors (Protection of Livelihood and Regulation of Street Vending) Act, 2014. This came in December 2014, a few months after the Central Government's Act on the same issue was passed.[2] On the other hand, there was the widespread organization of the hawker community in 2016 which resulted in the formation of the Meghalaya and Greater Shillong Hawkers and Street Vendors Association (MGSHSVA). At this juncture, it is also important to mention the ongoing case at the Meghalaya High Court, *E. H. Chen and ors v/s State of Meghalaya*, later impleaded by the MGSHSVA as third party in November 2016. This case is monumental in the larger framework of the hawkers' situation in the state because in the past two years, the various evolving orders of the High Court have been instrumental in determining the practice of hawking all over Meghalaya. The swift arrival of the state Act (2014) is not a cause for celebration for hawkers in Shillong primarily because it was this legislation that strategically removed many provisions of the central law which sought to offer reasonable protection of their businesses. Some of these were: (a) a substantial reduction in the representative membership of hawkers in the Town Vending Committee from 40 per cent of the total members (as specified in the central law) to the suspicious "not less than 2 members" (as specified in the state law) regardless of the size of the TVC, (b) the non-availability of a criterion through which the "holding capacity" of a vending zone is to be defined and (c) the removal of key terms like "natural markets" and "heritage markets" which the central law has identified as spaces where "sellers and buyers have traditionally congregated for the sale and purchase of products or services and has been determined as such by the local authority" and hence are areas which cannot be declared "non-vending zones." Through a hawkers' rights campaign that was first launched by a collective called Thma U Rangli-Juki (TUR), the hawker community in Shillong and other adjoining market areas began to organize themselves and collectively demand the amendment of the Meghalaya law and the implementation of the central law on hawking; the latter would ensure immediate relief to the hawkers from the plethora of unrestricted and indiscriminate eviction drives by the state authorities. The repeated negotiations with the government and the High Court have so far been futile, and the hawkers continue to be met with antagonism and even violence from the state apparatus.

2. Street Vendors (Protection of Livelihood and Regulation of Street Vending) Act, 2014

Hawkers and Cities

The question of hawkers' rights in the twenty-first century is located at the centre of social and philosophical debates about the idea of the city and the "urban". The history of hawkers' movements has been intrinsically linked to the politics of the city, and to the changing processes of urban planning and urbanisation together, not just in other Indian cities but the world over. Within the discourse of hawking is the contestation of space and the clash of various ideas of business, hygiene and urban aesthetics. In fact, in Meghalaya, the discourse of hawking has interestingly subsumed even the conflict between the hawkers' "right to earn a livelihood" and the pedestrians' "right to walk freely". The hawkers' movement in Meghalaya is thus not only pitched against the antagonistic manifestation of the state but also a large part of the public. When Thma U Rangli-Juki, of which I am also a member, launched the hawkers' campaign, there were a series of articles and Letters to Editors in many local newspapers by citizens who articulated the need for hawkers' eviction from certain locations. The dominant narrative from the public against hawkers primarily revolved around arguments like congestion of streets and the lack of cleanliness of roads and markets. Both points raised here seem to hint at a lack of awareness, not only of the lived reality of the streets but also the basic responsibilities of state and non-state actors in public spaces. A letter to the editor, published in *The Shillong Times*, dated 29 June 2016 reads:

> Anyone of these so-called champions should walk up and down the stretch between Motphran (Bara Bazar) area up to Police Bazar and see for themselves whether pedestrians are able to walk freely in the crowded midst of cars, buses, vendors and beggars all around. Another point to make is, a number of these vendors on the road have doubtful antecedents and many, I presume, are illegal Bangladeshi migrants from parts of Assam and across the border. Can representatives of TUR and other champions verify this or what responsibility do they have towards social security? None pay taxes to the municipality or to the KHADC while those who rightfully have a shop on the same stretch continue to pay taxes of all hues.[3]

The writer seems to lack clarity about what causes congestion — cars, hawkers or beggars; he also confidently plunges into an irresponsible, unsubstantiated assumption that not only are the hawkers troublesome but perhaps more so because the majority of them are "Bangaladeshi immigrants". Thus, the streets of Shillong cannot by any means be for non-tax-paying lower-income citizens, let alone non-citizens or "outsiders". Interestingly, the membership registration drive that Thma U Rangli-Juki have been conducting for a year now, along with the MGSPHSVA, has recorded no Bangladeshi candidate so far. I will get back to this question of ethnicity later.

3. Wankhar, *The Shillong Times*, December 2016

When one travels in Shillong, the primary source of worry is often the dread of being stuck in horrible traffic jams. Several reports have categorically underlined the upsurge in the numbers of automobiles in Shillong, a city where road construction is severely limited by the hilly terrain, making roads steep and narrow. A report published in 2013 by Centre for Science and Environment critiqued the pro-car policies of Meghalaya and emphasized the need to improve public transport and pedestrian infrastructure instead. Another report by the Centre for North-East Studies and Policy Research at Jamia Millia University published in 2011, also put forth the same observations and even detailed the vehicular traffic density: "Likewise in Shillong, Malki Point has the highest traffic intensity of 90 vehicles per minute followed by Police Bazar, (75 vehicles per minute) and Fire Brigade (70 vehicles per minute)."[4]

These studies raise very serious doubts about the argument of congestion being created by hawkers when most of the available public space in Shillong city is consumed by vehicles. Interestingly, these "right to walk" activists articulate nothing against the avalanche of cars getting onto Shillong roads every day. As for concerns over hygiene, people seem glaringly ignorant of the malfunctioning of the Shillong Municipal Board and also of the fact that most hawkers have their own systems of cleaning. Shane Thabah, General Secretary of the MGSHSVA, constantly retorts to the questioning of the press as well as the public on social media that hawkers do engage in the post-business waste disposal methods or else hire somebody to clean every evening. In fact, according to the interviews I conducted, there were many allegations that owners of the big shops in markets like Lewduh and Police Bazaar dispose of waste in the streets, for which hawkers are blamed. Pedestrians too contribute to irresponsible garbage disposal in the city and blame the hawkers for the waste epidemic of Shillong. This is just a convenient way of overlooking the larger breakdown of waste management by state authorities as well as the undeniable failure to problematize the apathetic response of civil society to it. Doesn't this constant association of the hawker with dirt disturbingly reveal a very problematic middle class perspective on how the public perceive people from the working community in Shillong city?

What is public space? The hawkers' demand for a right to conduct their businesses in a public space takes us to the heart of the urban predicament in this century. Historically speaking, a public space is one marked by open access, freedom to occupy, freedom to be and even freedom to trade. These qualities of the space are protected

4. C-NES Report on Air Pollution Released, 22nd October, 2011

by the absence of ownership by one or more individuals; space of this kind is most commonly owned by the state, thus ensuring the citizens' and public's freedom, safety and liberty within that space. Markets, streets, squares, bus stops, stations etc., all fall within the description of a public space. Hawking has always been an occupation specific to the geographical and physical precincts of the street and other kinds of public spaces in the South Asian, European and Middle-Eastern contexts. Even the legal definition of a street vendor states, "a person engaged in vending of articles, goods, wares, food items or merchandise of everyday use or offering services to the general public, in a street, lane, sidewalk, footpath, pavement, public park or any other public place or private area, from a temporary built up structure or by moving from place to place and includes hawker, peddler, squatter and all other synonymous terms which may be local or region specific."[5] Hawking is an organic element of a public space and hawkers are indeed organic specimens of its fabric.

A lot of the debates surrounding the expulsion of hawkers from city spaces are closely linked to the way twenty-first century cities are being imagined. The world over, cities are gradually losing their unique local identities as a result of being subjected to neoliberal policies which seek to make cities the breeding ground of global capital, finance, banking and trade. Adding to this is the move towards a type of urban planning which is informed by the mid-twentieth century American concept of huge shopping centres heavily shaped and designed by class and socio-economic divisions of space. This is characterized, most noticeably, by the large expansion of privatization and corporatization of land (growth of real estate, gentrification, malls, etc.,), and the subsequent transformation of the nature of public zones. Within the new imagination of the city, heavily drawn from the logic and ethos of the "global city"[6], public space is increasingly being moulded into one segregated by socio-economic backgrounds. The encroachment of big brands and chain businesses, mall phenomena, and the like in growing cities like Shillong, is redefining access and mobility, as well as the whole phenomenon of buying and selling, and social life in general in streets and neighbourhoods altogether. Public spaces are swiftly getting structured and rearranged along class lines.

5. According to The Street Vendors (Protection of Livelihood and Regulation of Street Vending) Act, 2014.

6. I borrow the concept of "global city" from Salkia Sassen who argues that the global city is one marked by "the ascendence of information technology and the associated increase in the mobility and liquidity of capital"(27). Unlike nineteenth century cities, global cities like Dubai and Miami do not function through the mediation of nation states. Their identity is shaped by global capital and information.

Like other cities in northeast India, Shillong is in a huge transformative stage, both in terms of size and character, albeit with the challenges provided by the topographical composition of the hill city. The expansion and multiplication of big businesses, local and otherwise, exists alongside the increasing migration of people from the rural areas to the city. Big businesses not only antagonise hawkers in terms of providing competition in the exchange of goods and services but also in their encroachment on spaces previously occupied by hawkers. This can be clearly observed in Laitumkhrah, Laban and other large localities in Shillong. A recently announced project funded for Rs 23 crore by the union Ministry of Housing & Urban Poverty Alleviation and flagged by the current Chief Minister, Dr. Mukul Sangma as the Polo Market Times Square project, is a plan through which he seeks to rebuild Polo Marker in the image of New York City's Times Square. Polo Market Times Square is envisioned as a marketplace with a shopping complex and widened roads, built over the demolished old Polo Market and the square which presently accommodates a huge hawker population. Dr. Sangma has also used the term "smart city"[7] to describe the project.

Polo Market Times Square is a specimen of the larger epidemic which does not overtly destroy the public space but transforms it. Polo Market, as it exists, is a hub for a very diverse population, not only in terms of class but ethnicity as well. There we find hawkers coexisting peacefully with small shops and big shops, and hawkers from various communities: Nepali, Garo, Bengali, or Khasi. Even the customer and pedestrian population is diverse here. Indeed the market requires some infrastructural renovation but to redesign it along the lines of New York's Times Square is to carelessly impose an alien concept to a space, erasing all of its local elements. The planting of huge commercial buildings would heavily alter the organic nature of socio-economic interactions in the area; apart from hawkers possibly getting removed from the market, the social composition of customers will change as well. An expulsion of hawkers who usually provide less expensive goods and services would ultimately result in a huge transformation of the social experience in these spaces. The Times Square project is a deeply flawed idea even in terms of practicality, since a Times Square in Polo would compulsorily require a complete make-over of the landscape, including the removal or shifting of one of the biggest rivers in Shillong, the Wah Umkhrah, which flows right next to the market. Government plans like these are examples of the problematic ways in which the urban is imagined in the twenty-first century in third world contexts,

7. Under the current NDA government, the Ministry of Urban Development introduced the smart city concept through the Smart Cities Mission; smart cities are ones which provide "core infrastructure and give a decent quality of life to its citizens, a clean and sustainable environment and application of 'Smart' Solutions."

where the various local situations are not even understood by the authorities. The local needs are sidelined and buried under the lofty first world dreams of the leaders. The non-inclusive nature of a space like Polo Market Times Square would not only dismantle the culture of open markets which freely accommodate hawkers and people from all kinds of socio-economic backgrounds, but would also perpetuate a different kind of market and public space experience, dictated largely by a capitalist ethos.

The rhetoric of livelihood emerges as a real and pressing thrust in the debate about hawking in Meghalaya. In fact, it is quite fascinating that in third world cities, hawking has been very efficient in directly addressing the predicament of job scarcity in the formal sector. Contrary to what many people assume, hawkers heavily contribute to state and national income. Their businesses are very much actors in the national economy and the larger flow of goods and services.

There is also the phenomenon of intra-state migration in Meghalaya, especially to Shillong, because a huge percentage of the hawker population are people who have moved to the city in the past decade for reasons such as agricultural failure, quest for different occupations and sources of livelihood and the like. The informal sector in general and hawking in particular have become crucial avenues through which unemployment and poverty in the state have been curtailed. Several reports, including a survey conducted by *IndiaSpend.in* of 2016 which highlights Meghalaya's high growth rate of 9.7 per cent also attributes the relatively high employment percentage of the state to the informal centre.[8] The phenomenon of hawking is thus deeply embroiled in the web of all these socio-economic situations in the state of Meghalaya.

Domestic v/s the Street

Although there are many parallels in the conditions, confrontations, histories and experiences of hawkers in Shillong and those in other cities, there are a few characteristics specific to Shillong. As mentioned earlier, a large part of the hawker population consists of women. This adds an interesting dimension to the hawking politics in the city. Hawking is a profession which pulls women out of domestic space and places them at the very crux of the public space - the street. While women hawkers make use of the democratic principle of the public space, they also challenge its historical and cross-cultural gendered quality. As we know, public space has always been marked by male domination as opposed to the private, which is identified with

8. "India's Fastest-growing State: Meghalaya (And Other Northeast Surprises)" published in *www.indiaspend.com*

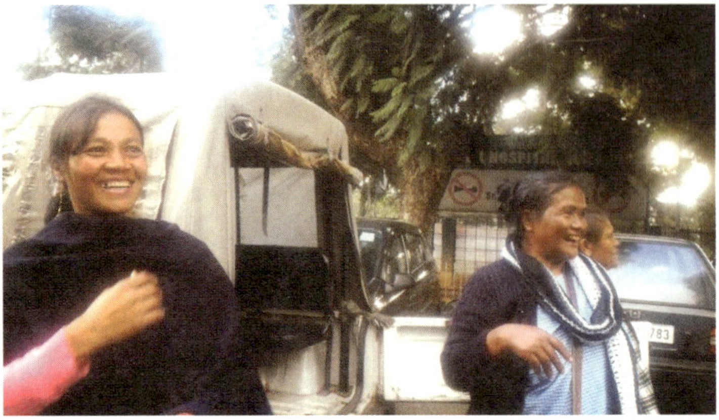

Saralin Pariat and Ribalin Pariat

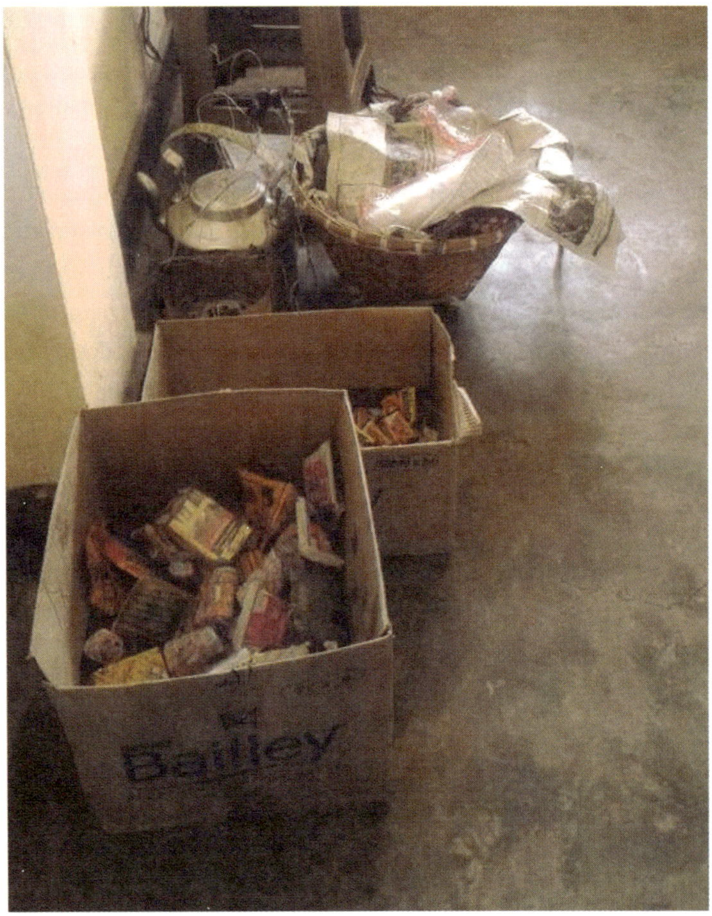

Goods belonging to Ribalin, Saralin and Idraini, which were seized by the Municipal staff, displayed at the police station. These were never returned to them.

women. The relationship of these women with public space is hence very fascinating in the context of a patriarchal and potentially violent world. In fact, the presence of women hawkers in the streets plays a huge role in creating a safe and secure space for pedestrians in these spaces. Further, hawking engenders a sense of economic independence and firm entrepreneurial experience. The choice of hawking (as opposed to being a part of the domestic service sector in cities and urban centres), by working class women is often deliberately made to avoid having an authority figure at work, to escape being part of a systemic workplace hierarchy and in the process maintain a clearer ownership of their own labour. The site of the reclamation of labour is a male-dominated space — the street — one which houses many elements of patriarchal violence, both coming from the state and the public, which qualify as direct threats to the safety and well-being of women hawkers. The act of women hawking is a strong challenge to the association of work with men, the kind of work removed from the domestic and rooted very centrally to the public platform of economic and cultural exchange — the street. Here, women become the non-peripheralized active subjects who impact the movement of goods and services in Meghalaya and who greatly contribute to the state and national economy as well.

Saralin Lyngdoh (on the left) and Ribalin Pariat (on the far right) sell kwai, cigarettes, bidis and various paan masalas at the Shillong Civil Hospital entrance. Idralni Syiemiong (the one in the middle) sells tea and snacks. This was 30 November 2016, the day they were picked up by the police and taken to Laban Police Station. On 26 November 2016, the Meghalaya High Court passed a "status quo" order, thereby not relieving the threat of hawkers' eviction. The three women were picked up under this order. By this point, members of MGSHSVA and TUR were already alert, because hawkers across the city were being evicted, taken to police stations or their goods seized, most times without them being returned. When the three women were taken to the police station that day, I rushed there to ensure that they were not locked in and also to see that the municipal staff did not take away the goods. Everything was done relatively smoothly that day but the next morning, we woke up to the news in local dailies of FIRs being filed against the three women by the municipal staff for having "resisted arrest".

Here in the first picture, the beaming faces of the women hawkers are a result of the sight of their children, most of whom are adolescents, at the Shillong Civil hospital compound, where the three women were brought back for the mandatory police medical examination. The children, after their mothers were arrested, took over the businesses for that day and continued selling the remaining items.

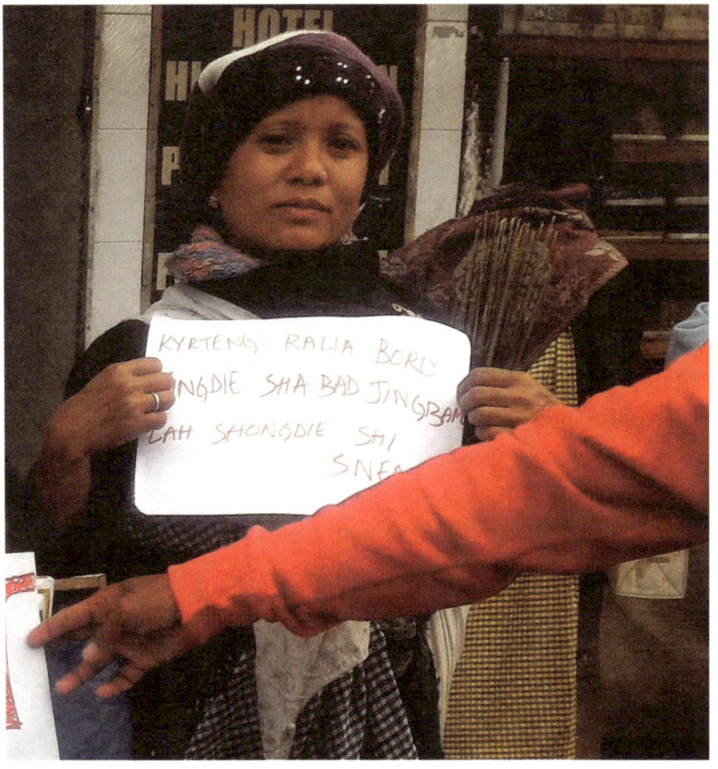

Ralia Boro

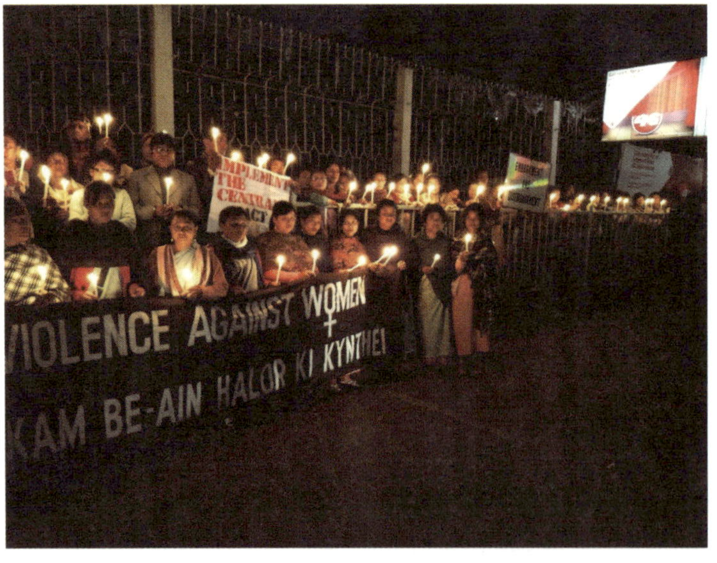

The Violence Against Women Hawkers Protest at Police Bazaar, Shillong on December 6, 2016

Now all three women have stopped setting up shop and carry their goods in small baskets, usually hung around their necks. This provides them with easy mobility and also helps them escape the accusation of "obstruction of pedestrian and car movement" from the authorities, a provision even the law and court order cites to legitimise an arrest. However, despite not having defied either, the police, along with officials of the Shillong Municipal Board still arrested them. Hawkers at the Shillong Civil Hospital provide an immensely important service, not only to hospital visitors but also to the workers. Having accompanied them to the hospital, I was very amused to see an intimacy between the three women and the doctors who examined them. They gleefully told me that the nurses and doctors in the examination room would order tea, kwai and other kinds of tobacco products from them.

Ralia Boro is a Nepali woman who sets up shop at Police Point, Laitumkhrah, Shillong at 5 in the morning and sells tea and snacks. Ralia's primary customers are people working nights in nearby hospitals, or the families of patients and also morning walkers and joggers from time to time, who without her, would have almost nothing else to eat at that hour. Ralia closes shop at 8AM, after which she goes home to take care of her children. "This is what I do," she says. "I only sleep for four or five hours every night because I have to prepare the snacks to be sold the next day. I wake up at 4AM to prepare the tea and make sure I leave by 4:30AM to get here at 5AM. It's hard but I have no choice, and once I'm here, once I start selling, I'm quite happy about it even if it is very early in the morning." In times of rain, which is often, Ralia says she uses a blue plastic sheet as shelter, that which she suspends on sticks; under this canopy, tea-drinkers gather in the wee hours of the morning to quench their thirst for the brew. Interestingly, the presence of women hawkers like Ralia at this time of the day makes the street a little bit more welcoming to women pedestrians and also children who go for morning walks and runs. In a way, the claiming of the street by women hawkers effectively leads to its claiming by women members of the public as well.

In the past year, Meghalaya, a state largely known for the matrilineal indigenous communities of the Khasis, Garos and Jaintias, has been in the limelight for the upsurge of reported cases of crimes against women. The popular notion that women in the state are empowered, and do not bear any gender-centric hurdles in everyday life, was thrown into question by these incidents. In response to this phenomenon, the Hawkers Association organized a public candlelight gathering at Police Bazaar on 6 December, 2016. The event was not only a strong statement against violence against women in general but also against the abuse of women hawkers by the state authorities. Women hawkers from different communities spoke up and were united on the issue of the violence unleashed against them by police officers and municipal staff. The speeches also touched upon the right of women hawkers to sell, as it is their only source of livelihood; several of them spoke about the fact that they were the sole bread-earners of their families and that the prohibition to hawk is a direct assault on the lifeline of their families and their individual economic autonomy as women.

The hawkers' movement has been and continues to be one of the most powerful grassroots struggles in Meghalaya, one which has incorporated intersectional politics at its core. MGSHSVA's fight for hawking rights and freedom includes within it women's demand for economic independence, equality, safety and access to public space. Moreover, the Association is representative of a principle of inclusiveness because it has embraced people of various religious and ethnic backgrounds as well. Indeed the emergence of MGSHSVA is of colossal importance in the larger political landscape of Meghalaya because for once, the thrust of the political energy does not reside on identity politics and instead, issues of gender and class have been allowed to define and redefine the texture and direction of the movement.

untitled

ZUBENI LOTHA

FROM THE SERIES "DIMAPUR 797112"

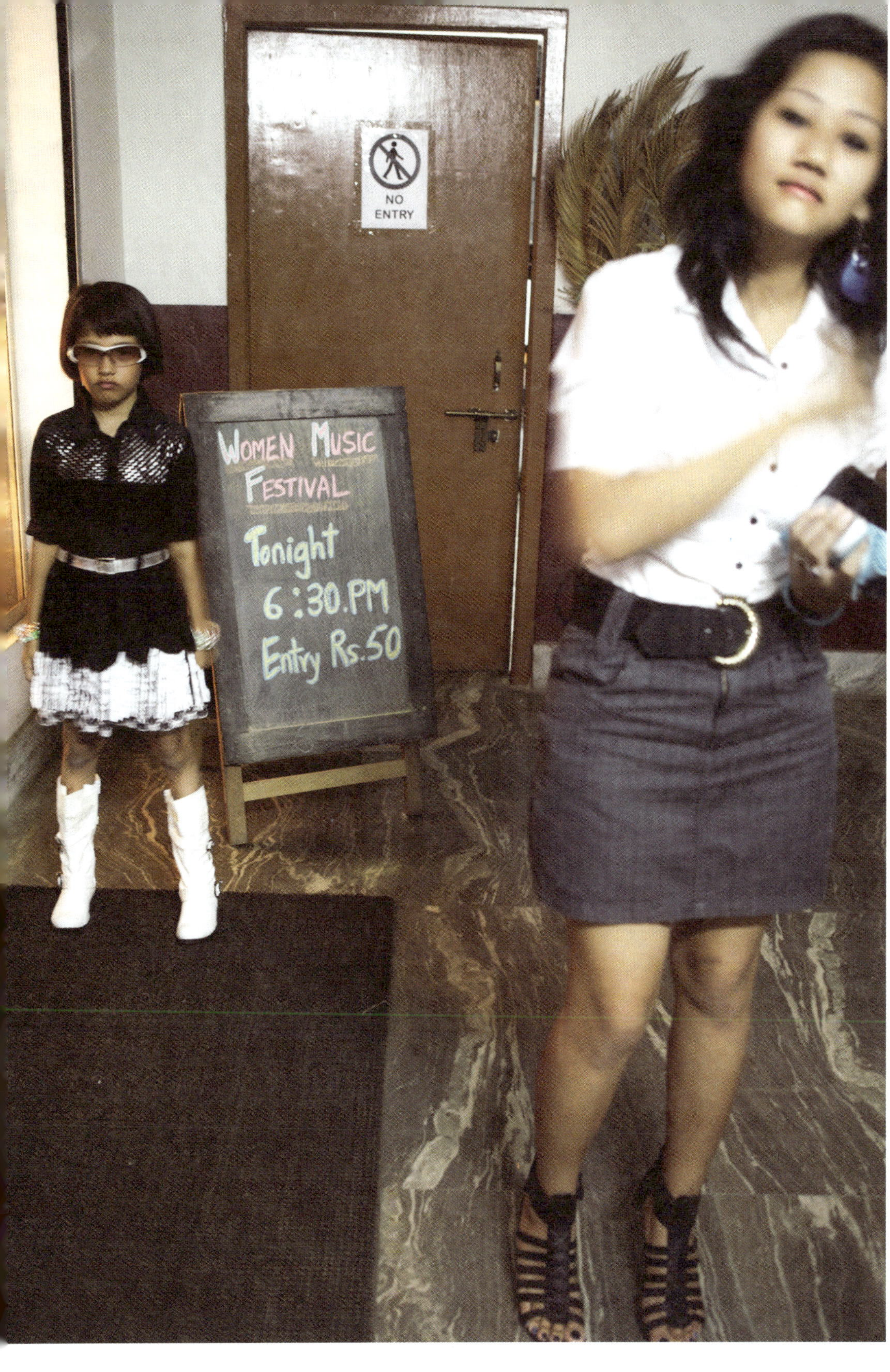
NO ENTRY
WOMEN MUSIC FESTIVAL
Tonight
6:30.PM
Entry Rs.50

transit work

SOIBAM HARIPRIYA

The sky is blue
from the glass airport wall.
I do not know
if it is actually blue
or superimposed from many such
similar scenes.
Maybe blue is just a nice backdrop
for goodbyes and arrivals
and temporary embraces
of all sorts.
I hold a book;
I am not reading.
I am writing
a paper napkin poem
about the janitor's heart
heavier than luggage;
this woman
whose workplace
is a toilet
accumulates the disdain
of sundry passengers.

II

A middle aged man
staggers to the woman
at the Air India counter.
'Madam you are beautiful.'
She hates it.
Hates it.
Smiles and says
'Thank you.'

III

People peopling the evening
after-work hours.
Is there an hour after work though?

hands that brew

RINI BARMAN

When I enter Upar Deori Gaon, it is only the cattle and birds under bamboo groves that are at leisure. Situated 12.5 kms to the north-west of Jorhat, its landscape is surrounded by four frontiers. To its north lie the majestic Brahmaputra and Kareng Sapori and to its south, Elengmara and Sonarigaon. Deka Sattra Bhakot Sapori and Naamdeori Gaon border it on the east and west respectively. The womenfolk here are constantly occupied with chores like feeding the pigs, sweeping the muddy courtyard, and various types of kitchen work. Accomplishing a day's aggregate labour with sweat brings solace to their families, the monotony of which they cynically call "letha". Words in Deori language, with its Tibeto-Burma origins, have also fused with Assamese, and as such, a lot of Deoris are fluent speakers of both languages. Letha is one of those nuanced words which has a range of meanings: work, embarrassment, encumbrance, responsibility, trouble and so on. No wonder, then, that it is used to denote the act of menstruation as well. To the average patriarch, all this — and more — is the baggage that comes with menses.

The act of brewing rice beer, too, comes with a wide range of implications—moral, economic, social, even sexual. In years gone by, pitchers of good rice beer have been the company of many Deori women after tedious work hours. The relaxing drink is locally called suzen and in the course of my conversations, I saw how carefully women present it to the males in the household. The dominant belief is that traditional drinks ought to be preserved unadulterated and the onus of doing this lies with the women. Although urban mobility has changed the roles of women, a new Deori bride has to be taught the skill of brewing; it is not something she can choose "not to learn". In lieu of the custom of bride price in tribal societies, it is imperative that labour be rewarded when weddings are fixed. Deori fathers, who typically head the house, believe that women not only keep the fire burning at home but are seldom thanked for the rigorous chores they do within the confines of the house.

While traditional drinks are eulogised as repositories of culture to visiting guests and outsiders, I have had the privilege of seeing some of the less romantic aspects of this practice. In this essay I would like to address the complexity of female labour in the making of rice beer across three tribal societies, Deori, Mishing and Adivasi, in Jorhat. Female labour is extracted not necessarily by force or violence, but vis-à-vis the nostalgic retreat to one's ancient past. Elderly women and grandmothers have perfected the art of preserving rice beer, in pots and in folk stories. For them, this creates an alternative knowledge system, in scattered sites of gossip, away from the systematic genealogy which their males have internalised, largely by coming to terms with the Assam intelligentsia. To this effect, these women may not know their individual ages accurately, but when it comes to estimating ingredients for rice beer, they are inimitable geniuses. This fact has often been used to exploit women. The local beer is made from rice, and rice is also the staple food. This becomes the reason for many conflicts related to food security and labour. By definition, a 'staple food' is something essential to your survival — and rice is precisely that. At the same time, it is the main source for making beer. When male family members get addicted, larger quantities of rice need to be used for making alcohol, leaving less and less for consuming food. This becomes a vicious cycle.

I

From a clean, washed Dison (pitcher), Jinti Deori hands me a cup of suzen and continues to filter a large amount in anticipation of other guests. It is thick and pale white in colour, quite different from the rice beers I had tried before. Jinti explains the intricate process of fermentation for the preparation of suzen — it is largely dependent on the procuring of medicinal plants. "First we grind the herbs with rice powder to make the balls of rice cakes. The dheki is used for a fine crush. When the rice cakes, known as the Perankusuri, dry up, rice is boiled and mixed with the yeast cake. It is kept aside undisturbed. After a week, we taste it; it requires experience to be a good judge of the taste. Thereafter we remove it from the dola, (bamboo tray) and a distinct smell shows us the way. If the mixture gets spoilt, we are cautioned from the dola stage itself."

A resident of Upar Deori Gaon, 29-year-old Jinti Deori often goes with her sisters-in-law to pick herbs in the wild and also helps prepare the brew. She's a strapping, healthy woman, but her hands are wrinkled. She had a witty comeback to my question of how many hours of work she puts in on a daily basis. "Bosoror barota maahot terota xakaam kora" which translates into "In twelve months, we, the Deoris, observe thirteen festivals!"

In the days of yore, suzen was used as an offering to the Deori gods. In festivals like Bihu, this custom is still visible and venerated. Some people call it Deo-ras (elixir of the gods). It is tough to exactly say how a sacred ritual began to occupy a domestic space among the Deori tribes. In the case of neighbouring Arunachal Pradesh, Mamang Dai's *Mountain Harvest* (2005) tells us that existing folk narratives point out that mankind assisted the gods and acquired the expertise of making rice beer. The family head is served suzen on first day of Bihu; he must approve of the taste, for things to not go haywire.

Jinti is familiar with most medicinal plants required for the process and can't recollect the ones she knows only by appearance. Jura, Romakhaku, Bonjaluk, Jomlakhoti, Kothal leaf, Jibasi lota... the list is endless. An elderly lady of her house joins us; she begins to list a few more. "Sharing herbs is very common, in the past we would fetch around 108 medicinal plants," she says, "but with deforestation, wild plants aren't available that easily anymore". Similarly, they used to brew 40-50 kg of rice in the time of their forefathers, but this has gone down now. The women tell me that bora saul and motong saul taste better, the former being famous for its sweet flavour. For storage purposes, Jinti's mother-in-law uses the pitcher but Jinti herself prefers plastic vessels for better longevity. In fact, I was quite astonished to see this in a lot of other Deori houses too; older clay vessels have been replaced by plastic.

In *Deorilukar Sanskritir Ruprekha* (2009), Nandeswar Deori writes, "According to older women who are more experienced, in order to make the perfect suzen, a total of 101 herbs (bon-dorop) are necessary. Purity of mind and soul is very essential to prevent the concoction from getting spoilt." Women in Jinti's age group showed concern for the scarcity of herbs. Venturing out to the forest for collecting herbs breaks the monotony, albeit temporarily, of their everyday chores. They carry their bags and their children along with them. Many fields in their area have been taken over for building houses; additionally, frequent floods drown the small plants they need. Jinti's brother-in-law too helps occasionally with the herbs. The task of brewing suzen comes with certain responsibilities. Climate change and natural disasters are constant challenges—adverse weather can upset the brewer's best laid plans. The female brewers in Naam Deori Gaon (naam implying "lower" Deori village) are the worst affected.

Jinti took me to meet one such brewer about 2.5 kms away, who has come to her native village. She is more than fifty years old, and her stern eyes have the spark of a matriarch. Back home, she has taught her daughters-in-law how to meticulously brew suzen. As I sit comfortably on her bamboo-stilted kitchen floor, I see that I have interrupted her from peeling vegetables and areca nuts. "Here, have some suzen, it's freshly made," she says. Even before I can refuse, she laughs and says quickly, "Our guests will ridicule us if we cannot serve suzen. It has become a rule, even when we have a bride from a different tribe, Ahom, Kachari, or Chutiya, she has to mix with us and in due course, pick up the skill of making rice beer."

Every brewer is keen on exploring the most fresh and unique plants that are available. Nothing fits the bill better than yeast cultured from medicinal plants. The women bond over the vagaries of brewing, using their collective wisdom to optimize the process. "During winter it's convenient, but in summer, we get tired easily. On rainy days, we dry our cakes on the stove (in dhuasang), even share a few cakes to be dried elsewhere, the vapour and heat ease the process. We meet often for herb collection, and tease each other about the strength of the alcohol— did it have the target result or not [laughs]. It is always better if there is someone to co-operate because every hand can lend its own flavour."

It is widely believed here that rice beer offers plenty of health benefits. It removes urinary troubles, cures gastric problems, and keeps the body cool during humid summers. The women claimed from experience that the medicinal plants used in its preparation are cures for malaria, cholera and even menstrual pain. When Jinti was nursing her child, little drops of suzen would help her baby suckle breast milk with ease. "Older rice cake remains are mixed often, it makes the work easier. The sturdier the cake is, the better it is. With experience, we can even measure the strength of the final product through smell — we don't even have to taste it, our nasal instincts have become so strong!"

Ela Bhatt, the founder of Self-Employed Women's Association (SEWA), the world's largest trade union for economically backward and unorganized women workers in India, had revealed to *Quartz* that the female labour participation rate is roughly 27 per cent in India. A host of economic reasons aside, she points out how female labour that goes into tasks like milking a cow isn't regarded as economic activity though it adds to the GDP. "For those women, the perception is that this kind of work is not work, because men do not perceive this kind of work as a job," she states. For the Deori women, unrecognized and unrewarded labour such as brewing suzen and much more is just another way of life. They are also expert weavers of the gamusa, with which they cover their heads with as a mark of respect. It appears that the dominant masculine perceptions of labour are responsible for limiting employment opportunities for women in rural areas. For the Deori women in this village who go out to schools to work, it doesn't affect the distribution of labour as the domestic space is still the women's to take care of. Male involvement in chores is very marginal.

II

About 3–4 kms from Upar Deori Gaon, in the dense interiors lies a Mishing village. By the time I reach Mishing Gaon, it's close to dusk and I see many young women riding back from school on their bicycles. "The LP School nearby has a field that becomes a water pool on rainy days, you did well by walking to arrive here", says Mrs. Biju Doley (44), a kind host who agreed to show me local beer preparations the following day. I rest with her children in their sang ghor, a raised stilted hut, and the delicious pork dinner keeps us all warm.

Early next morning, Biju introduces me to her female companions—mischief makers—and excellent apong brewers. Apong being their signature local drink, it has acquired a larger-than-life status in their festivities and rituals. All of them are young mothers (aged around 18-20), carrying yelling infants on their shoulders and hips. They have accepted that domestic chores are their department and that even though men can learn how to brew, they do not do so. There are two kinds of apong: Nogin and Po:ro. For the Nogin apong, starter cakes called E'pob are made by crushing rice with medicinal plants, each providing a unique health quotient (and sweetness) to the drink. Biju also tells me that some flowers are used, though she doesn't know their names. Cooked rice is laid out on leaves of banana or bamboo and after it cools, crushed E'pob is added to the rice. Then the entire mixture is put inside a pitcher or a plastic drum, the latter more commonly visible these days. I am told that in summer it may take upto 5–6 days for a proper fermentation. After that the mixture is filtered and the waste is used as pig or poultry fodder.

Mili Pegu, a young woman of about 20, shows me her fermented drums full of rice beer ingredients. They are covered carefully with bih-dhekia (*Cyclosorus dentatus*) leaves that form the upper layer of the mix. One of the drums contains black coloured rice; it is kept separately because this recipe is slightly more demanding and labour intensive than Nogin apong. Also known as Sai Mod (Sai=ashes/Mod=liquor), Po:ro apong is best for the winter; Mili tells me that it does wonders in healing urinary tract infections. She comments, "The ash needs to be collected with an expert hand after burning rice husk and dried rice straw. It tends to scatter easily, on windy days, it is very challenging. Thereafter, it is mixed with cooked rice and E'pob — say, a 6cm

× 3cm cake for half kilo of rice, with variations as per choice. Filtration is done by using a conical bamboo basket generally lined on its surface with banana leaves."

Biju and Mili both agree that it was after their marriages that they learnt how to brew apong. As Mili's sister-in-law joins us, they tell me in chorus that in their natal homes, they picked up the rudiments of the process by observing their mothers brewing. But, they hardly ever participated in the task, *"jiwori kalot eman kora nohoi"*. These experiences further throw light on how knowledge and labour skills are passed down orally and transmitted by women in order to facilitate the larger network of patriarchy, which they imagine holds them together. They act as mediators for community subsistence; brewing beer acts as a cathartic outlet from their everyday tasks. But, it can also be argued that such outlets are "permissible" only because any complete subversion might be crushed. In that respect, merry women producing better beer is a part of myth-making. Forms of carnival laughter[1] such as this, are made available to women only temporarily because the fruition of counter-knowledge in the process is perceived as the real threat.

When the women come together, there are small moments of transgression. Biju says, "In folk festivities, when the pressure is higher, we brew together to divide the labour." Sisters from Majuli, Dergaon and other places fetch the herbs for the one who is too bogged down by chores to do so. "Even at 44, I am sturdy enough to go and cut firewood, not to mention that the urban ladies who come for Ali-i-ligang[2] order Sai Mod secretly. I have a fair share of fans from the city..."she laughs.

It is usually believed that merry minds can brew better apong. So Biju and her companions remain in good humour while picking herbs. Plant knowledge and awareness is shared en route to the forest; herb gathering effectively allows an outlet from other kinds of laborious work. This is an area where women have mastered their skills with lived realities providing them better modes of survival as opposed to textual/formal learning (where there is hardly any room for teaching domestic skills). Their voices seep through these little uncared-for areas like picking herbs, making it a subterranean exercise of power.

Other rules include keeping sour or bitter fruits, greens and menstruating women at bay, all of which are believed to turn the drink sour. Women are supposed to refrain from eating sour or bitter fruits and even farting while brewing. Biju says, "Initially, menstruating women were supposed to rest hence they were kept from working, but

1. Mikhal Bakhtin, *Rabelais and his world* (1965)

2. Harvest festival held on the first Wednesday of the month of Phalgun (spring).

gradually this fact became more stringent, with the rest factor taking a backseat. Now my husband is irritated when I menstruate for he has to help with chores. All these taboos are directly connected to the larger spectrum of gastronomic beliefs about purity and pollution." It is worth noting that I got easy access to kitchen space, because I was "clean" and the women did ask me *that* question as I got closer.

Apong khaute tika uluwa or to be bare-assed while consuming apong is a popular idiom among the Mishings—it alludes to the capacity of liquor to reveal the naked truth, as it were. Repeatedly invoked in varied forms by Mishing women, the metaphor of nakedness provides a window to how liquor came to be ostracised in the attire of an imported colonial modernity. The private–public divide has also been influenced with the colonial encounter. For instance, in the Dobur Puja, where Mishings worship their ancestors for curing diseases, apong is brewed by men. Villagers believe that if women are allowed to brew in public, it will make the gods angry. Female labour participation is therefore restricted and this ritual substantiates the rift between the public and the private.

Ratneswar Mili refers to a Mishing folk song in "Mishing Loka Xadya"[3], which stresses the importance of apong by alluding to the "taste" of wooing women. In fact, a large number of Mishing women told me that eloping with one's lover while drunk is hardly surprising:

> *Bohut paani khaleyu*
> *Apong khuwar spriha beleg*
> *Bohut suwali dekha paleyu*
> *Tumak suwar spriha beleg*
>
> I have drunk myself a river,
> But getting drunk on apong tastes out of the world,
> I may have wooed a thousand girls,
> But wooing you tastes out of the world.

It is interesting to observe subversions by the women themselves in real life as opposed to the women being invoked in poetry and folk songs such as the one mentioned above. To an outsider, who is unfamiliar with the context of apong, these idioms and riddles act as a permanent conundrum. I recall one such situation, present in one of the first novels in Assamese about the Mishings[4] — called *Miri Jiyori* — written by Rajani Kanta Bordoloi in 1892. This epic love story about Panei and Jonkey looks at the structure of

3. From Angsuman Sarma, "Axomor Janagusthiyo Loka Xadya"

4. It is very clear that Bordoloi's position is that of an observer who documents the cultural life of Mishings, which places him outside of the system.

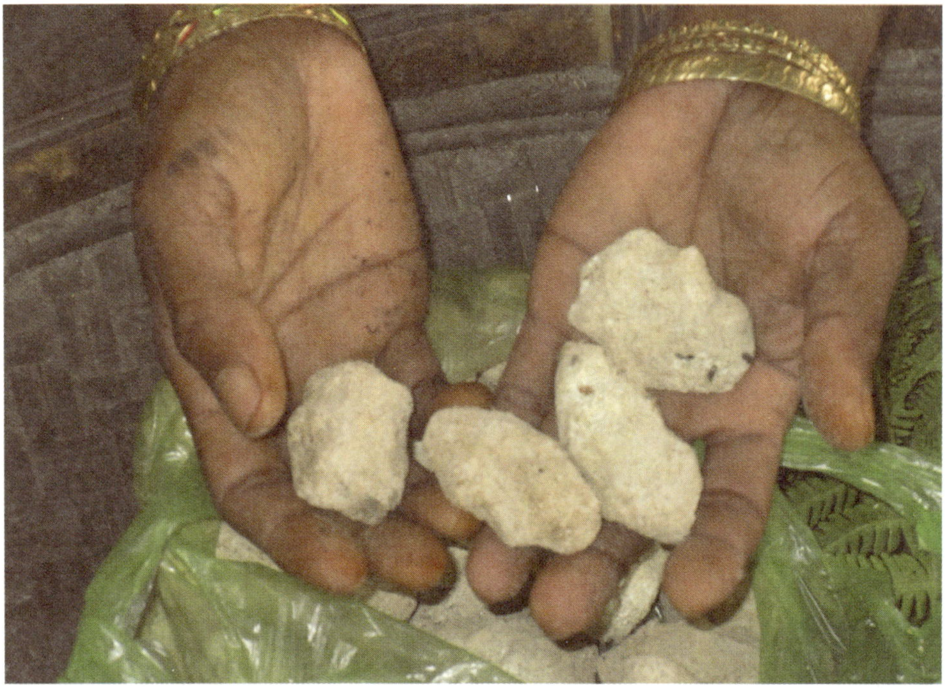

Biju holding her mod pitha or dorop (medicinal rice-beer cake)

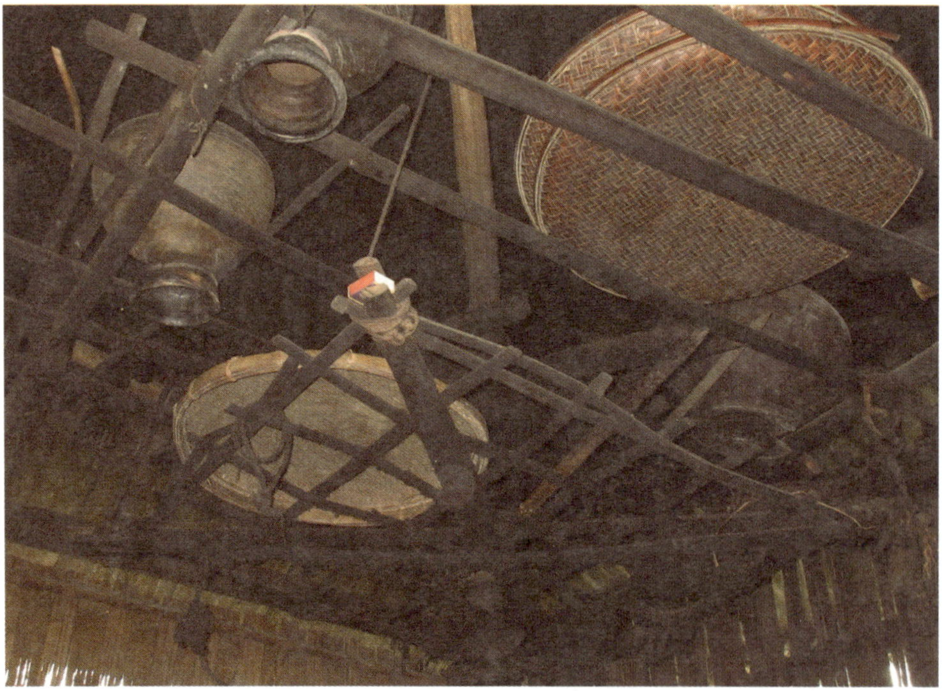

The dhuasang above the clay-stove or where the rice beer cakes are dried on rainy days in a Deori house

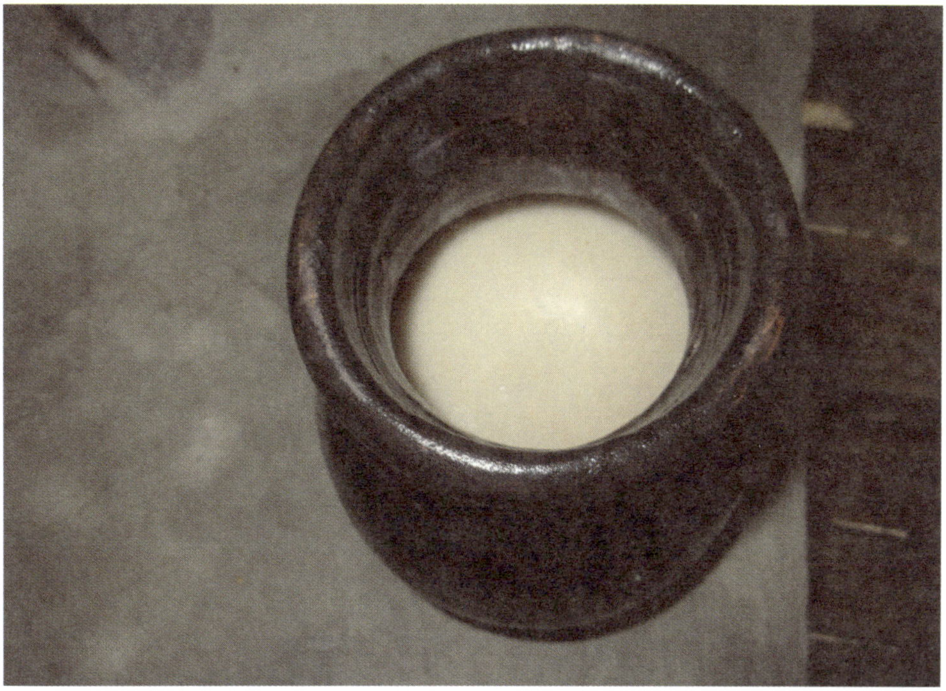

Thick, flavourful suzen ready to be served

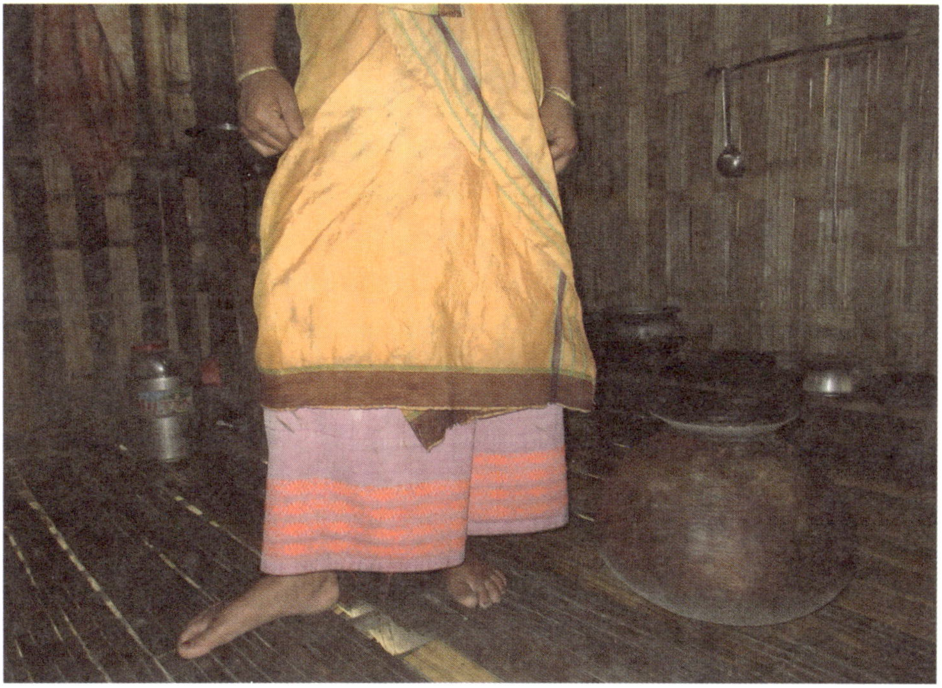

Jinti, in her traditional Deori attire, standing beside her kitchenware

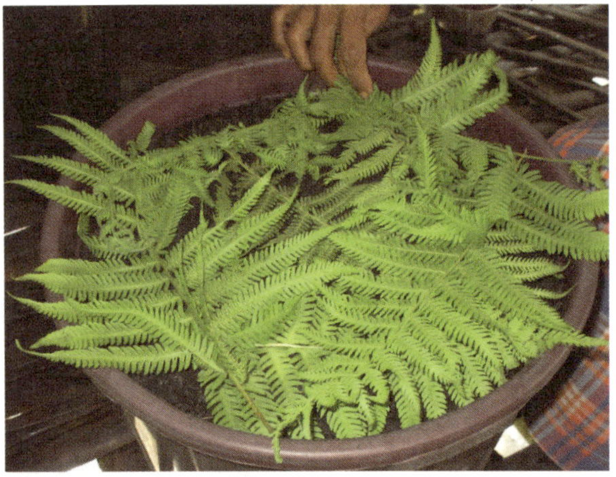

Sai-mod requirements in a drum preserved with bih-dhekia at Mishing-gaon

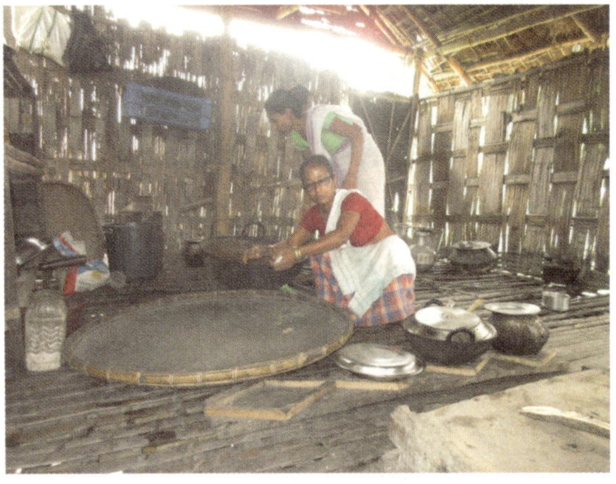

A glimpse of Mishing women at work

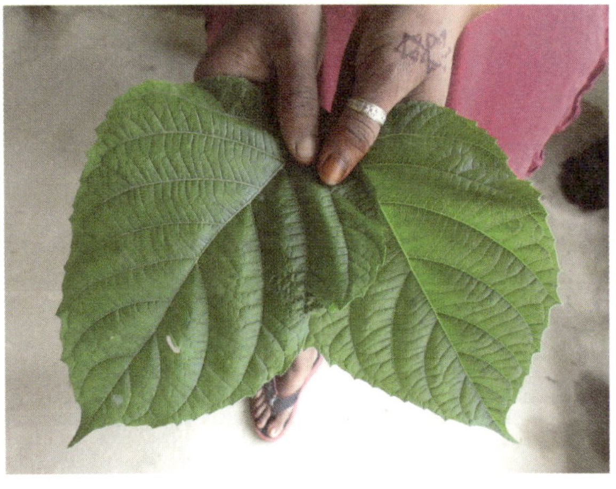

Bhatou-paat (parrot-coloured leaves) used for making the haria starter cake

civil society in those days. In chapter 13, Panei, the miri damsel, has to flee from the clutches of a "proper Babu" (who is not the "rustic type"and "consumes English liquor"). He takes it for granted that because she consumes her ethnic rice beer (apong), she will give in to his amorous advances.

As Mili and Biju converse with each other, I ask them what kind of drinkers the men in their lives are. Mili says, "Women and men are both ridiculed ('Which tribe do you belong to that you can't even handle beer?') if they can't control themselves after having apong. So there is a natural tendency to stay sober, though this is not always the case. But, the bagania women have a tough time, most of their men beat them up. I run into them in the nearby haat."

III

Mishing women sell rice cakes in nearby haats of the village. The haats function as communal sites for the women, where bonds are forged and often, left in media res. It allows them to exchange surplus produce and ideas every now and again. Locals typically get a flavour of the changing countryside as the Sohorer Sahabs (rich urban-goers) drop by to buy organic goods cultivated by the villagers, including but not limited to rice beer.

It was a joy therefore, to see some of the Mishing yeast cakes in the households of Adivasi women who make their living by plucking tea leaves [5] —I stayed with a couple of them for about a week. Sokolatinga Pothar Gaon tea estate is where the labourers go to work and they live at a walking distance from Kaziranga University, Jorhat. Small pandals of Durga and Kali covered by tropical trees await the arrival of autumn. Taking me to be a cop in disguise, or a media person, most of them shut the door on me. Liquor is a particularly complex domain for the female residents—it determines/influences their everyday life and suffering. Many of them have migrated from the Chotanagpur pleateau in the British times and have since assimilated with the native culture and customs. They speak the Sadri [6] language—which also contains some Assamese and Bangla words, the two languages which they need to use officially, I am told.

Hema Tanty, 41, was already tipsy when she shows me her secret godown of rice cakes and herbs. "Individually consuming these plants might be fatal and poisonous,

5. Adivasi is a political identity used by the descendants of migrants who were brought to Assam during the Colonial period for work in the plantations. They comprise of Santhals, Mundas, Oraons, Saora and others.

6. Sadri is a link language popular among the communities of Santhals , Mundas, Oraons etc., who migrated to Assam during the Colonial period. Their language is sometimes colloquially refered to as 'bagania' or 'the language of the bagaans'.

but when mixed with rice grains, they magically turn into elixir," she laughs. Locally called handia, it is still a part of everyday consumption and taken in the right quantity, it is known to elevate energy levels required for plucking tea leaves. In the summer, it provides nutrition and helps cure alimentary diseases. Like with the Mishings and Deoris, handia brewing is an all-women performance for the Adivasi women, albeit within the confines of their homes.

The primary medicinal plants used for handia brewing are biholongoni (*Polygonum glabrum*), mitha paat and bhatou paat among others. Hema and her friends collect herbs while working in the tea gardens. Though the process of making handia is more or less similar to other kinds of rice beer, there are some differences too. The yeast cake for example is inserted in between layers of hay in a huge bag and taken outdoors into the sun. Next, the rice is roasted before being used for fermentation. A white-coloured drink, safely kept in bottles, its strength is strategically controlled by the women.

Debatree Majhi, who is about 65, is a retired a tea garden labourer. She says, "Herbs are difficult to procure in the rains. Younger and older women prepare the brew together and learn from each other. We try to sell the yeast cake (Pitha guti) alongside pigs, goat and cow milk. Handia cures dysentery and acts like sharbot. It is excellent for summer but if you overdo it, sloshing is what you deserve!"

Hema and Debatree are worshippers of Manasa—the snake goddess. Apart from this, during Tusu Puja, they are supposed to prepare a huge quantity of handia for the male guests. It is drunk like prasad. Inside their bedroom and kitchen lie a treasury of yeast cakes, and it leaves me astonished. They repeatedly tell me to be secretive about the extra rice cakes. They make a few extra and sell them in order to earn a little more for their livelihood. Wages are fairly low and the women are unable to feed the many mouths in their families.

The domestic space for them has been a perennial source of gender rift. This is largely due to the conflicts between "licit" and "illicit" liquor. While handia is constituted as a "lighter" drink, it is Sulai mod which is potentially harmful. Piya Chatterjee's account "An Empire of Drink" examines some of these features. She writes, "...women workers were also viewed as 'better' workers than their male counterparts because they are usually not matals (drunkards). Such idealized constructions of women's 'passivity' are belied by the fact that women are primary producers of the local brew handia. Women make and sell handia, on plantation market days to supplement their wages. Some also consume it though they don't do so publicly like men."[7]

7. Piya Chatterjee, "An Empire of Drink: Gender, Labor and the Historical Economies of Alcohol", *Journal of Historical Sociology* Vol. 16 No. 2 June 2003

The circle of Sulai mod (distilled liquor) sellers and brewers is largely controlled by men unlike handia. According to Hema her man often feels a sense of emasculation when she goes out in the market to sell her handia. Because female tea-garden workers already access the public space (i.e. the tea gardens), they seem more aware about their rights. They bravely and repeatedly articulate how insecurities among men are an indication that they are not comfortable with women taking control of the fruits of their labour. Besides, the ones who get addicted to sulai never end up making it to work. Consequently, the pressure to manage both household work and work in the gardens piles up on the women.

As per the recent World Employment and Social Outlook: Trends for Women report 2017 by the International Labour Organisation, East and South Asia are the only two regions where female labour force participation rates have decreased over the past two decades.[8] This statistic indicates that the toiling away with household chores does not add up to the economy.

IV

In April 2017, the Assam state cabinet approved a budget proposal to take the state's array of home-brewed, rice-based liquors from homes to factories. The attempt is to place these local brews on shelves alongside their IMFL (Indian Made Foreign Liquor) counterparts. For the first time in the region's history, locally brewed alcohol can now hope to gain a market, post their labelling as "heritage" drinks.

Though this news is to the liking of some consumers in urban areas, major questions about labour empowerment surround expansionist endeavours like this. One has to question whether these newly-branded bottles will make a difference to the lives of the women who continue to brew in their homes. It will always suit the interests of liquor corporations to have a readily available workforce that also has low levels of organization and therefore, less negotiating power when it comes to wages and worker rights.

Things have definitely come a long way since the 1990s, when tribal liquor was seen as a social malaise—it created social fissures among the rising bourgeoisie and the tribes (for whom drinking is an essential part of culture). Uddipan Dutta's "Creating Robin Hoods: The Insurgency of the ULFA in its Early Period, Its Parallel Administration and The Role of Assamese Vernacular Press (1985-1990)" discusses

8. *World Employment and Social Outlook: Trends for women 2017*, http://www.ilo.org/global/research/global-reports/weso/trends-for-women2017/WCMS_557245/lang--en/index.htm, Web. Accessed 17 June 2017

some of these developments that trace the political map of the state. He refers to Debabrata Sarma's analysis of ULFA's blanket ban of alcohol—how this move had further marginalized the tribal peoples from the dominant mainstream. He wrote, "Wine is part and parcel of the cultural life of many indigenous communities in Assam, who preserved their culture inspite of all odds [...]. It is the Vaishnavite influenced middle class morality which traced liquor as the source of all evils". [9] My grandmother for instance, would share her folktale wisdom, where couples did crazy things with liquor.[10] A popular idiom I learnt from her, warns the patriarch against three things in alliteration: "mod, maati aru maiki" (alcohol, land and women) lest he fall into oblivion. Myths around alcohol and women are not limited to one region, culture or language. Women are not just supposed to abstain, they are also supposed to support their men's drinking habits—financially as well as emotionally.

Alcohol was a fortune maker for many wealthy industrialists in Assam in the 1990s. While locally brewed alcohol was pushed to the periphery, there was a large hue and cry about giving licenses to foreign liquor. The game has everything to do with class politics and little to do with the popular version of alcohol being injurious to health. The state's measures to pacify the SULFA members by granting soft loans and liquor licenses failed to take into account the larger repercussions of liberalising the liquor trade. As such, monetary trends like this continued with both the Asom Gana Parishad and the Congress and for them, social problems took a backseat.

When capitalism enters a hitherto unorganized sector such as home brewing, regional sentiments take a Janus-faced turn. If previously, the unorganized workers had even a slightly equitable, almost fair deal with vendors, this is taken away from them. For capitalism, cheap labour is the dream, so women brewers are preferred—easily dominated, even unremunerated in many cases. As collective drinking by the tribals will now be seen as a "rustic" custom, a more urbane product differentiation will establish the politics of taste, which will influence labour patterns. In the late nineteenth century, when tea estate owners were beginning to make their fortunes, they imitated the British colonial trick of getting labourers drunk on local liquor to more easily exploit them and extract labour from them. Now that we meander in a post colonial tapestry, vestiges of market imperialism (one that took tea to the empire)

9. Dutta, Uddipan. 2008. *Creating Robinhoods:The Insurgency of the ULFA in its Early Period, Its Parallel Admistration and The Role of Assamese Vernacular Press*

10. In the tale "A Clever Old Man", a witty old couple who regularly consume rice beer get rid of thieves who come to steal their valuables. The old couple put up an act of drunken oblivion which the foolish thieves buy. For a written version of this tale, see: *Folktales of India* (1987), edited by Brenda E. F. Beck, Peter J. Claus, Praphulladatta Goswami, Jawaharlal Handoo

seize the labourers by the throat. Only this time, their drink suits the direction that the market seeks—it provides the perfect commodity fetish the upper middle classes want to identify themselves with.

Will the diverse contexts and the contribution of the female brewers be gradually erased? Will branding local beer further add to the inequalities already rampant in society? In the essay "Inconspicuous Consumption: Sake, Beer, and the Birth of the Consumer in Japan" Penelope Francks gives us an insight into the evolution of sake, the rice beer of Japan. Taking the example of pre-industrial Europe, Francks goes on to analyse how the act of drinking sake became a way of defining and adhering to class hierarchies."The 'peasant pattern' of drinking, involving large amounts on special occasions, alongside regular consumption of weak forms of alcohol as 'food,' gave way to the urban 'middle-class pattern' of smaller amounts of stronger and/or more refined products drunk more regularly in small and more private gatherings." I see more than one parallel to this story of sake with that of local brews in the state. If formerly local beers constituted a marker of identity and cultural background, they would now be branded for the same. Due to this, a glass of apong or suzen would be equivalent to any other drinking product, and the upper classes will simultaneously lose out the ritual of collective drinking with the tribes.

In small scale industries like cottage industry around the world, a system called "outwork" or "putting out" is followed. It involves travelling businessmen who buy raw materials in bulk. These people travel from village to village, handing out (not selling) raw materials to domestic manufacturers. After the products are made, these businessmen collect the finished products and keep travelling, selling them everywhere. The domestic manufacturers are paid wages for their efforts. This system is yet to pick up in Assam. So if the "bottled rice beer" trend grows beyond a point, big processed food companies will start playing a pivotal role. The fates of millions of people will be handed over to a handful of big companies. Their salaries, their working hours, their lifestyles will all be guided by the policies of these few companies. If selling was formerly handled by the families who brewed, now middle-men are going to take over the trade.

There is also the danger that taking rice beer to factories may introduce a large number of preservatives which will change the taste of the final product. When you look at Assam and the pros and cons of liquor consumption, it gets more and more complicated with the introduction of every new variable. Brewing often makes some money for the families. Lack of education limits their alternatives, so blanket "rehabilitation" attempts will not succeed unless backed up with really deep pockets and a super-efficient bureaucracy; neither a hallmark of the state.

Taken to its extreme, commercialisation of locally brewed alcohol has brought a bad name to the tribes. Biju's husband told me that within Mishing society, rules exist to prevent such abuse of intoxicating substances. This prevalent discord and apprehension has been discussed by Dr Punya Lata Gohain's in her comprehensive book *Axamar Janagushthiya Laupani* (2015). She digs deep into the conflicts involved in commercialisation of rice beer, traditionally a sacred offering to the gods. Foremost among them is the homogenisation implicit in the craze of equating rice beer with IMFL products. It has already created a network of easily available "Assam excise" which permits rice beer to be sold in places where formerly it would have been forbidden. This has led to plenty of trouble and chaos for economically downtrodden classes.

Jinti and her elder companions tell me that they are aging and find urban changes in the realm of local liquor tiring, to say the least. *"Ami tu aru burhiye holu, amar jiwori buwari bure jiyai rakhibo mod bonuwa poddhati, xeiye aasha koru..."* (We have become old in the trade of making rice beer, our daughters and daughters-in-law will keep it alive, it is our hope...). The idea that the organization of a sector automatically leads to economic parity for women is dangerous and one that both state and central governments would be well-advised to abandon. Capitalism has little use for the home brewer's rights and even less for the cultural context. In such a tug of war, stories of Jinti, Biju, Hema and the bonds they cement with every cup fade away in broad daylight.

Names have been changed to protect identity. The author is grateful to Tanmoy Sabhapandit (Kaziranga University, Jorhat), Sumana Mukherjee (former food editor at Mint Lounge), residents of Upar Deori Gaon, Mishing Gaon and Sokolatinga Pothar Gaon for their help.

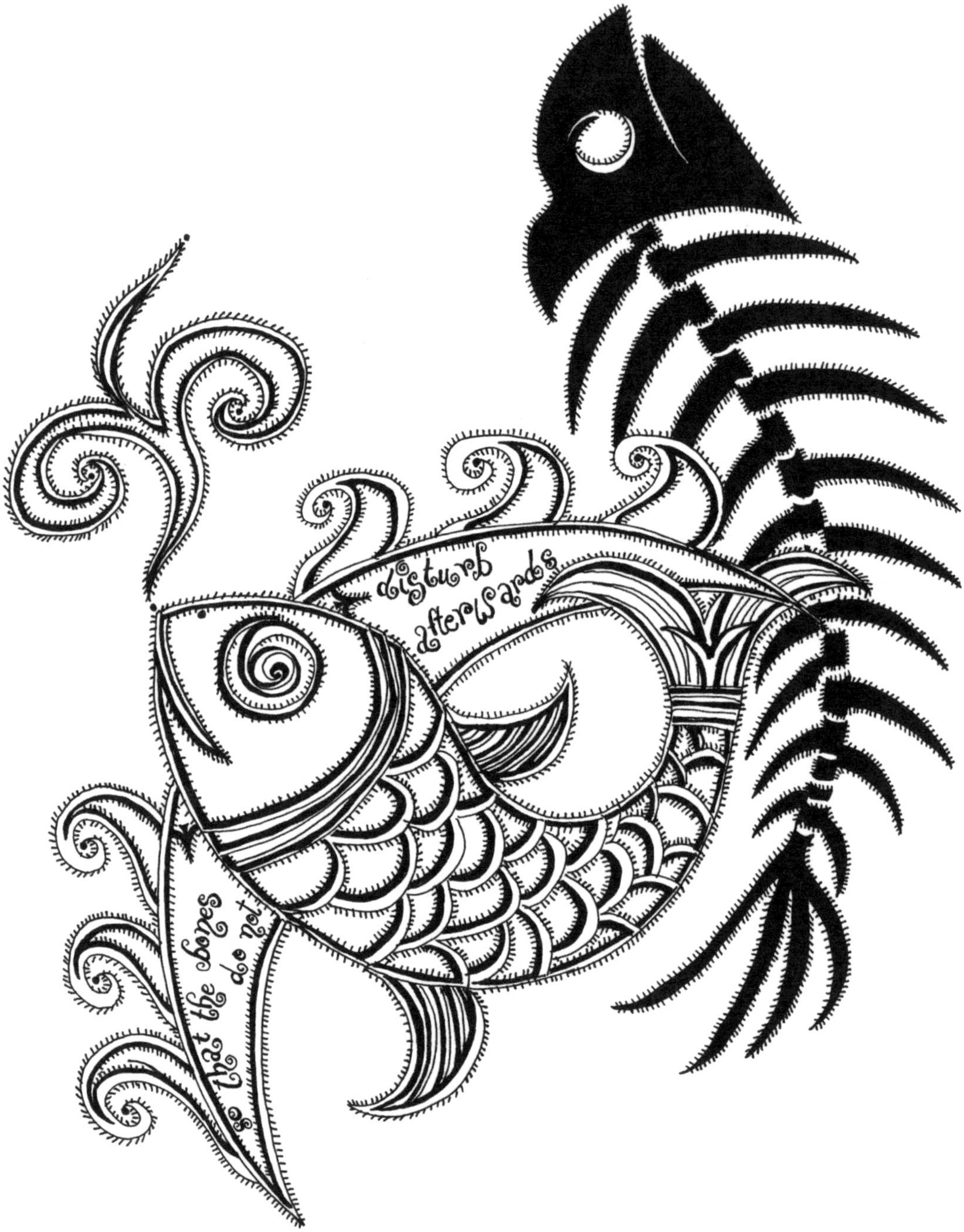

so that the bones do not
disturb afterwards

how to cut a fish

POETRY AND ILLUSTRATION BY **NITOO DAS**

you have to sit
                    properly
woman-like on the floor
put   one foot
strongly gingerly
on the base of the blade
hold the fish with firm hands
head and tail   and swing
him quick leftrightleftright
to remove the scales check
beneath the gills red fans
cut them swift and
then fins here there up down
and tail
feel that perfect line
where the head ends and the body
begins choose it fine and move
slow over the edge
feel the resistance of white flesh staring eye
and open mouth but keep at it let him feel the pressure
of your fingers until it is done and the head sits isolated with a hole
dripping with stuff and then halve
him down his body and pull out the red mess
make equal pieces cutting him so that
the bones do not disturb
afterwards.

terminal

SOIBAM HARIPRIYA

My father, an oncologist,
says, the first time
a patient died,
my mother insisted
he cleanse himself
of death
at the gate
with a bucket of water
she dragged through
the mud courtyard.
Many deaths later
the act seemed redundant
for someone who deals
with terminal diseases.
Yesterday, I read
of an encounter specialist
whose wife, likewise,
dragged buckets of water.
She too stopped
after too many deaths.
The apron and the uniform
a little too stained
with blood
and body filth.
The body after death
is too often a rotting filth.
My father grasps the uniform
sometimes
mending blood
mending bad blood.
Are they any closer
to each other?
They stay in a place
that is terminable
all lives are terminal,
We, bodies, imprinted
with either of their fingerprints.

untitled

ZUBENI LOTHA

FROM THE SERIES "DIMAPUR 797112"

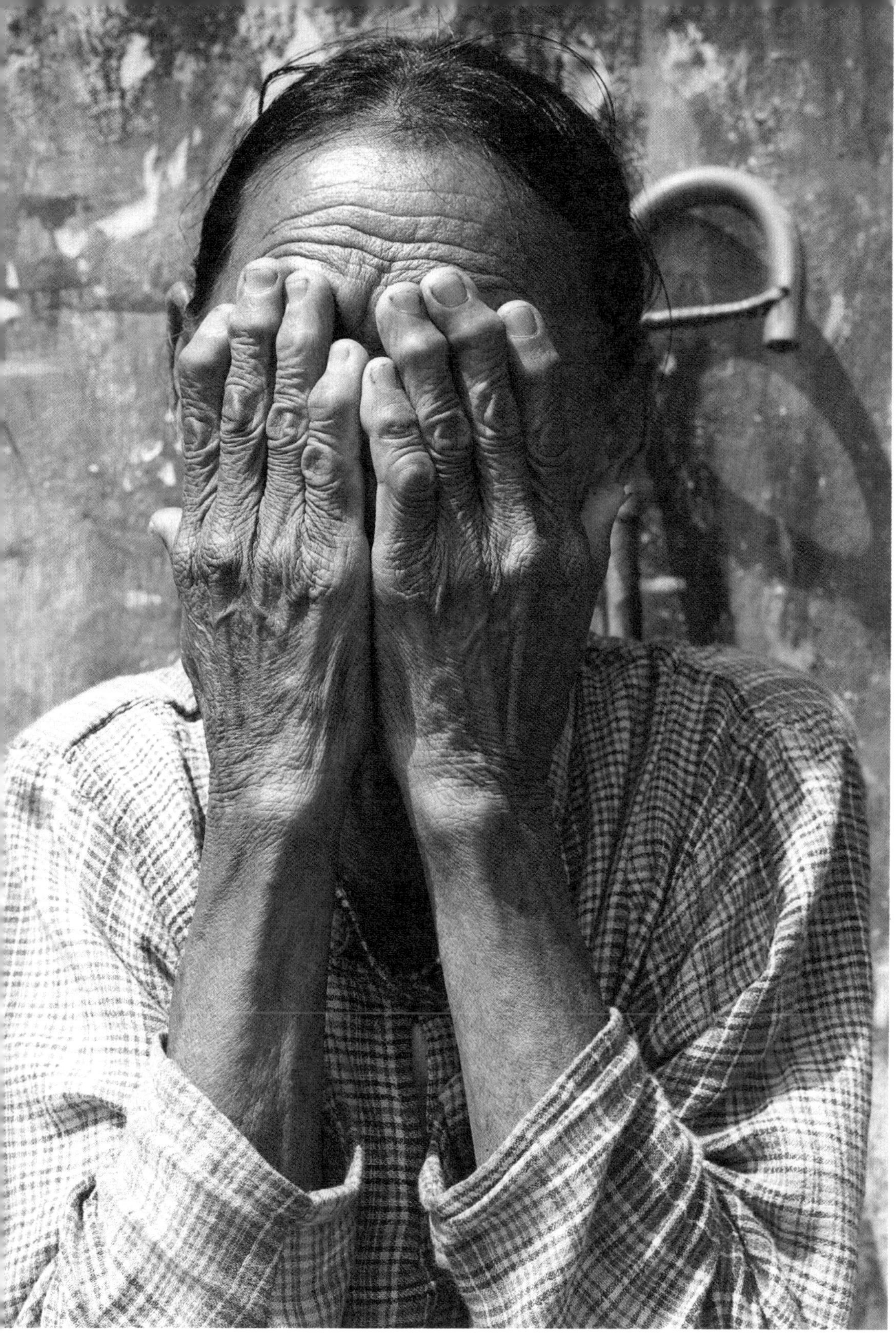

#hashtagpoetry

THINGNAM ANJULIKA SAMOM
ILLUSTRATIONS BY **TAIBANGNGANBA AND PUNSHIBA**

Lines to a one-sided crush, emotional lyrics from greeting cards and songs, limericks during a boring class. Those were creative days.

And then college, job, family and kids. If that was not enough, there was the journalistic exposure to real-time Manipur. The extrajudicial killings, the endless days of bandhs and protests, the multi-layered conflict narratives and blurring manifestations, the self-justifying, otherizing and prejudicial rhetoric emanating from all sides, the customs-conflict double burden on women. Writing a story or article for a publication is always a wire-walk, a balancing act without safety nets. The tears and the vitriolic atmosphere seemed to suck out all creative imagination.

And then slowly, I found a new muse (a slightly problematic one, no doubt). With lessons from the new generation, it started with a few people on my Facebook friend list and posts about birthdays and children, flowers and vegetable gardens. Soon, the captions became as important as the pictures themselves. Phrases became sentences and before I knew it, the words became poetic on their own.

Anger, love, frustration, joy, the Manipur political climate, the gender equations... .I couldn't stop once I'd started. This didn't take gut-wrenching planning-ahead to steal time from the cooking, driving or even meeting people. A stray thought, a momentary image, a gush of emotion and few minutes of finger-dancing on the smartphone were all it took. The likes and emojis in response. The words poured out and became my own hashtag poetry.

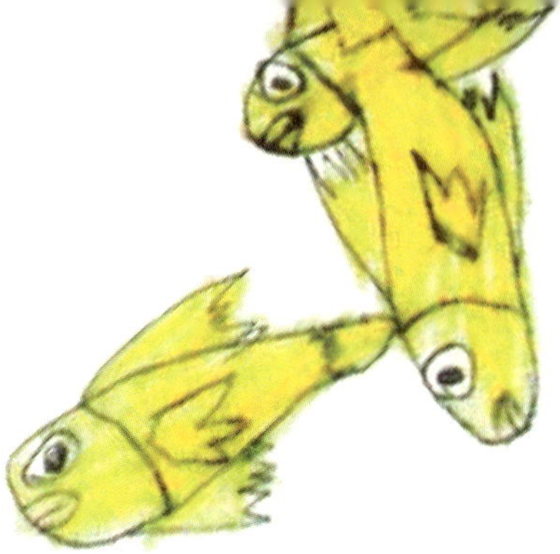

#moontrip

If I do not want
To bring myself back
From my trip
To the moon
Just to sort the rotten chives
And put out the soggy dried fish
In the sun
Would you call me less
A woman?

#wordprostitute

I am a word-prostitute
Pimping the stories
Of a dead society
I am a word-prostitute
Scavenging off the remains
Of trust lost and faith broken
I am a word-prostitute
You have made me one

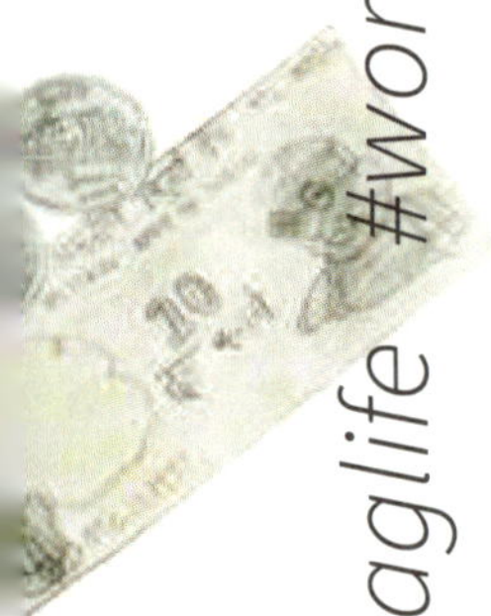

#hashtaglife

I am your calendar girl
The muse of your poetry
The songs of your patriots
I am your scenic beauty
Silhouetted against the orange sky
Knee-deep amongst the green fields
Hashtagged My Beloved Motherland
Hashtagged Tranquility
Hashtagged Scenery
Why then did you crop me out
From your selfie,
Hashtagged Roadtrip?
Is it the leeches crawling up my thighs?
Or my sun-burnt face and unkempt hair?
Or the hunger of my children drawn across my forehead?
Or your fear of lived lives?

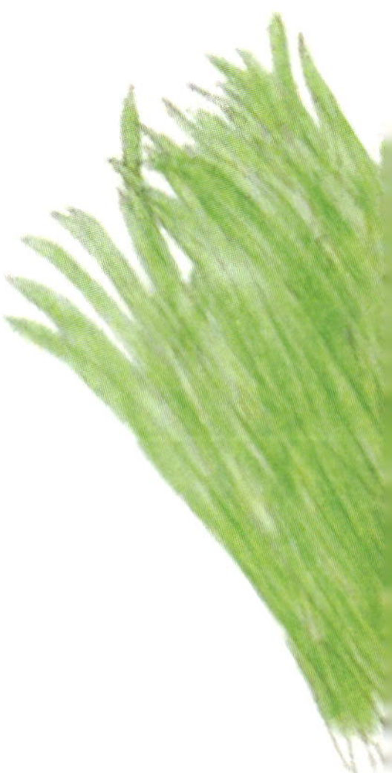

#kitchenlines

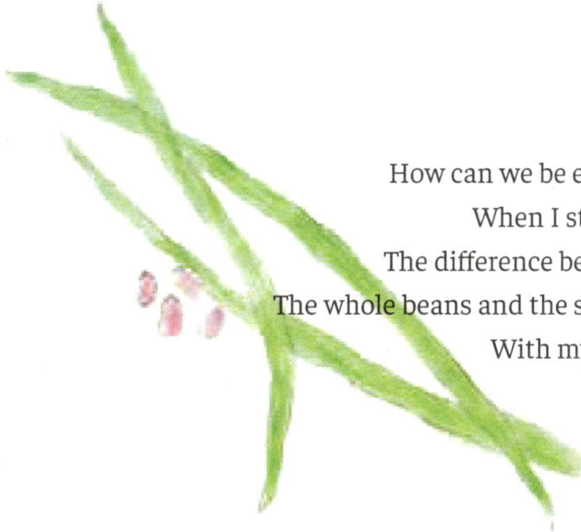

How can we be equals?
When I still pay
The difference between
The whole beans and the shelled
With my time.

#empressofnonsense

I painted my walls with shit.
Dog shit, Bull shit
Man shit, woman shit, baby shit.
I smeared the yellow, the black
And the in-between browns
Scooping up handfuls and handfuls
Drawing patterns and designs
That I alone created.
In this house decorated with shit
I alone reign supreme
An icon, a queen.

#solutions

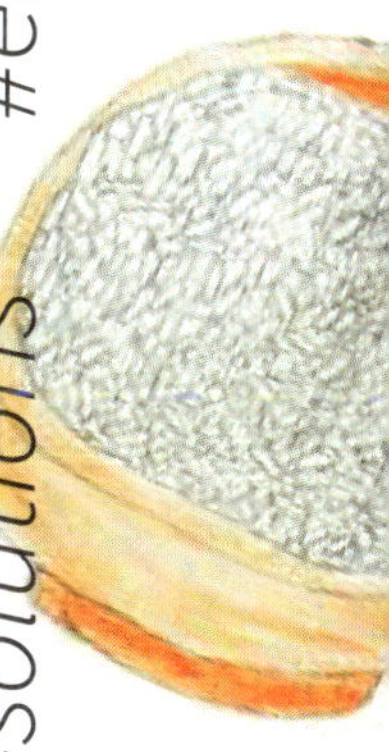

Writing a recipe
At a safe, cocooned distance
From the kitchen fire
Is somehow
More colourful, more productive
More politically correct
And less messy
Than actually cooking
In the kitchen.
Even if the taste
Does not suit the eaters.

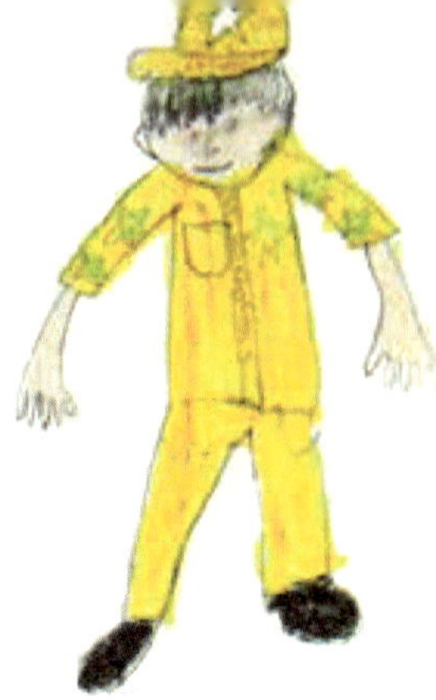

#khwairambandkeithel

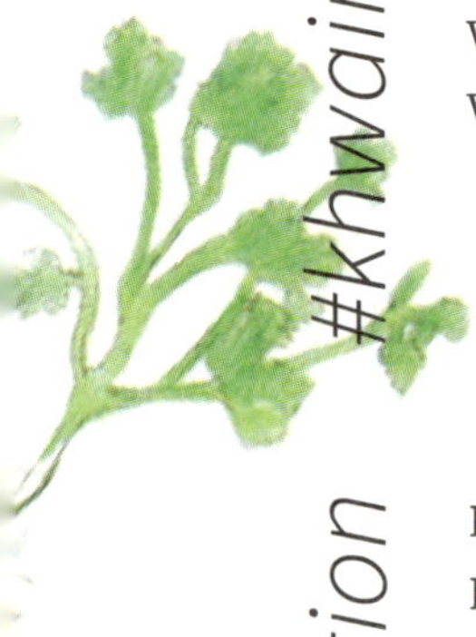

Why do you come to Khwairamband Keithel, Mother?
Here, the rich man's cars will smoke you slowly
Like the charcoal-turned Meitei ngamu
Curled up in little rows on your lokmai.
Here, the policeman's gun is pointed at you –
Everyday you have to feed the khaki-clad
With ten-rupee notes and sprigs of coriander
Though it leaves none for your nine children at home.
Here, the protestor's stones and the tear-gas canisters
Love you alike, equally, with no prejudice.
Why do you come to Khwairamband Keithel, Mother?
Why don't you drown yourself in Loktak?

#appropriation

I make my rhythm
From the pounding of paddy,
The winnowing of rice,
And the cries of my baby.
You come,
Listen to my lullabies,
And compose your PhD.

#untitled1

Democracy is homegrown
In my kitchen garden
Where the poor man's sougri
Competes for the sky
With the heinous.
I wonder
What the little tendrils of gourd
Have been saying to one another.

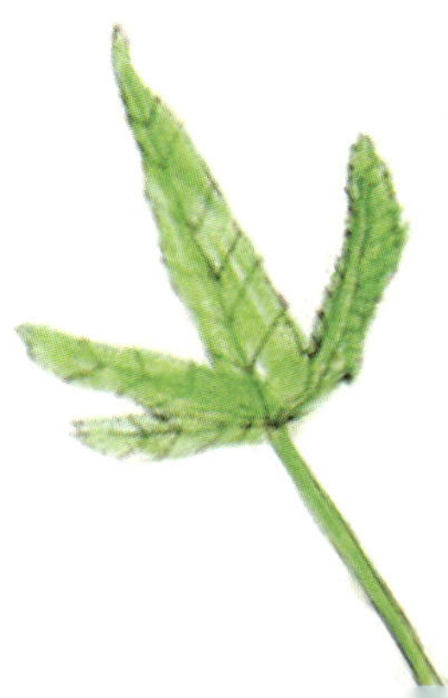

#untitled3

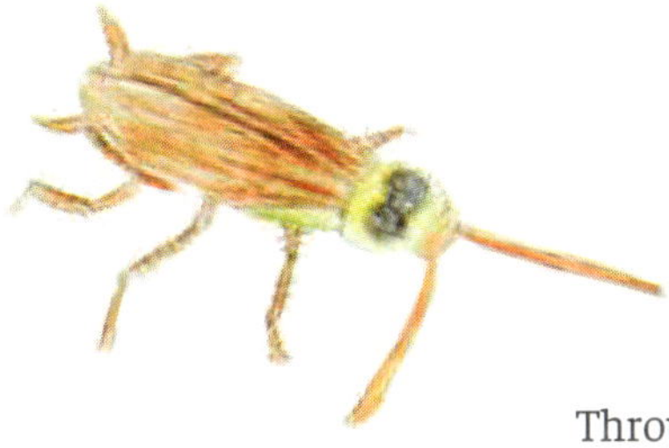

Clearly, my sandaled foot
Was not the first one
To aim at your brown body
Your innards half out
You weave your way
Up and down
Back and forth
Through the pebbled market road
Clearly, the din of the market made you crazy
Just as it did me
The struggles of living
Dear Cockroach,
Of hating, loving, eating and killing.

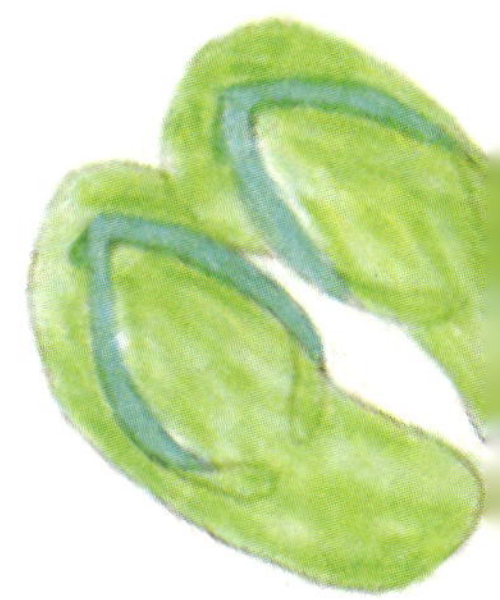

#men #women #war

The men went to war
Stomach filled with rice
Cooked by the women
In the middle of the night,
Back bent over the smoking hearth
Food is strength, they said.
And the speech of the patriots
Came in an A4 sized page.
I tore it in half
Exactly where Tikendrajit and Thangal
Were hanged for their bravery
And rolling it all around
My menstrual blood-soaked napkin,
Threw it into the dustbin.

in the market

PARISMITA SINGH

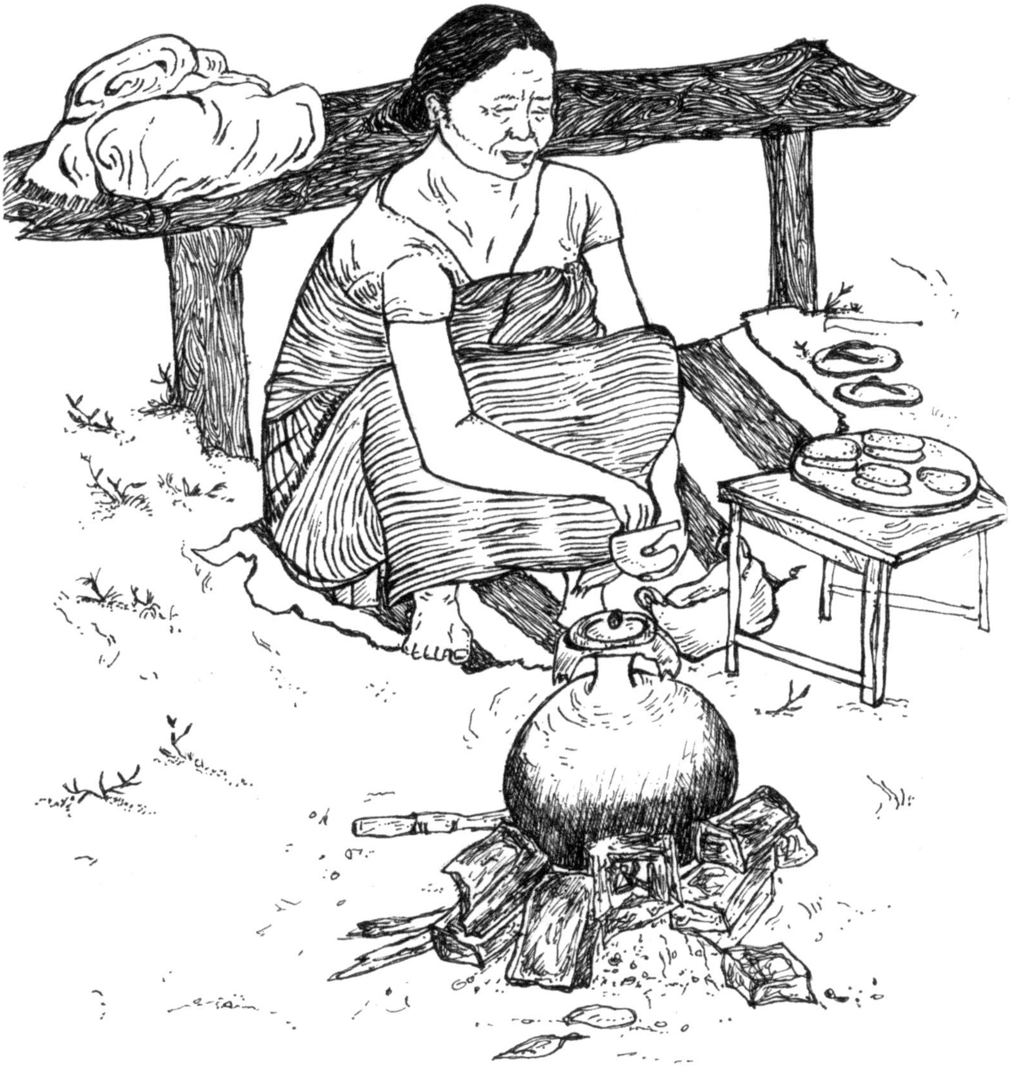

breakfast

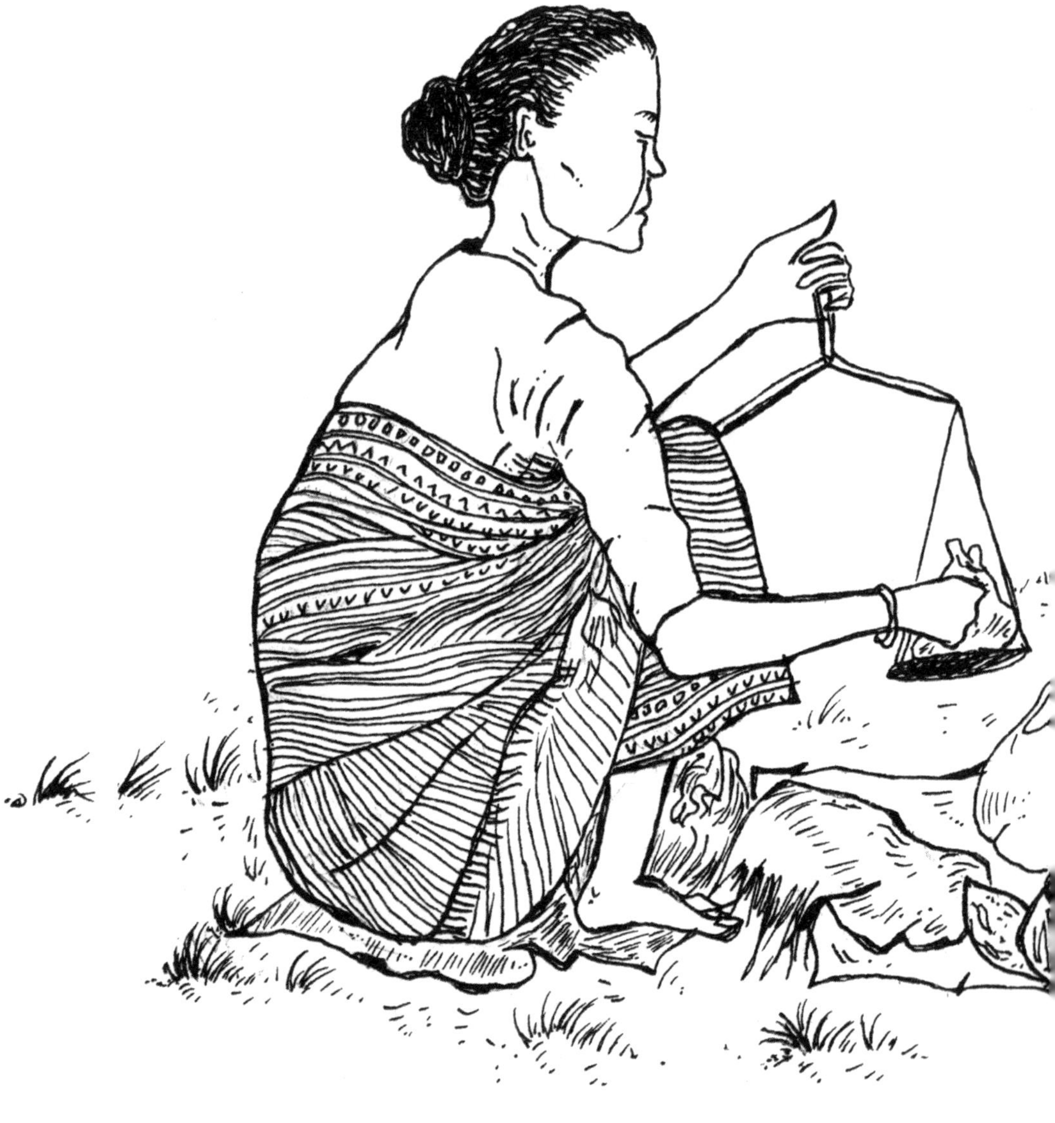

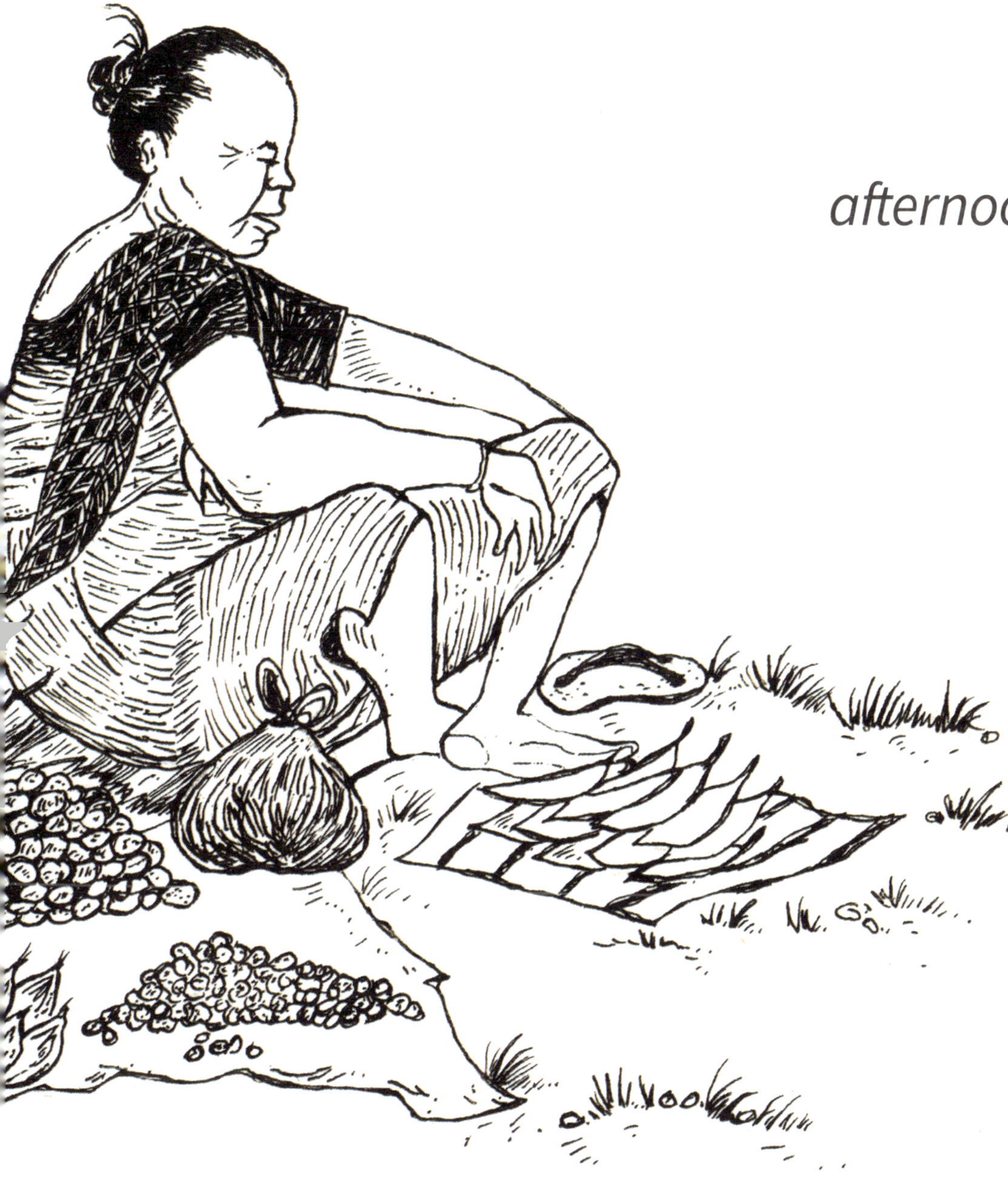

afternoon

women at work: the gender, culture and customary law debate in nagaland

DOLLY KIKON

Introduction

Through the winter of 2016-17, Nagaland, its urban centres and rural districts were restive, with tensions over the elections to the urban local bodies. Since 2006, when the first Amendment for the Nagaland Municipal Act was enacted, tribal bodies dominated by men had consistently opposed the affirmative action policy passed by the Government of India. In January 2017, many of these tribal bodies stepped up the opposition to implement 33 per cent reservation for Naga women and brought the state to a standstill. The violent protests that shut down educational institutions, public offices and shops across the state were aimed at stopping the urban local bodies election scheduled for February 1, 2017. After the initial protests, church elders and civil society leaders were called upon to broker a temporary peace, where the government decided to defer the elections while the organizations called off their civic strike campaign. However, the administration allowed the elections to take place in districts that were not opposed to the reservation, leading to a call for return to the streets by the protestors. Three deaths, destruction of property, closure of government offices and educational institutions, including the censorship of social media and the Internet were widely reported and enforced. The protesters blamed the government of Nagaland for failing to consult "the people", in other words, the male tribal bodies and authorities. Condemning the government of Nagaland for being "anti-Naga people" and disrespecting customary practices and culture, the protests intensified. As a result, the urban local bodies election was postponed indefinitely and the Chief Minister of Nagaland, Mr. T.R. Zeliang was forced to step down and hand over power to his colleague Dr Shurhozelie Leizitsu. Some normality was restored only after the decision to implement the 33 per cent reservation for women was indefinitely postponed.[1]

Opposition to affirmative action

Nagaland is the only state in India where there has been a sustained opposition to the 33 per cent reservation for women's participation in public office. And the dramatic events of the last winter have raised serious concerns and led to debates about gender justice in Naga society. Nagaland, in Northeast India, with a population of 1.9 million, has managed its own civil and legal affairs since its inception as a federal unit within the Republic of India in 1963. Customary courts and traditional tribal organizations have functioned as the administrative and moral authorities in the state. Although there is a Legislative Assembly where members are elected through the Indian electoral system every five years, the traditional courts and organizations enjoy a degree of influence that is unprecedented and barring a few other states of Northeast India, cannot be found in other parts of the country. A provision within the Constitution of India, known as Article 371 (A) guarantees protection of Naga culture and customs, land ownership, including preservation of local, social and religious practices.

These functions have given immense power to the male tribal councils and associations in Nagaland. However, their power and authority needs to be understood against the backdrop of the Indo-Naga conflict, an armed struggle that had started in the 1950s to demand a Naga homeland. Spanning over 60 years, the conflict ravaged homes and lives across the Naga areas in Northeast India. Given the long conflict, state organs and public offices in Nagaland are struggling and Naga society is extremely militarized. Leaders of parliamentary political parties who hold important positions are often accused of corruption and of instrumentalizing the conflict for their political gains. Given the political instability, the tribal organizations and associations have emerged as a powerful public forum with a strong and resolute leadership. As in other indigenous societies around the world, these bodies were revered in the past and

1. In July 2017, Nagaland witnessed another change in leadership. Dr. Shurhozelie Leisitsu was replaced by Mr. T.R. Zeliang as the Chief Minister of the state. Refer to: *http://morungexpress.com/offices-struggle-get-back-track/* and *http://www.firstpost.com/politics/tr-zeliang-is-new-nagaland-chief-minister-after-former-cm-shurhozelie-liezietsu-skips-floor-test-3830125.html*

Naga culture and customs were propagated as practices handed down "since time immemorial" through these tribal institutions.

Justice and Customary Law

Like many nationalist societies around the world, the issue of gender justice and rights in the context of women's work has remained marginal for a long time in Naga society. But this iteration of Naga culture as pure and unique has come to be contested in the ongoing debate about women's rights. Advocates of 33 per cent reservation have argued against the notion of a static and masculine Naga culture. They have argued that customary laws and practices that continue to exclude women from positions of power cannot be upheld as instruments and institutions of justice. This issue about justice and equality lies at the heart of the gender debate in Nagaland. The irony of the ongoing debate around gender justice and women's work is that even though the male-dominated tribal bodies exclude women's participation, Naga women hold important positions in almost every other field, as administrators, doctors, engineers, academics, and successful entrepreneurs, to name a few. It is significant that none of these positions or professions is within the ambit of Naga cultural and traditional institutions. Therefore, the processes of negotiating for women's rights in Naga society are often regarded as a demand outside the traditional customary set-up. It is by this logic that Naga women's assertions for gender justice have been tagged as an "anti-Naga" move by some of the activists during the agitation. The "anti-Naga" slur used during the 33 per cent reservation agitation can be seen as a tactic to shut down dialogue and debates about gender justice. This reiterates the practice of restricting women's access and participation as decision makers in the apex tribal bodies and customary institutions. Here, traditional bodies that argued that supporting the 33 per cent reservation for women was an "anti-Naga" position defined the existing practice of tribal male bodies as an inherent part of Naga culture. These debates exposed the contradictions that exist in Naga society about gender equality and work culture. For example, Naga women and their labour are glorified as intrinsic qualities of Naga society as long as they are traders, officers, waiters, or choose to pursue any career that generates an income for the family. Their work ethics represent Naga values and culture. Naga women can toil and labour, yet they are denied the authority and power to become decision makers as equal members in the traditional assemblies and customary courts. In this context, any assertion to participate as decision makers in the traditional institutions is immediately seen as an opposition to Naga culture.

Reflecting on the acrimonious situation in Nagaland, Sanjay Hazarika, a political commentator noted, "Prominent Nagas say that women's groups have failed to understand the larger issues, although one influential tribal group has acknowledged that men have not accepted women as equal partners. A case in point is the fact that customs lay down that Naga women do not inherit ancestral property".[2]

From comments like these, we can assume that irrespective of the visibility of Naga women as successful professionals, they continue to be excluded from all traditional decision making bodies on the assumption that men and women are not equal in society. These positions of the Naga male bodies and traditional councils reveal a deep nexus of patriarchy, culture, and law. It is a case in point that well into the 21st century, neither the Nagaland state assembly nor apex tribal councils have ever elected a woman as a member with the exception of Ms. Rano Shaiza.[3]

If Naga customary law is seen as the foundation of justice, the exclusion of women from these powerful decision making bodies like the traditional councils and assemblies negates the entire notion that these are pillars of justice. The Indian state and the male traditional bodies alike are responsible for excluding the Naga women from all spheres of representative political processes. Article 371(a) is a prime example of the patriarchal nature of the Indian Constitution that bestows on Naga male bodies the full authority and power to interpret customary affairs covering social, religious, and criminal cases.

But what is Article 371(a)? I reproduce the clause 1 of article 371(a) below, so we can understand it better.

371a. Special provision with respect to the State of Nagaland

(1) Notwithstanding anything in this Constitution,

(a) no Act of Parliament in respect of

(i) religious or social practices of the Nagas,

(ii) Naga customary law and procedure,

(iii) administration of civil and criminal justice involving decisions according to Naga customary law,

(iv) ownership and transfer of land and its resources, shall apply to the State of Nagaland unless the Legislative Assembly of Nagaland by a resolution so decides;

---

2. See Sanjay Hazarika's piece: *https://thewire.in/108277/nagaland-gender-divide-womens-rights/* (Last accessed March 1, 2017).

3. See *http://morungexpress.com/first-woman-mp-from-nagaland-state-rano-m-shaiza-passes-away/*

Besides Clause 1 which has four slim lines about protecting Naga customary practices and land rights, it is noteworthy that a larger section of Article 371(a) of the Indian constitution actually defines the power and functions of the Governor to the extent of laying down the qualification and salaries of the regional councils like the autonomous councils. Therefore, if people argue that all Naga rights "since time immemorial" are determined by this article, the social and political transformation in Naga society is in serious question. Article 371(a) does not even define what is "customary law and procedure" or "social and religious practices". These processes which were regarded as enabling instruments for Naga people to become citizens of India, have in fact become the basis of violent contestations and debates today.

Here I would like to make a detour to look at some other circumstances when the article 371(a) has been invoked. For example, the ongoing coal mining operations and the oil exploration negotiations in Nagaland have rested on multiple interpretations of this constitutional provision. Naga politicians, landowners, village councils, and business families have all interpreted the provision for their benefit to mine for minerals and not be held accountable for the environmental degradation. Today, rivers, paddy fields, and forests across the coal belts of Nagaland suffer high levels of pollution with serious consequences. Article 371(a) has indeed favoured a male interpretation, and goes on to reinforce Naga patriarchy and exclude women from positions of decision making in several other spheres too, such as environmental matters and peace processes. What it has done is to continue to propagate a male hegemonic power and authority in Naga society. Naga male bodies have acquired the language of justice to retain the order of Naga male heritage and patrimony. It has nothing to do with retaining the customary law and culture of the Naga people.

This kind of historical struggle for justice has been vibrant and real, and women, including tribal and non-tribal women have been part of these alliances in Northeast India. These movements were significant because they captured the experiences of the people's movement that became centres of activism, and intersected with different conversations about rights and justice at the grassroots as well. In an odd travesty, over the decades, men and women activists, interlocutors, intellectuals, and organizers have become virtual prisoners of human rights. They have been pressured and pushed into professing exclusive rights along lines of ethnicity, territoriality, and gender. We have to address this fracture in the foundation of our political history in order to situate our conversation about tribal feminism and gender equality. Feminism and equality are synonymous.

The politics of Naga feminism: ***So how did things come to this point?***

Where and how do we begin crystallizing the everyday experiences and journeys through a period of militarization and violence of the last one hundred years or so, starting from World War 1 till today? The years of the British colonial administration (especially the periods of the WW I and WW II) and the postcolonial administrative period in India (after 1997), as well as the experiences of war and violence in this region have intimately shaped the social, political, and gender relations today. The voices of Naga women demanding justice and equality emerge from experiences of hunger, hardship, and humiliation. As in many armed conflict situations, granaries and paddy fields were burnt down as part of the Indian counter-insurgency operations leading to starvation and hunger across the Naga villages in the 1950s and 60s. The overwhelming responsibility of the women-headed households in Naga society has seldom been acknowledged in the political and public sphere. Instead, women continue to have no representative rights or visibility in the Naga traditional councils and customary assemblies. Naga women face the danger of being subsumed within an exotic cultural trope as non-speaking subjects, passive development programme participants, tea serving smiling figures waiting to be integrated into mainstream projects to become good Indian citizens.

Perhaps the gendered political distinctions that emerged over the decade were so deep that even movements that fought for freedom and independence deviated from a collective understanding of history. This was present in the Naga national history. Only Naga males became martyrs. Women were always victims. How can we talk about equality as a foundational pillar when justice, equality and freedom in Naga society have remained the prerogative of the few? Can a society be called democratic when a minority have defined such a heroic and masculine militarized past? Today the Naga poor, which includes orphans, widows, the unemployed youth, old people, and a large section of the disenfranchised public, cannot take part in this debate. These are inherent contradictions. These are flaws that cannot be integrated into the vision of a just Naga society by simply including women who have been excluded. Here, it is important to acknowledge the feminist ideology of what it means to embrace gender equality and justice. Feminist philosopher Angela Davis wisely cautions us that the Black power movements were dominated by male leaders although a substantial number of women were involved as organizers. At the same time, she notes that we cannot imagine incorporating women into a misogynist society and dream of justice and equality. In the Naga context, like any other society around the world, it calls for the transformation of society from patriarchy, economic injustice, racism, homophobia, and gender violence.

If the Naga movement for the right to self-determination, or the civil and political rights movement, or the solidarity alliances have meant anything at all, it is, quite simply, the quest for justice. We must take into account the solidarities of the past few decades, the work done by organizations such as the Naga People's Movement for Human Rights, the Naga Women's Union of Manipur, the Naga Mothers' Association, the Naga Students' Federation or the solidarity alliances like the North East Human Rights Coordination Committee, Northeast People's Alliance on Trade, Finance, and Development, the North East People's Alliance, to name a few.

Of course, justice is not a goal that can be achieved by simply implementing 33 per cent reservation for Naga women alone. It is not a thing to be coveted and possessed alone by individuals – be it Naga men or Naga women. The Naga feminist dream of justice is based on a collective consciousness of a world where male, female and queer will march together and build a just society together. During the agitation against the reservations, instead of engaging with these voices and the particular history of gender violence and injustice in which they are located, there were continuous attempts to discredit them. During a public protest, a Naga male leader said,

> The only women demanding change are spinsters and divorced women, other women accept our system in which decision making is done by men. Women can only take kitchen decisions. We take the big ones.

Should Naga women seek permission from the male members to speak about gender justice? The schizophrenic image of the Naga woman remains a fictitious figure that is nurturing, courageous, sacrificing, moral, hardworking, and docile, carrying baskets on her head, feeding the family, or perpetually serving tea and cooking in the kitchen. They would never be fit as political subjects to enter the tribal councils and customary courts. Naga men adorn their proud bodies with colorful shawls, jackets covered in beads, and neckties with tribal motifs whenever they assemble in hundreds of tribal councils across the hills of Nagaland. These fabric and designs are created by women: the yarn spun around the weaving loom, the designs created with the skill and precision of years of work, and the tassels of the shawls rolled by coarse hands that works the fields and chop the cattle fodder at daybreak.[4] Naga women remain a token

4. In big weaving centres and factorise, migrants from Assam, Bihar, and even West Bengal work as weavers and produce various designs and patterns of Naga shawls and mekhalas. There are also cases of outsourcing the designs and patterns to factories outside the state where Marwari traders employ workers to weave the Naga designs and sell it back to Naga consumers across Northeast India and beyond. Therefore, the complicity of adorning tribal motifs and designs to perform a tribal political identity generally leaves out the political economy of how these cultural materials are created.

representative ornament in a photo session after public meetings and are not seen as fit to occupy a chair next to male leaders in the tribal assembly.

In the backdrop of these dominant cultural frameworks about gender relations, the debates about justice and equality during the 33 per cent reservation debate in Nagaland were interpreted as attempts to shame society or shame Naga men. How can the cry for justice and freedom from the lips of Naga women be read as shameful? Today, what kind of justice and freedom do we choose at this crossroads in Naga society? One that excludes the poor and speaks the language of exclusive economic benefits for Naga individuals? One that includes the rich and their network of families and friends? One that solely sees people through the prism of class, ethnicity, and entitlements? What is it that we should call for at this moment in Naga society?

To begin with, if Naga women have to be included within the 33 per cent reservation for political participation, then the existing practice of Naga customary law, practices, and processes that are defined as "democratic" or at times "egalitarian" need to change.

What kind of change can we call for? We can begin a process of working towards a Naga democratic system that calls for an end to militarization, violence, and demand the repeal of Armed Forces Special Powers Act (1957). The existing militarized Naga society we have come to accept as normal is an exceptionally soul numbing system that Naga men and women alike have had to endure every day.[5] During the 33 per cent reservation debate and agitation in Nagaland, Naga youth patrolling the streets with sticks and other weapons, destroying public buildings, and using aggression and violence to humiliate and subjugate voices of dissent, exposed how experiences of militarization under extra-constitutional regulations like the AFSPA had been internalized by the Naga public to regulate and control their neighbours and friends.[6] This included the fear, digital censorship, apathy of the state authorities, and the charged violent atmosphere across the state. The political crisis witnessed during this period underlined the foundations of Naga militarization.

One of the issues about the violent protests around the 33 per cent reservation was related to the media coverage. Irrespective of the criticisms against national and international media who covered the issue in Nagaland, we need to recognize that the issue of gender justice did come up. Naga people have to engage with the national and

5. See Inotloi Zhimomi's reflections about why Naga society needs an honest discussion about the 33 per cent reservation in Nagaland. *http://raiot.in/nagaland-needs-to-honestly-discuss-33-reservation-for-women/* (accessed on 14 August, 2017)

6. To read the fear that such youth patrolling provoked from the opponents of the 33 per cent reservation, read Vizokhole Ltu's reflections *http://raiot.in/in-the-name-of-the-customary/* (accessed 14 August, 2017)

international community as our interlocutors and allies. We cannot afford to push away and ignore the disturbing issues about Naga society that some journalists wrote about. I would instead argue that the 33 per cent opposition and the culmination of the violent protests in Nagaland made us realize the importance of feminism as an ideology. Naga men and women alike who participated in the debates about gender justice felt the need to extend these conversations. At this hour, we need to recognize the importance of tribal feminism, justice and the need to conceptualize these terms and processes. The debates that have emerged though the agitation should push us towards a political tradition in Naga society that shakes the foundation of inequality and unjust practices that exist under the cloak of Naga culture. This is the time to create a form of Naga gender justice that becomes a norm and ignites conversations about addressing many more political issues such as racism, discrimination, and the rights of tribal migrants in contemporary India.

This is not the time to be ashamed as Naga people because of the crisis.

It is a time to reflect and connect; examine our political foundations, build alliances and solidarities to talk about justice across the region and beyond. To be honest, we cannot expect a radical change in Naga society through electoral politics. History stands as a witness. Even if we implement the 33 per cent reservation, unless the municipal council as a system embraces the principles of gender justice, includes the Naga poor, single mothers, widows, unemployed youth, and speaks for the old and the marginalized from all backgrounds including the poor non-Naga migrants and traders, the moneyed groups and power hungry elites will continue to dominate Naga lives. Despite this, I feel that this is a wonderful moment in Naga society when every man, woman, and youth has read the Nagaland Municipal Act, the Constitution of India – especially Article 371 (A), and has knocked at the door of the Bar Council of Nagaland to hold discussions about the legal implications of the act. In every locality, there are small groups of men and women sitting together rebuilding trust and reaffirming their support for gender justice. Imagine hundreds of such small groups coming together to form a joint common vision for a just Naga society! However, failure to recognize the existing militarization and violence will obstruct a shared vision for a Naga just future. How can we live under extra-constitutional regulations like AFSPA, have ceasefire camps with stagnant peace talks, and pretend to fix our society? Until we continue our demands for a political resolution of the Indo-Naga political conflict and demilitarization of Naga society, we cannot rebuild Naga society.

The logic of protecting Naga women from the dangers of politics, public office, reservation, and all kinds of activities cannot be based on an Indian state-like

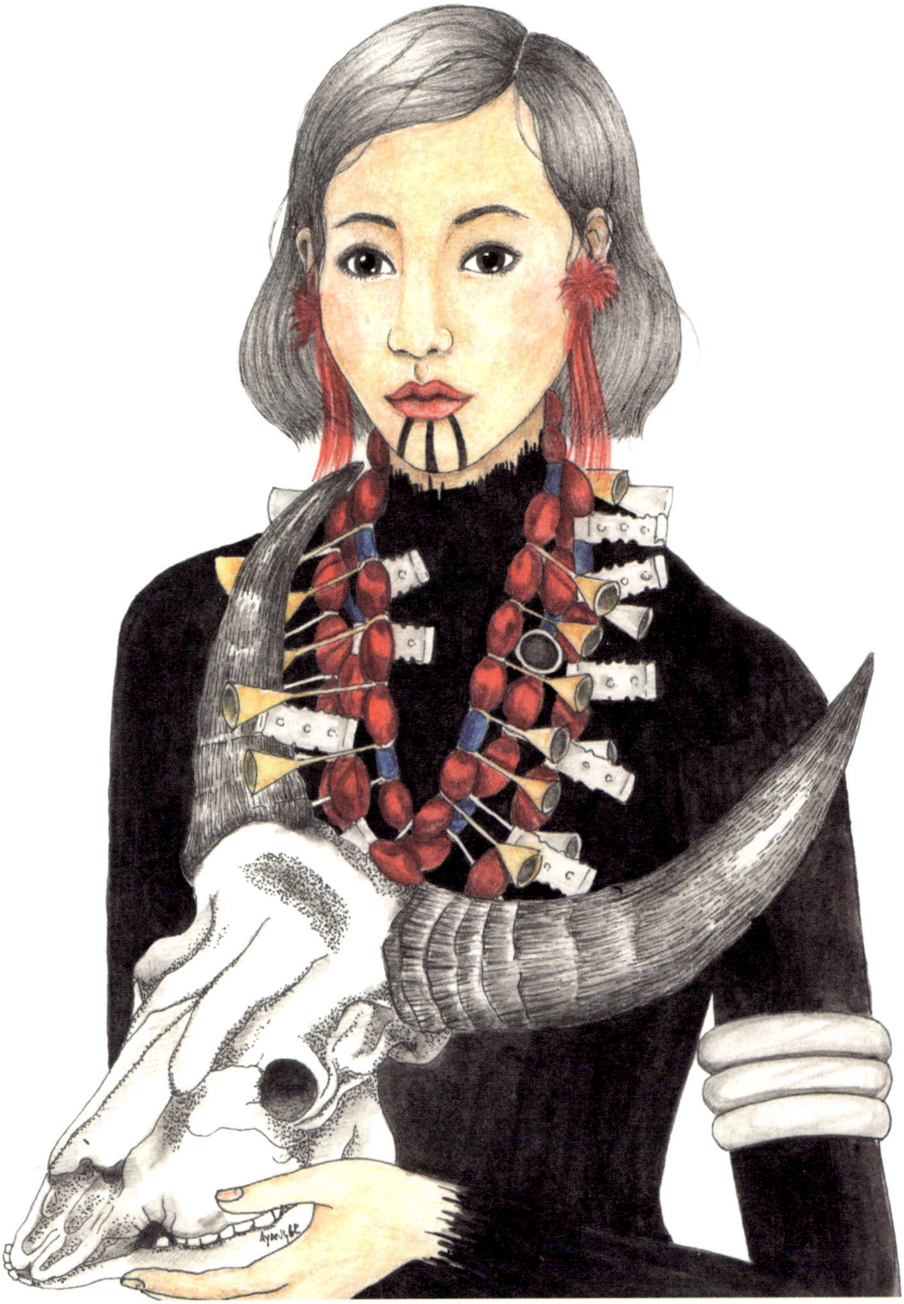

portrait
AYANGBE MANNEN

militarized strategy; to impose a cultural and traditional curfew and incarcerate them within the limits of the four walls. Lest we forget, let me remind you of the logic of the Indian state. Today, Naga women can work for charities, as volunteers, or household heads but purely for utilitarian purposes. As long as the face of the political sphere in Naga society is a Naga male who outlines and defines what constitutes Naga culture and tradition, the patriarchal status quo is observed. Such hierarches, among other things, define what is "important political work" and all other things, thereby reiterating how understanding of tribal power and authority is extremely masculine in Nagaland. For long, Naga people were defined as emotional, childlike, barbaric, wild, and savages. Only guns and bullets from the Indian state could tame them. If this same logic is used by the Naga leaders and male tribal bodies on the Naga women/the poor/ and marginalized sections of the society to rule them, we have successfully adopted the master plan and replaced the vision of a just future with a broken and violent mechanism. Today, we are yet to hear the name of a Naga woman who will lead the Indo-Naga ceasefire talks, become an advisor to the Naga Hoho, the arbitrator at a Naga customary law proceeding on divorce, the wise head in a property dispute between two brothers, the head of the Naga Forum for Reconciliation, the Chaplin who prays for the Chief Minister, or the leader of the Christian churches (across denominations).

Naga people (both men and women), scholars, activists, and practitioners across the fields (churches, education, government offices, cultural associations, and women's bodies including youth clubs) need to recognize that a feminist tribal ideology can achieve a meaningful framework of gender justice and peace. Feminists in the women's movements across the region have shown us the courage and wisdom to create political alliances across class, ethnicity, race, caste, generation, gender stereotypes, and beyond territorial and nationalist boundaries to dream of a new just world based on equality and a habitable future. As a Naga feminist, I remain hopeful that we are able to resist the money, power, and attractions of authority wrapped in Naga patriarchal and traditional cloaks.

How should I articulate this hope? What is the foundation of this tribal feminist politics?

These questions take me back to the memories of my mother in the kitchen preparing for my departure to Delhi for my undergraduate studies. In the days preceding my departure, my mother would become obsessed with making pickles and smoking beef and pork for me. Roasting chillies and frying the dry fish, she spent a considerable amount of time in the kitchen working and making my food parcel. As a single mother in her 50s who worked at the Department of Information and Public

Relations, she kept to herself and avoided the Naga public sphere where males and females participated, which was predominately the tribal church gatherings, weddings, and festive occasions. I read her action as a mark of individual protest. Institutions – be it religious assemblies or cultural bodies – that humiliate the poor, widows, divorcees, and the dispossessed – are best avoided, her actions seemed to indicate. In the last twenty years since then, my mother and I have continued our conversations about what it means to be a Naga woman. Can the kitchen be part of the public sphere?

Domestic work such as making pickles, cooking, and cleaning is not defined as work in Naga society. The labour of Naga women that goes into feeding the family, preparing a feast, or the routine sessions of serving are naturalized as feminine qualities that women ought to possess. Such conceptions of domesticity and labour add a layer to the traditional divide of the private and the public sphere. For opponents who argue that Naga women should not be allowed to have equal decision making powers in the apex tribal councils, they perceive the domestic world as an extension of tribal femininity and erase it as a site where important decisions and activities take place. But the presence of working Naga women in the paddy fields, markets, public offices, and the professional world of research, engineering, business, and media, means that the public and private divide created and upheld by male members in the traditional councils is continuously blurred. Instead of rejecting the private sphere as a realm of domesticity and femininity, Naga women have embraced the security and comfort of being at home after a long day at work. In this context, the home has become an important place to locate new political debates about sexual violence, unemployment, livelihood issues, and emerging forms of masculinities and insecurities in Naga society. For instance, the figure of the unemployed male member in the family attracts more negative comments from relatives and neighbours as compared to the female siblings. In this respect, the assumed expectations of the Naga male members to live up to their traditional duties as prescribed by a dominant tribal patriarchal framework only seem to obstruct a democratic dialogue about gender justice and equality. Therefore, the moral reasoning and values of Naga society cannot be founded on inherent principles of gender inequality. If Naga men and women alike are considered as subjects under customary law, the cultural and traditional argument from their opponents I have elaborated in this essay to uphold the existing practice of all male membership simply falls apart.

the objects of everyday work: a photo essay

AUNGMAKHAI CHAK

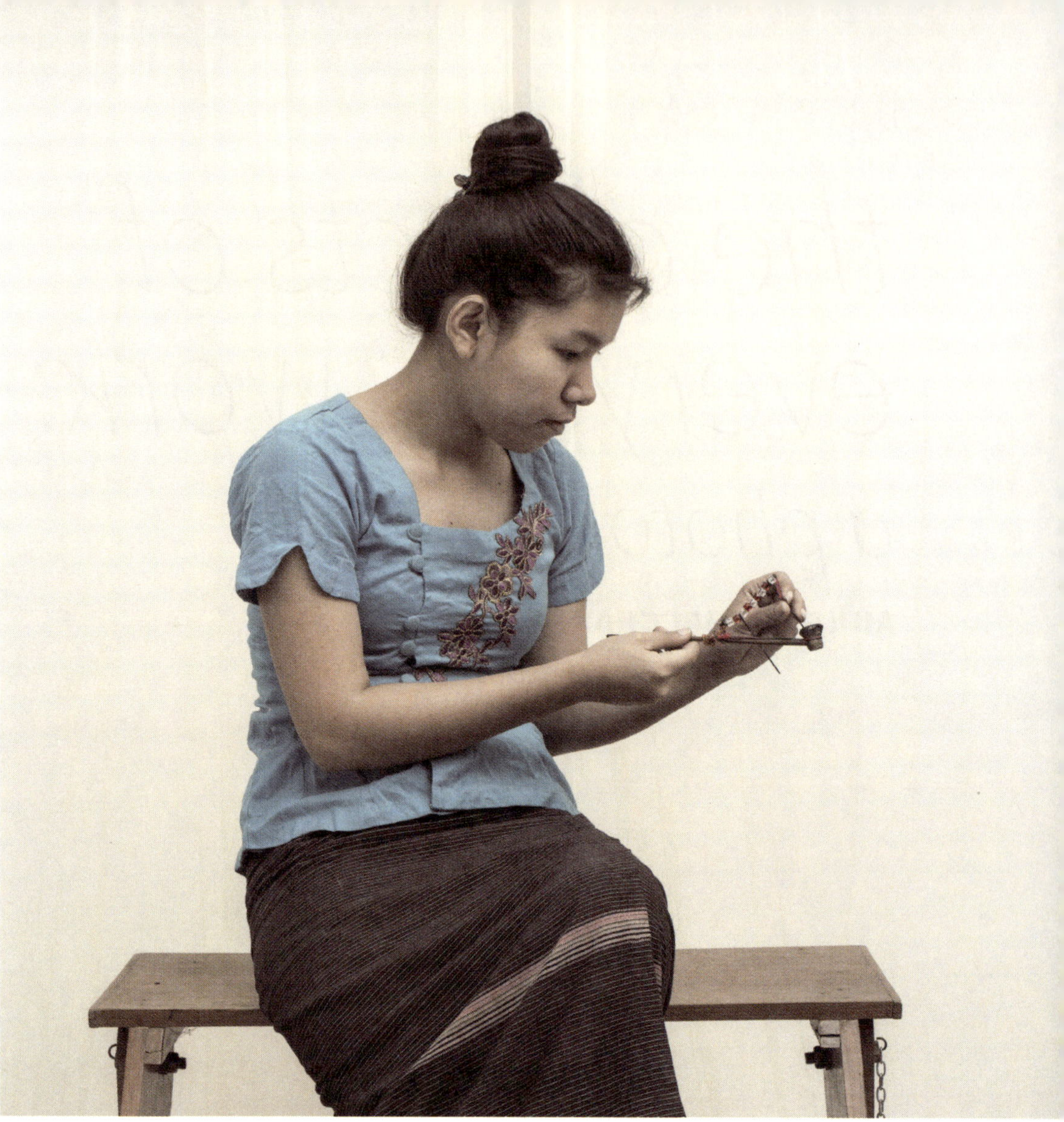

I reject the idea that work is only related to money or food.

The Paing-du or pipe is made by the women of the Chak community for smoking tobacco. A Paing-du is different in shape and nature for men and women. For women, it is not simply for the pleasure of smoking, though that is there. It is also a form of self- expression.

When a woman makes one, it reflects her taste and personality through her choice of beads and other objects that decorate the pipe. Unlike our "modern" capitalist society, the concept of beauty and art for indigenous women in my grandmother's generation was intimately related to objects that were part of everyday work.

For them, beauty meant the beautification of objects that are closely related to life.

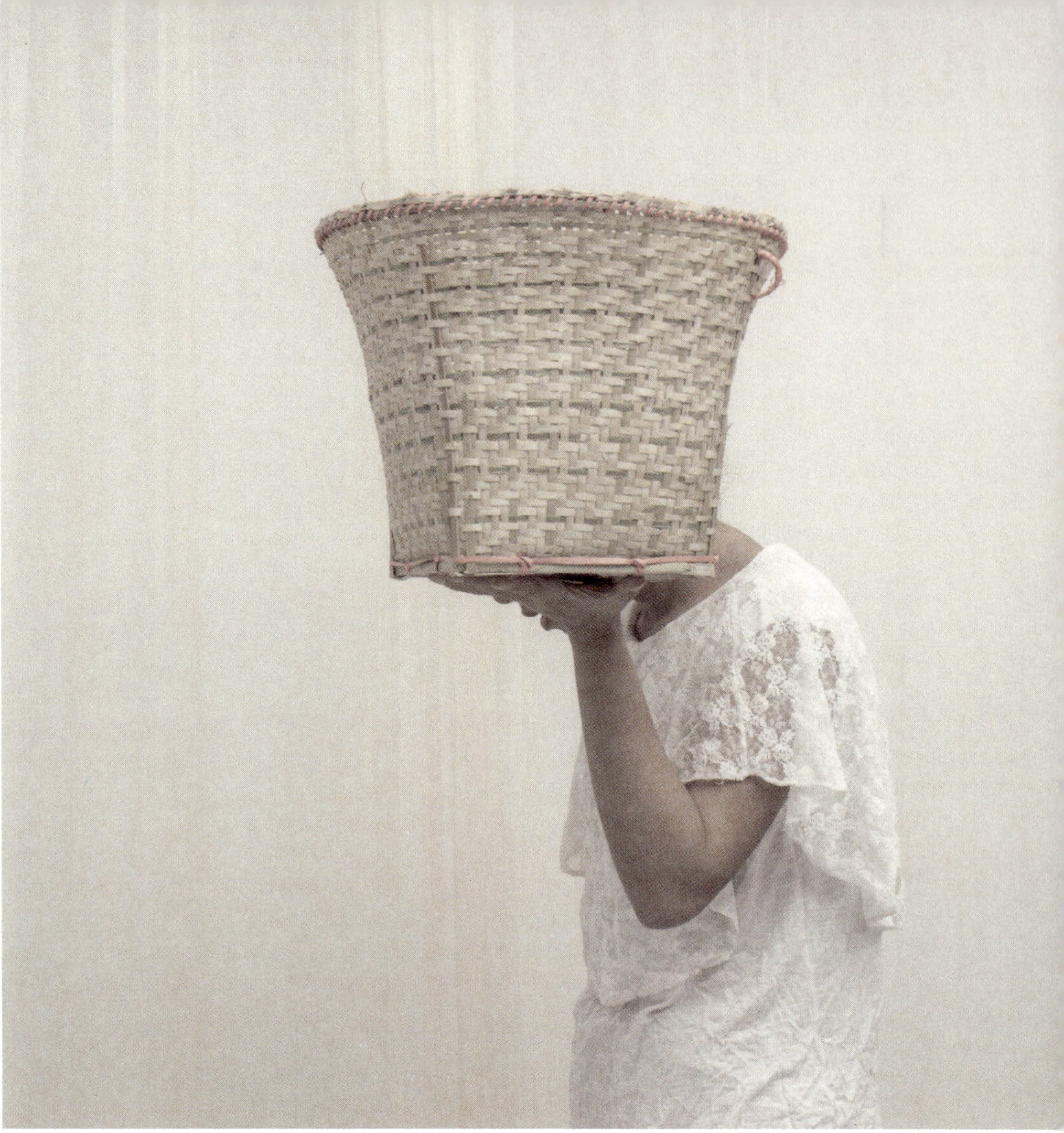

II

The established iconography for indigenous women at work is a woman with an indigenous face, carrying the “kung” full of crops or vegetables. Her face is usually different from the women from majority (Bengali) communities.

In those representations, the face is often more important than the work itself.

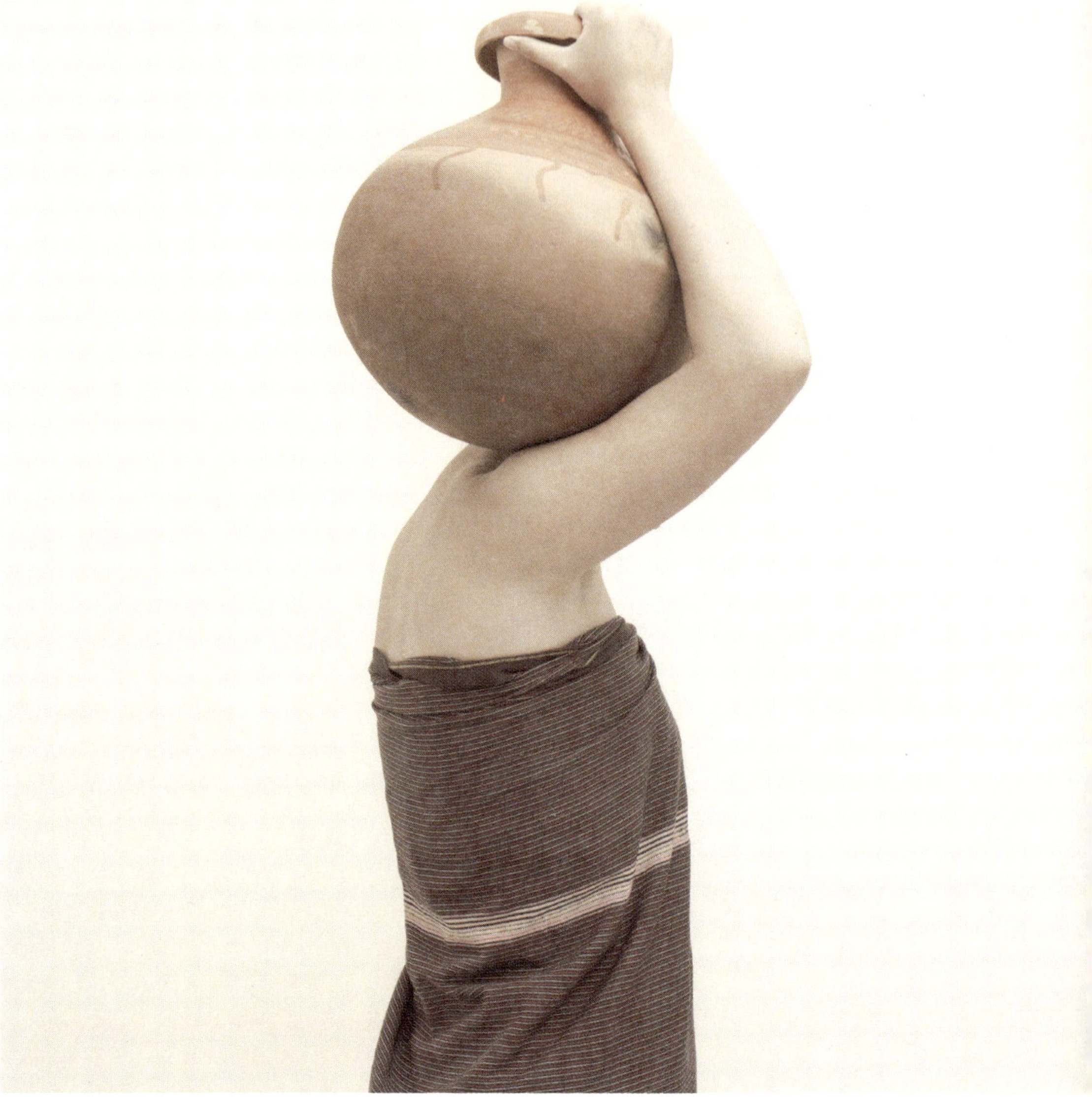

III

There is a common misconception that indigenous societies are free from gender discrimination or do not follow patriarchal norms. My experience of growing up as an indigenous woman was different. Being the youngest among four sisters in our family, I along with my sisters, faced numerous challenges from the "moral policing" of the community. Like other societies, many indigenous communities have different roles for men and women. If they are playing the same role, there are unwritten regulations for men and women on the way of carrying out the same role. I carry the earthen jar for water in a manner that is often a man's way of carrying a jar. Men carry the water jars on their shoulders, projecting their physical strength as opposed to women who are often seen carrying the jars on their waist.

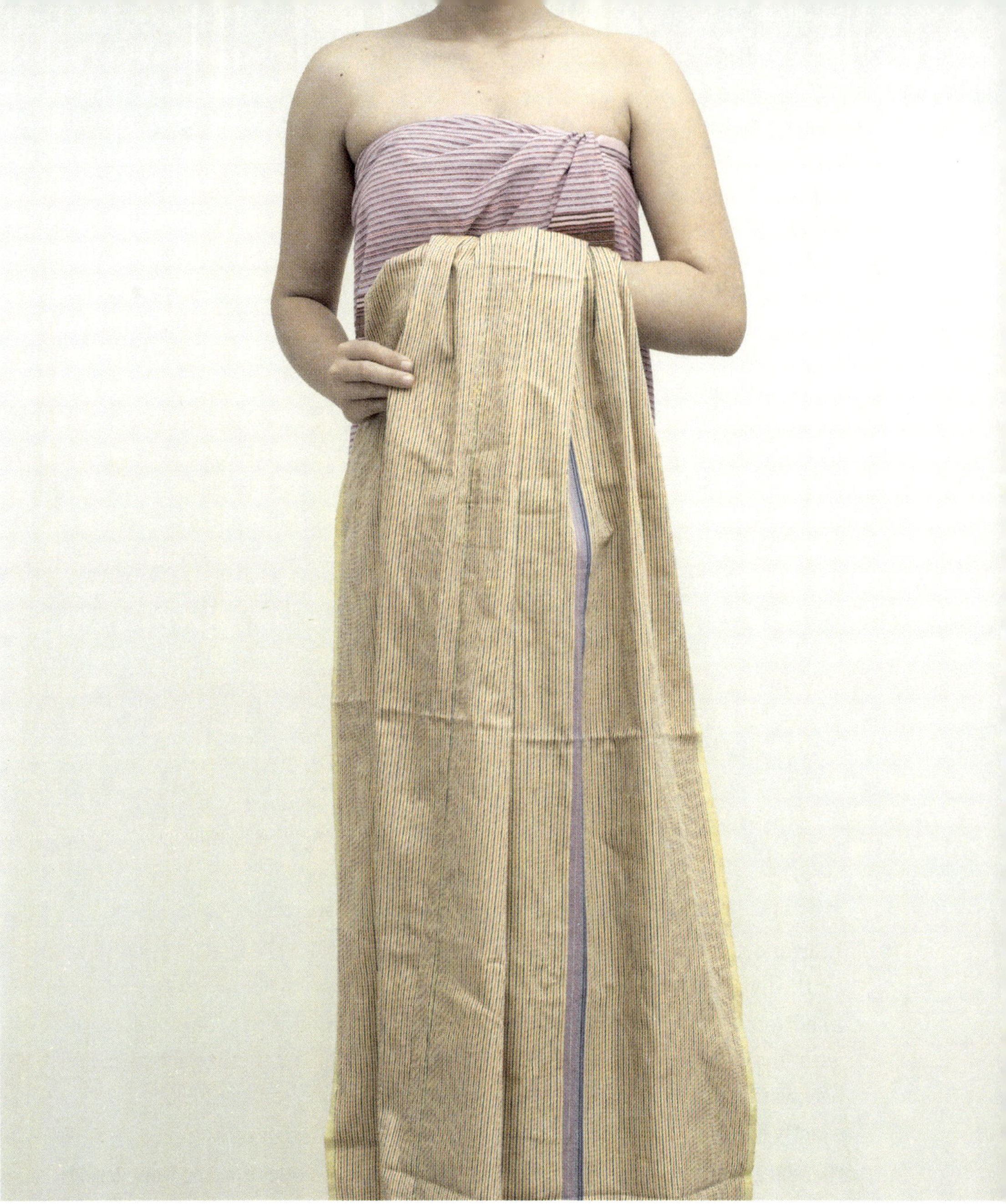

IV

Indigenous women in my community used to weave the Na-phing, a skirt-like outfit for the lower part of the body. In my grandmother's generation, they used to wear a shorter version of the Na-phing. With time, our communities came in contact with "mainstream" society. Women wearing a short Na-phing turned into a sign of backwardness and savagery. In my mother's generation the Na-phing became longer, exactly double in length. My mother and others would weave them and stitch two similar pieces together to make it longer. The work has doubled over time and with the influence of "modernity".

Unlike my grandmother and mother, I have grown up in a mixed society. Ideas and perspectives of the "dominant" society are constantly trying to change ours. Wearing a Na-phing in public is not "normal" anymore, we are ridiculed. However, this dominant society loves to see us in our attires occasionally. For example, singing, dancing or other performances for their entertainment. Then, not wearing a Na-phing would be criticized by both the "mainstream audience" and indigenous males. Therefore, indigenous girls of my generation (especially those who live in urban or semi-urban settings) wear these traditional skirts occasionally, when we need to perform as 'indigenous'.

the other side of the looking glass:

retelling of mizo folktales

JACQUELINE ZOTE

Mawii gazed at the burning candle in front of her, carefully observing the movements of the flame. There was a power cut again and they had to make do with candlelight. Power cuts were frequent in her mountainside town. Normally, Mawii would hate it when there was no electricity because she couldn't watch TV or read her comic books.

But tonight, she felt, would be different though she didn't know why. She was sitting on a mat on the living room floor. The night was warm but there was a cool breeze blowing from the open window, making the white chiffon curtains flutter.

Her father was sitting on the couch next to her, strumming his guitar, and singing to the tune of his favourite country songs. To Mawii, he looked as if he'd fit right in if you threw a cowboy hat on his head and placed him inside a western movie. Her little brother was curled up next to her on the mat, gradually falling off to sleep. He was 4 years old and the day had been long for him.

On another couch, her teenaged cousin Pari sat reading a novel under the light of a torch. Pari was staying with them for a few weeks while her parents travelled to Kolkata for health treatment. She read a lot and would be lost in a book every chance she got. A simple power cut wasn't going to stop her from following the adventures of a little boy in Hogwarts.

Mawii had always been fascinated by Pari, although the latter didn't pay her much attention. The teenager's quiet demeanour and intelligent eyes impressed the little girl immensely. Mawii believed her cousin knew everything about everything and would often bombard her with random (and sometimes absurd) questions. This was annoying to the introverted 16-year-old, who often tried to avoid any kind of social interaction.

Mawii's attention shifted to the figure entering the room. Her mother had been washing the dishes from dinner. "'Finally, Nu! I've been waiting since forever,'" Mawii whined.

"'I have to finish my work first, you know that."

"I hate that you have to work so much."

"I know, honey. But sometimes it's necessary. Who's going to do all the work if I don't, huh?"

Sensing her mother's agitation, Mawii thought it better not to respond.

Mawii's mother went by the name of Sangi. She was a petite, middle-aged woman with kind eyes and an even kinder voice. Even if Mawii tried with all her might to remember a time when her mother shouted at her or lost her patience, she wouldn't succeed.

But today, Sangi had had a particularly tiring day as she had to get ready for a small feast they were hosting the next day. It was to celebrate her husband's promotion. She immediately regretted snapping at her daughter.

"And what exactly have you been waiting for?" Sangi said teasingly as she made herself comfortable beside her daughter and rested her back against her husband's leg. She was trying to lighten the mood.

Mawii replied enthusiastically, "I want a story. Please please, Nu! I'm so bored. There's nothing to do."

Sangi smiled as she pulled her daughter close and held her head against her chest. Evenings like these set the mood for storytelling but she sometimes wondered if she wanted her daughter to be brought up with the same stories she heard as a girl. Would it be wrong to change things around a bit?

She glanced at her husband who had begun to nod off. Sangi couldn't help but feel a slight resentment, an irritation. Men have it so much easier here, she thought. That settled it. It was time for a story – the story of Sichangneii.

"Sichangneii was a woman of the skies," Sangi began. "Women of the skies are popular in the stories our ancestors told. They might be similar to angels and are often described as beautiful young women with majestic bird-like wings.

"The story begins with a young man who built a small pond from a natural spring. Every morning, he would go to check on the pond. But to his dismay, the pond would always be murky and dirty. The man found this puzzling and was unable to figure out who could be behind it.

"So he decided to ask around the village to see if anyone knew anything about how his pond got so murky every morning. He went from house to house, only to discover that no one could point their fingers at the culprit. Just as the man began losing hope, he met an old woman who claimed to have seen the people who dirtied his pond.

" 'It was Sichangneii and her sister,' she said confidently, 'they fly down from the skies every morning to bathe in the pond. That's why it gets so dirty when you get there.'

" 'But beware,' the old woman added, 'if you're planning to catch them, make sure you approach them from behind. Else you'll be blinded by their beauty and you won't be able to catch them.'

"The next day, the man waited behind the bushes near the pond for Sichangneii and her sister to appear. As dawn approached, he saw two magnificent creatures flying down from the skies. They looked like women but they also looked otherworldly. He was awestruck by their bright glow that lit up the pond and its surroundings as they bathed in it.

"By this time, the man had forgotten all about the old woman's advice. He rushed in to catch them but as he looked at them, he was blinded by their light. This gave the sisters enough time to escape to the skies.

"Having seen the sky women, the man could barely sleep that night. He was enthralled by their beauty and couldn't think of anything else but them. Finally, he decided that he would catch one of them and make her his wife.

"The next morning, he hid near the pond again and waited for the creatures to appear. This time he would follow the old woman's advice. Soon, the skies started to open and he saw the same two women floating down.

"He waited for them to be at ease so he could catch them unawares. After a while, the maidens started splashing the water playfully at each other, their laughter ringing melodiously in the man's ears. He took this chance to slowly creep up behind

Sichangneii and jump on her, grabbing her tight to make sure she wouldn't escape, even as her sister flew back to the skies.

"The man then took Sichangneii home to make her his wife. To prevent her from flying back home, he clipped her wings and tail feathers and then hid them from her. So she was trapped with no option but to marry her kidnapper."

"That's so sad, Nu." Mawii said.

"Yes," Sangi responded.

"What happens next?"

"The two of them get married and have seven sons."

"Seven? That's a lot!"

"Yes, believe it or not it was the norm back in those days. It wasn't until recently that it became acceptable for women to have fewer children. Even your grandmother had six siblings."

"Oh! I didn't know that. And then what happens?"

"While Sichangneii wasn't home, the man would entertain his sons by taking out his wife's wings and tail feathers from hiding. But he warned his sons to never tell their mother about it because then she would leave them."

"Why doesn't he want her to know?" asked Mawii.

"Even after so many years of being together, perhaps Sichangneii had a hard time with the man. If you remember, he had caught her and married her by force."

Sangi wistfully looked at her daughter and wondered if it was too soon to tell her all of this. But she soon snapped out of it when she heard Mawii ask, "What happens next, Nu?"

"One day, Sichangneii had to take care of the kids while her husband was away from home. But unlike the times when her husband looked after them, the kids were cranky and uncontrollable. Exasperated, she asked them, 'Why is it that you're so well-behaved and quiet when your father is at home but not with me? Why do you want to stay inside with him but when I am around, all you want is to run around the fields?'

"'There's a reason why,' was the youngest son's reply, which was quickly followed by his brothers shushing him.

"This stirred Sichangneii's curiosity. 'Please tell me, son, what is that?' she nudged him. 'Well, father takes out a beautiful pair of wings and some tail feathers. So we wear them and dance around the house pretending to be birds. It's really fun!' the kid answered.

"Sichangneii felt a wave of relief rushing through her as she heard this. Could this be true? Would she finally find her feathers?

" 'Do you know where he keeps these things, son?' she asked. The youngest son pointed towards the bamboo basket in which he'd seen his father putting their feathery toys back before his mother got home.

"Despite her others sons' attempts to stop her, Sichangneii rushed towards the basket, took out the plumage that once adorned her, and immediately put it on. She ran out to the porch but halted to take one final look at her seven sons. She then called out to them and said, 'Goodbye, my sons. You're all grown up now and you can look after yourselves. Take care of your little brother.'

"Before she could change her mind, she spread her wings and flew back home towards the skies. What a relief, don't you think?"

"But she has children...seven of them! Why would she want to leave them behind?"

"As much as she loved her children, she was still in entrapment. It's possible that she dreamt of being free and going back to the skies."

"I see..." Mawii responded but you could tell from the look on her face that she was still somewhat confused.

"Look, Mawii," her mother said in a firm but patient tone, "marriage and children aren't the ultimate source of happiness for many people. It's like that, sometimes."

"Oh," Mawii replied in a tone that said she was still mulling over it.

"My point is people don't enjoy doing things that they've been forced to do. And for Sichangneii, she was forced to marry and live with someone she didn't love. She then had to bear seven children on top of that. Would you be happy if you were forced to do something?"

"Well... Is it like when I don't feel like going to school but Apa forces me to go?"

Sangi giggled, "Yes, a bit like that but much more serious."

"I don't know... I feel bad for her but I'm also sad for the sons. They no longer have a mother. You'd never leave us would you, Nu?"

A faint smile spread across Sangi's face. Her daughter's question reminded her of that night a few years ago. She was so close to walking out the door. A few months of virtually endless fights with her husband combined with post-partum depression had taken their toll.

Something set her off that particular night. She was on the verge of giving up. She couldn't bear it any longer, and hastily threw her clothes in a duffel bag. She doesn't remember much after that, but she didn't go. She had sat by her two sleeping children. They had looked so peaceful, so untouched by the evils of the world.

The sight calmed her.

"Nu?" Mawii had grown impatient to hear her mother's response.

"You know I won't, Mawii. Besides, Sichangneii was a sky woman, remember? She could still keep watch over her sons and protect them whenever they needed. She just couldn't stand living with her awful husband anymore. "

"Oh, okay then. So what happens after that?"

"When the man got home and discovered his wife gone, he was distraught. Unable to bear the loneliness, he takes a hammer and cracks one of his testicles."

"So he's practically trying to emotionally blackmail Sichangneii by hurting himself. What a manipulative bastard!" Pari fumed. She seemed to have been immersed in a book but was evidently listening to the story intently.

"Language, Pari," Sangi responded, half-amused at her niece's anger but also impressed by her perceptive reading of the situation. When did she grow up so much?

"Sorry, so what happens afterwards?"

"The man writhed in pain after he cracked his own testicle. But his youngest son was unable to see the gravity of the situation. He laughed as he watched his father, who looked as if he was dancing.

"The man, after realizing that his self-inflicted pain couldn't compel his wife to come back to earth, decided to crack his other testicle. So he did and ended up dying from the pain."

"I love Sichangneii. I'm glad she finally got her wings back and flew back home," Pari declared.

"Me too! I wish I had wings as well so I could fly wherever I want to," her little cousin added.

"I think it's time you fly off to bed," Sangi joked.

"But I'm not sleepy yet, Nu."

"Me neither, aunty. Besides, we don't have school tomorrow so we can stay up a little longer."

"All right, all right. I can never win with you two, can I?"

Her tone was playful but there was a hint of tiredness in her voice.

"I'm sorry, aunty but can we please have another story? It's not every night we get to spend time together."

Sangi sighed.

"Yes! Another story! This time, make it a scary one," Mawii pleaded.

"Are you sure you want to hear a scary story? You won't be able to sleep," Sangi teased her daughter.

"What about Phungpuinu and Chhurbura?" Pari suggested.

"What's a Phungpuinu?" Mawii asked, her eyes sparkling with excitement.

"In olden day Mizoram, there were lots of stories about a creature known as a phung," replied Sangi, "it's a grotesque humanoid creature with wild bushy hair and pitch black skin. The bodies of phungs are entirely covered with matted hair, which adds to their sinister appearance. Some types of phungs even have teeth the size of cucumbers. And even if it's not specified, they're normally considered to be females.

"These creatures, possibly due to their bizarre physical appearance, have a knack for scaring humans. That's why there's a phrase '*phung hmu ang mai*', or 'as though they've seen a phung'. There was once a man who went hunting on his own. Unfortunately for him, he had had too much to eat that morning. So after a while, he felt the urge to relieve himself in the bushes. As soon as he began, he felt a small stone hitting him in the head. Confused, he looked around but couldn't find anything.

"So he returned to his 'task'. But as soon as he started again, a much bigger stone hit him on the forehead. He was livid. He stood up, took his gun, and pointed it towards the direction from which the stone came. 'Come out and fight like a man, I dare you!' he shouted.

"That's when he heard a blood-curdling cackle from behind the trees. And suddenly, a phung leapt into view, grinning from ear to ear and ready to attack. This sight scared him so much that he ran off without another word, forgetting his gun and finishing the rest of his 'task' as he ran."

Her two young ones roared with laughter. Once they were ready to listen again, she resumed, "They say that the Amaranthus bloom repels these phungs. That's why you'll always see the bright red blooms near the entrance of a thlâm. The Phungpuinu is the mother of these creatures and her name translates to 'mother phung'.

"Chhurbura and the Phungpuinu often appear together in Mizo folklore, always troubling each other and trying to outwit one another. There's the time Chhurbura sets up a swing at the courtyard of his thlâm. The thlâm, like traditional Mizo cottages, was made of bamboo with a thatched roof. It stood on wooden stilts so that the entrance was level with the hilltop.

"The hilltop served as a courtyard for the thlâm and had a few clusters of trees and flowers. It was among these trees that Chuurbura set up the swing. Along the slope of the hill lay the rest of his farm, where he grew tubers and vegetables.

"Every day during lunch time, Chhurbura would take a break from farm work and open up a bundle of food wrapped in banana leaves. After devouring the contents of the bundle, he would rush to the swing and spend the rest of his break time lounging in it.

"Sometimes he dozed off, serenaded by the chirping of birds and the warm summer breeze. And sometimes he would sing or whistle as he swung back and forth with daydreams of a more leisurely life.

"It was on one of these days that a Phungpuinu happened by Chhurbura's farm. Intrigued by the pleasant and unfamiliar sound, she decided to follow it and investigate. She crept up behind some trees and found a burly and somewhat awkward human being happily drifting in the air.

"As she inspected further, she found that the man wasn't levitating but was using some sort of rope to swing from the trees. This discovery amazed the Phungpuinu so much that she stood there with mouth agape for several minutes.

"She must try this strange contraption! She decided to wait until he was gone.

"So she waited and waited until the man finally set off towards home. As soon as he disappeared from sight she rushed to the swing and climbed on it. At first, she lost her balance and tumbled down head first on the ground."

Mawii suddenly burst out laughing, followed by a brief snicker from Pari.

Sangi grinned and continued, "After a few more failed attempts, the Phungpuinu eventually got used to the movements and mechanisms of the swing. Within a couple of days she started to enjoy the swing rides until that was all she could think of!

"She took pleasure in the cool wind blowing against her face and the leaping of her heart every time she took a swing. But one day, her thick bushy hair got caught in the ropes. Although she managed to break free, a few clumps of hair were still stuck in the swing. Not realizing this, she headed home to her lair after sunset.

"The next day, Chhurbura came to the farm. Like every other day during lunch, he sat on the swing and prepared to start swinging. But he immediately came to a halt when he saw the thick clumps of dirty, matted hair caught in the ropes of the swing.

"He hesitantly removed the hair clumps as he tried to figure out who or what had been using his swing in his absence. He eventually came to the conclusion that it must be a Phungpuinu, judging from how the hair looked.

"So that evening, he pretended to leave the farm like every other day. But instead of heading home, he hid behind some trees and waited for the Phungpuinu to appear. As soon as the coast was clear, the creature rushed out of her lair and hopped onto Chhurbura's swing.

"As she merrily swung on the swing, she started singing a song – 'Chhurbura awm ta love...' which means 'At last, Chhurbura's gone home.'"

Mawii and Pari couldn't help but find this amusing and all three of them dissolved into laughter. They could only stop after tears started flowing from their eyes. "All right, what happens after that?" Mawii asked, her cheeks aching from laughing so much.

"Lost in her own little world, the Phungpuinu didn't see it coming when Chhurbura jumped out from the back and grabbed her by the hair," Sangi continued.

"The creature struggled in vain to break free from Chhurbura's grasp. Finally, she tried to reason with him and offered him various magical tools in exchange for her freedom. The man eventually decided to free her after she offered him a Sekibuhchhuak.

"A Sekibuhchhuak is a magical horn that can produce an endless supply of food – rice from one side and meat from another – if you coax it with a certain chant. Even the name literally translates to rice-producing horn.

"Chhurbura then takes the Sekibuhchhuak home, pleased with himself for making the deal of a lifetime. Now he won't have to toil in the farm anymore because he can get all the rice and meat he wants. Although the Phungpuinu came up with plan after plan to get her treasure back, she couldn't act on them because Chhurbura never came back to the farm."

"I'd love to have a Sekibuhchhuak too. I'll never have to work," Mawii sighed longingly, which made her mother chuckle.

"They say Grandmother had a Sekibuhchhuak too. Even when there was an unexpected guest from another village, there was always enough rice for them to eat."

Mawii's face brightened up at this.

After a few minutes of silence, she asked her mother, "Do you know any stories about good ramhuai?"

"Of course, there are several. But my favourite among these are the khuavang."

"Isn't khuavang a mole on the skin?"

"Well a mole is the mark of the khuavang so it's called khuavang chhinchhiah."

"I didn't know that."

Sangi smiled and began, "They say that the khuavang are a group of magical creatures. They're like humans but they can turn themselves invisible so they live all around us, possibly in a different realm. We can't see them but they can see us."

"That's a bit unsettling, isn't it? They could be watching us in our sleep and we wouldn't even know. Who knows? They could even be listening to this story right now," remarked Pari.

Her aunt shot her a look that said, "Don't scare your little cousin with such thoughts," which made Pari giggle.

Sangi hastily resumed, "These creatures are normally considered as good spirits. Some even say that the khuavang sometimes guard humans.

"There are both male and female khuavang and they get married and build families just like us humans do. There are even stories of entire villages of khuavang buried beneath the earth. You can enter the village through a hole in the ground.

"You know how sometimes there's pin-drop silence even when you're in a group? That moment is called khuavang kal lai, which literally translates to a moment during which the khuavang walk among us.

"And the first person to speak after a pin-drop silence is believed to earn a new mole, marked by the khuavang. Our ancestors believed that the moles on our bodies are a way for these creatures to distinguish between different human beings.

"They also say that the khuavang have control over the formation of mountains, ridges, and the earth's surface. Some even believed they were as powerful as gods.

"The khuavang only bless or help humans if humans have done something good for them. And if you've done something to annoy them, they could curse you or cause you harm.

"When they do decide to make themselves visible, the khuavang often appear as old ladies."

"So you mean any old lady can be a khuavang? Even the ones on our street?"

"It's possible. They could be living right next to us and we wouldn't even know."

"What about the old lady who sells smoked fish from door to door? Doesn't she seem like a khuavang? She always keeps her head covered and she looks at me weirdly."

This made Sangi stifle a laugh. Trust her daughter to come up with the most outrageous assumptions. Though come to think of it, she did have a point.

"We'll never know," she finally answered.

"I wish I could meet a khuavang and ask them all about their world," Mawii mused.

"Who knows? You might have already met one. But I think they'd like to keep their world a secret from us humans."

Mawii didn't respond to this and instead seemed to be in deep thought. After a while, she asked, "Nu, do you think there are any good ramhuai that live in our world? I mean are there any that won't make themselves invisible or live in a different realm?"

"Wait, there's one that I think you're going to love."

"What's that?"

"It's called a pheichham. Have you ever heard of the term 'pheichham man', which means 'to catch a pheichham'?" Sangi asked.

"I have heard it but I've always been confused."

"It originated in Mizo folklore. According to the beliefs of our ancestors, if you catch a pheichham you could compel it to fulfil your wishes..."

"Like a genie?" Mawii interrupted.

"Yes. Very similar to a genie, or a jinn," Sangi answered.

"The pheichham is a creature that lives in the forest and looks very much like a human being in fact. But it has only one leg. So it hops around instead of walking or running."

"Wait... I've read about something similar in one of *The Chronicles of Narnia books*. They're called Duffers and they can make themselves invisible," Pari said enthusiastically.

"That's really interesting, Pari. You should tell Mawii about them some time," her aunt replied before she continued with the story.

"It's possible that these creatures don't have a specific gender identity. What they do have is the ability to grant wishes. Some say if you catch a pheichham it will grant you as many wishes as you can mention without taking a breath.

"Others say that since the pheichham only has one leg, it's prone to falling down and being unable to get back up on its own. If you chance upon one in this situation and help it up, it will bless you or grant your wishes.

"There's one story in which a man called Ṭhasiama managed to live a long and prosperous life after being blessed by a pheichham. The story goes that a mischievous pheichham had destroyed the crops in Ṭhasiama's farm. In an attempt to catch the creature red-handed, Ṭhasiama hid inside his thlâm long after it was time to go home.

"When the creature appeared, Ṭhasiama managed to catch it and threatened to take it home so he could use it as a decoration. The desperate pheichham tried to reason with the man and promised to grant his wishes if he let it go. The only condition was that he mention all his wishes in a single breath.

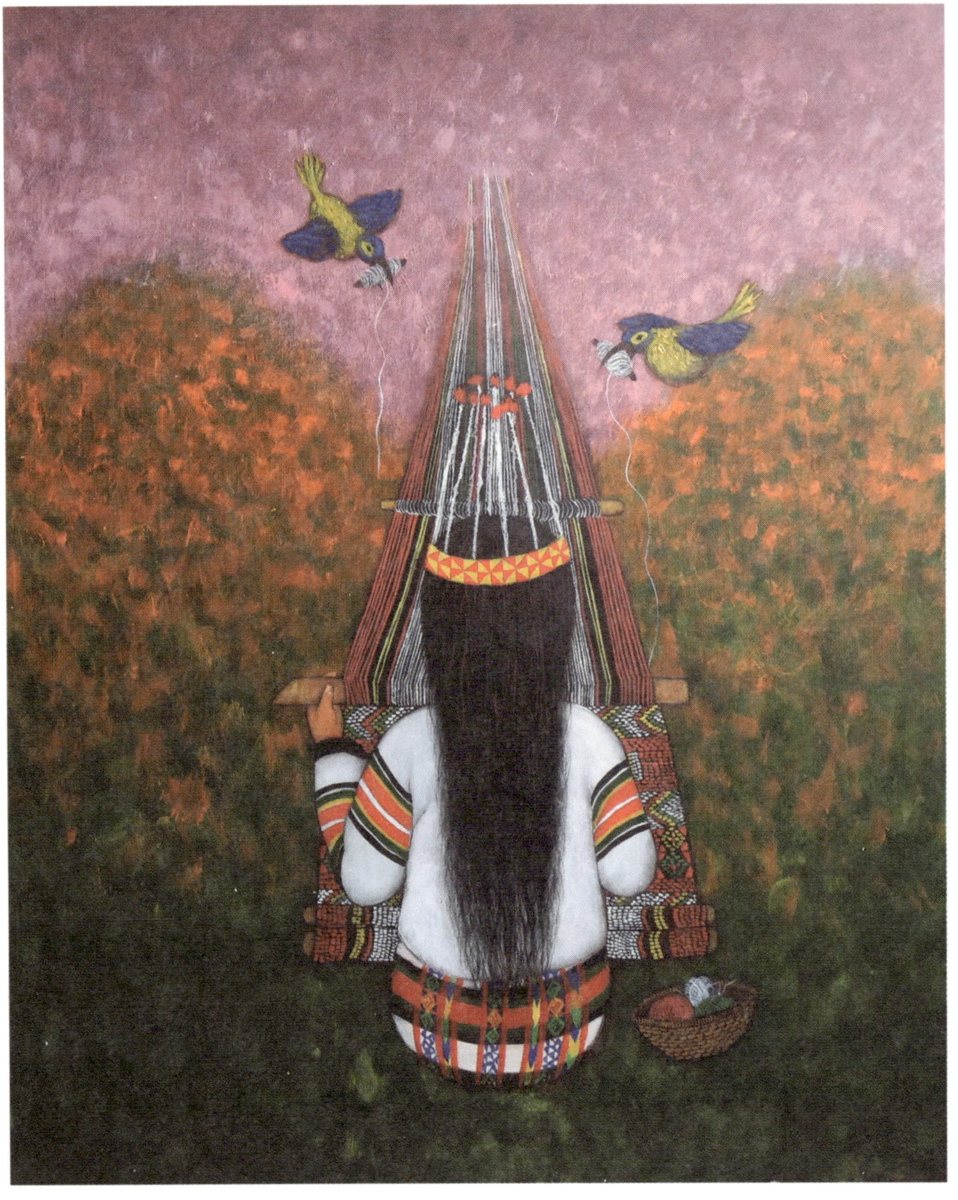

weaving between hills
MEENA LAISHRAM, ACRYLIC ON CANVAS (22×20 INCHES)

"Ṭhasiama then talks about all the things he wished for – wealth, fame, longevity, and so on. But before he could mention his wish for children, Ṭhasiama ran out of breath. So the man lived for hundreds of years in prosperity, never lacking food and never earning a bad reputation. But he never managed to have children.

"There are also variations in how people tell this story. Some say instead of a pheichham, it was lasis that blessed Ṭhasiama with long life and wealth.

"You might have heard several stories involving a lasi. And there may be some variations in what they can do and how they treat humans. But one thing is for certain...they always appear as women with bewitching looks and long, flowing hair.

"And they're said to live in the forests and enchant hunters. A hunter under a lasi's enchantment would get immense luck in his hunting expeditions, never going home without a kill. But he could never speak to anyone about his relationship with the lasi, or it could result in his death.

"In one variation of the story of Ṭhasiama, he manages to capture two lasis. In their attempt to break free from his grasp, the creatures shape shift into other forms like snakes and caterpillars. With no luck at escaping, they finally decided to grant him a boon if he sets them free.

"Though there aren't many stories about a male lasi, the story of Chawngtinleri talks about the King of the lasis marrying a beautiful woman named Chawngtinleri. This is the only instance in which there's a male version of this creature. But some people also described him as the king of the spirit world.

"The offspring of Chawngtinleri and the lasi king ended up with a human body and a goat head.

"When Chawngtinleri went to visit her brother in the human realm, the neighbours took a peek in her baby's cradle and were horrified to see the half-human half-goat creature. This angered the lasis, who accused Chawngtinleri of having exposed their true form. To punish her, they twisted her eyes so that they became vertical.

"Her vertical eyes made her forget her fellow humans. It must be because she no longer saw the world like she did before and she had become something else other than human. The lasis later granted her power and she eventually became queen of the beasts and is believed to be the creator and protector of all wild animals. Despite all this power, Chawngtinleri was often bored.

"To pass her time, she decided to start weaving again – something she excelled at as a human being. So she set off to collect the tools that she would need – a loom and a seat. She would also need threads to weave. Once she was done collecting these items, she began looking for the perfect place to set up her loom.

"Her search ended in a valley between the mountains of Lurh and Ṭan. She set up her loom here, surrounded by the trees and animals she created. But there was one problem – the loom was too tall so she had some trouble stringing the thread to it. Seeing their queen's struggle, the swallows and martins offered their help.

"They took the threads in their beaks and flew around the loom to string the weave as Chawngtinleri sat down to weave. Every day when she began setting up her loom, the birds would fly over from their trees and help her out. They say that even today, Chawngtinleri still weaves at the same spot between the twin peaks with her loyal birds by her side."

"That will be such a breathtaking sight," Pari remarked, "I think I'll try to do a painting of that scene later."

"That's a great idea, Pari. I'd love to see it once you're finished," her aunt responded.

"Nu, do you think people really saw Chawngtinleri weaving between those mountains?"

"Maybe they did... Maybe that's why we have the story today."

By now, Mawii's eyelids were growing heavier. She was trying to suppress a yawn, which her mother caught sight of.

"Sleepy?"

"A bit but can we just have one more story? I promise I'll go to sleep right after."

Sangi paused and thought for a while.

"When you were small, I had to make up all these stories about Mualzavata's wife Ramfangzauvi? Do you remember her?"

"Not so much anymore. Who was she?"

"Ramfangzauvi was a giantess. Her husband was a giant named Mualzavata.

"She could clear 90 ranges of land in a single day. There's a cave called Pukzing Cave, which was believed to have been created by Mualzavata using only his hairpin.

"The stories normally only describe the couple as humans of supernatural strength but I think you'd have to be a giant to cover all those hill ranges in a day. Even if you had the strength and energy to clear them, you'd still have to reach them fast enough to finish the job in one day."

She was about to go on, when she noticed Mawii in deep sleep. She could finally stop.

Sangi looked at her daughter sleeping peacefully. She treasured nights like these when she could go back to the nights when her own mother narrated stories of their ancestors. Where had all the time gone? Soon she was asleep too.

The house was quiet except for the occasional snore and the chirping of crickets in the garden. The only one who was still awake was Pari. She was still thinking of the stories – what would she do if she had been in Sichangneii's place?

What if the spirits lived in a different realm and humans couldn't see them?

All these questions made her breathless. So she sat up and opened the window for some fresh air. As she laid her head against the window frame watching the ink black sky, something caught her eye near the banyan tree opposite their house.

She could only make out its shadowy outline but it looked like a woman with a huge pair of wings. The figure was bent down as if it was picking something off the ground. Pari observed it for a few minutes and finally decided that it must have been a tree or a twisted bamboo pole because it seemed to be inanimate.

Just then, the figure rose and spread its wings. In one swift and graceful move, it headed for the skies with what looked to be a bundle of vegetables swinging from her arms.

Pari squinted to get a closer look and gasped in disbelief. Could it be...?

josie paris

PHOTOGRAPHS AND TEXT BY **PRASHANSA GURUNG**

Goa in March. It is a few minutes past noon and the weather is a pleasant 25 degrees. I am in Little Vagator and in front of me is a barren hill. Parked atop this hill is a vanity van, confirming that I am in the right location.

I'm here to meet Josie Paris, a renowned stylist in "Bollywood", who has been in Goa for the past two months, working on a web series featuring the who's who of today's Indian Cinema. Originally from Aizawl, Mizoram, her family moved to Goa in 2009. She has been in Mumbai since 2011. Though I have known Josie for a few years, and have had pleasant exchanges whenever we met at events, or online, this is the first time we are "hanging out" together. I know her to be a reserved person, who takes time to open to people; but more importantly as a glamorous person who has a simple and chic style. Josie does fashion styling, costume styling, as well as hair and make-up. Her job, on this particular project, involves creating the look for each character, based on the brief given by the director. On set, she is a taskmaster, confident about her work and highly organized. What becomes apparent in her interactions with the technical crew, as well as the celebrity talents, is the fact that they trust her. She has built a professional, yet friendly rapport with the people she works with. She says, the fact that she is Northeastern gives her clients confidence in her styling skills, as "people from the Northeast are generally more stylish - we carry off clothes well - we look good in anything."

While there is much glamour and fanfare when a film or series is released, behind the scenes, the working hours are long and gruelling, with shoot schedules stretched over ungodly hours. It takes a special kind of strength and patience to work in the industry. I got a taste of this, in the few days I spend following her around on sets. Shooting would begin at midnight and go on till the wee hours of the morning.

The icing on the cake was that Josie styled me for a small role I was offered by the producers since I was on set. We shot at 3am in the morning for what will become my television debut! I have found a friend in her - and I wish for her to achieve all her dreams – including opening her own boutique of wedding gowns. Good Luck Josie!

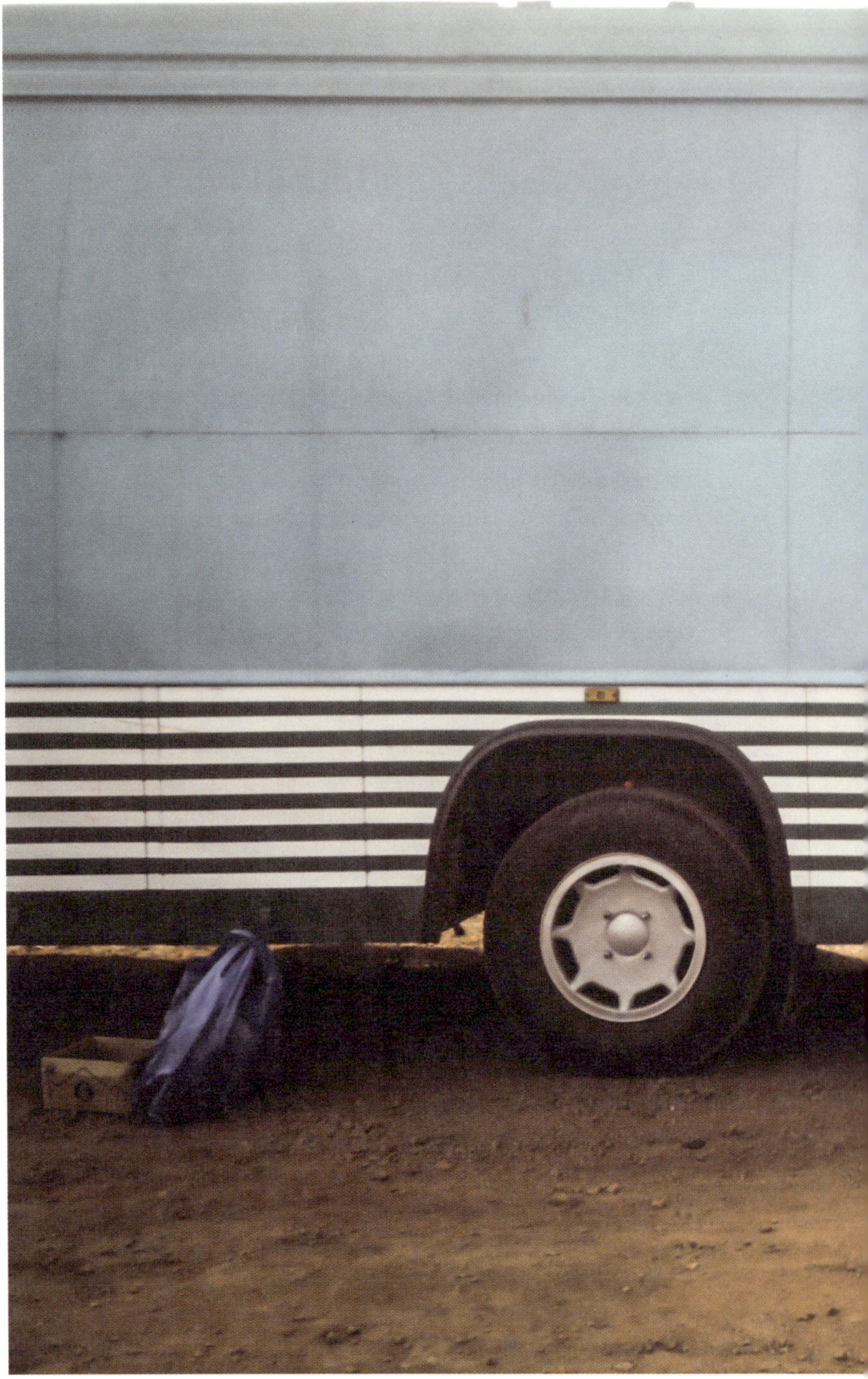

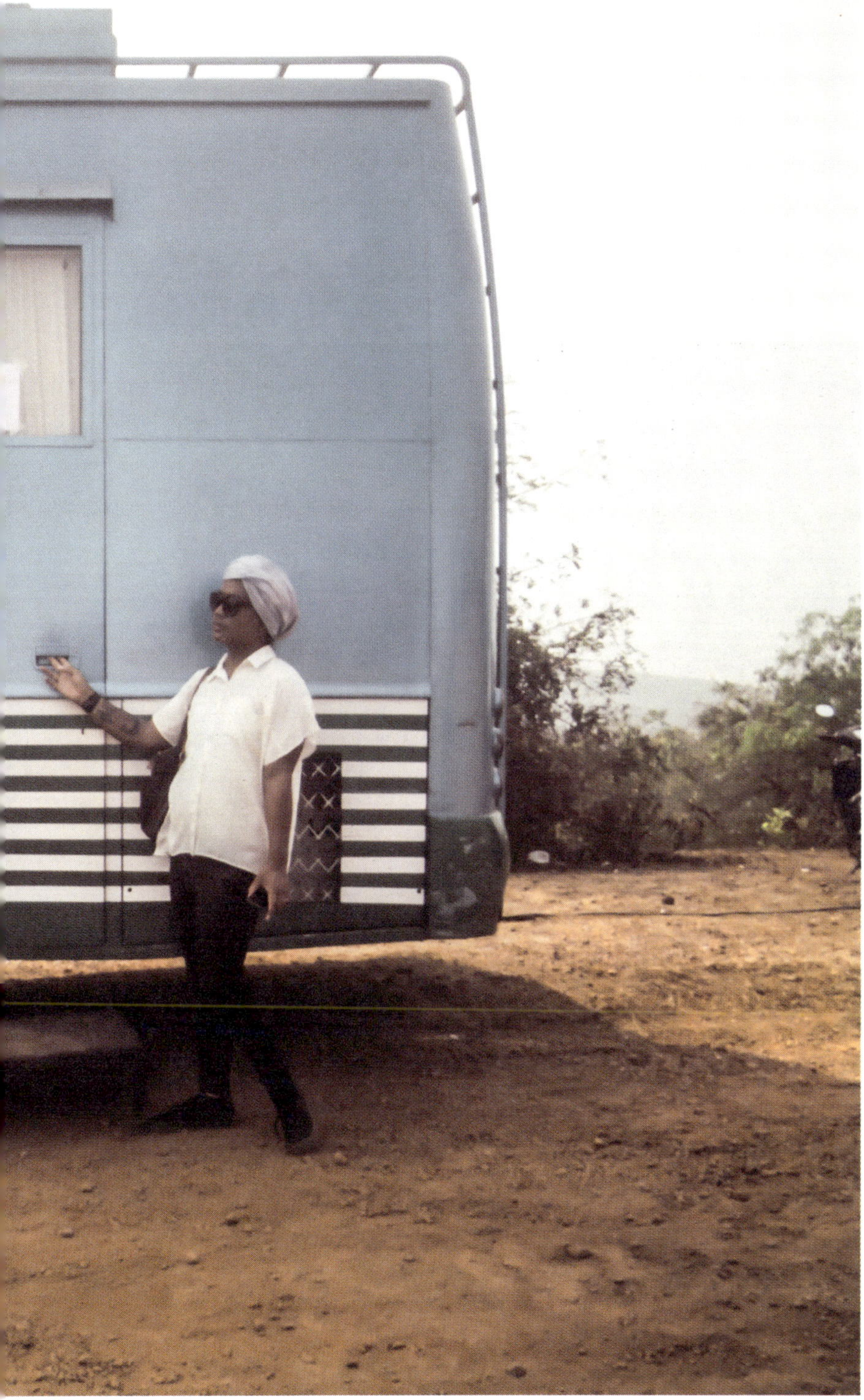

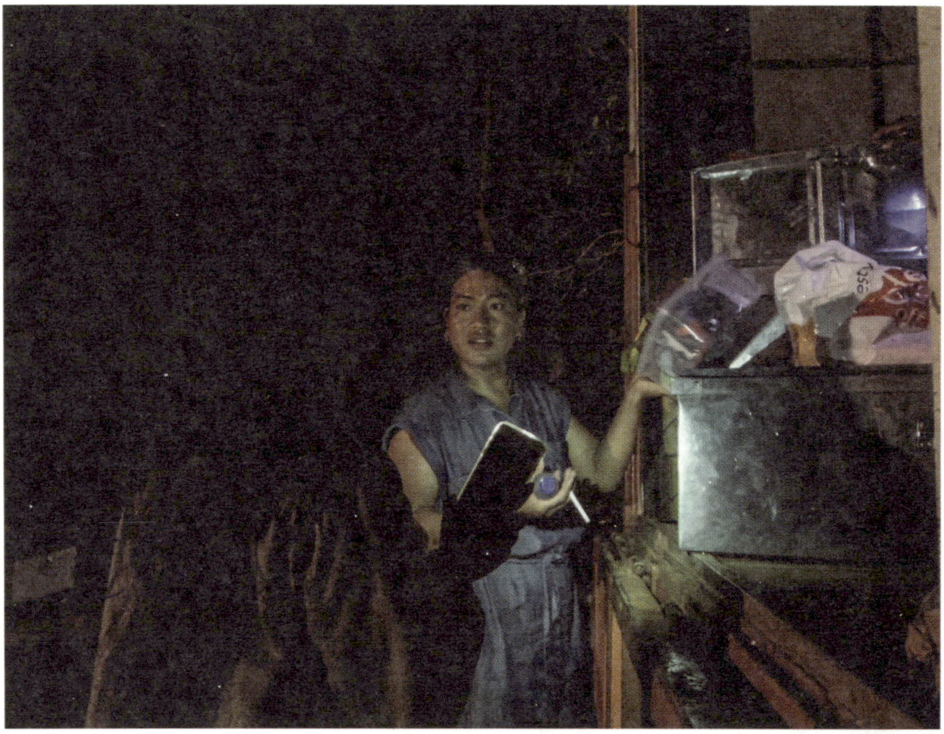

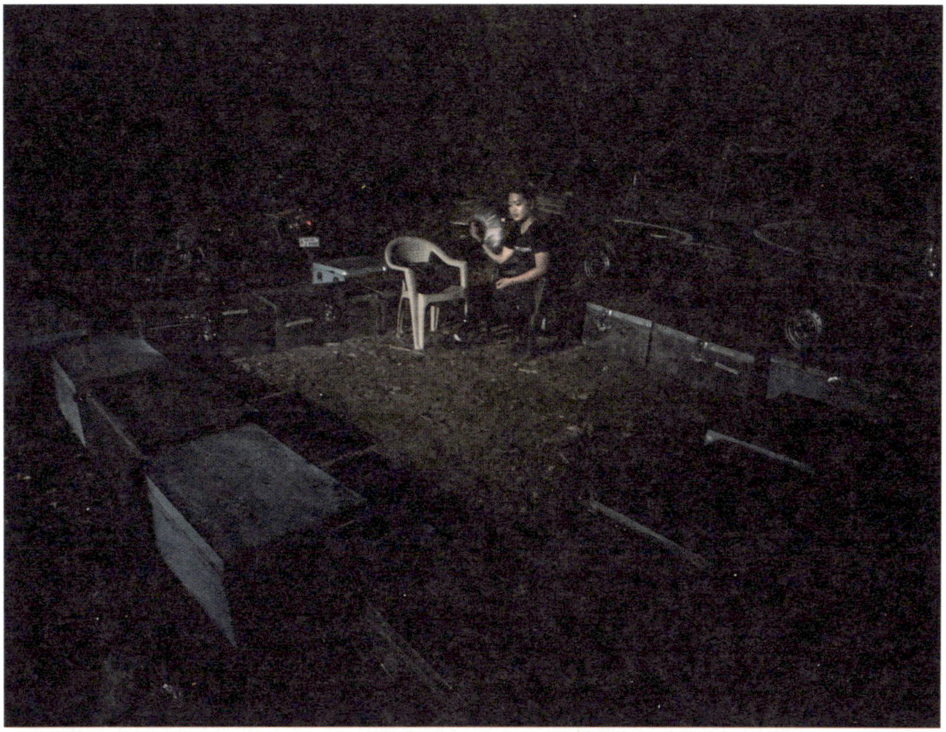

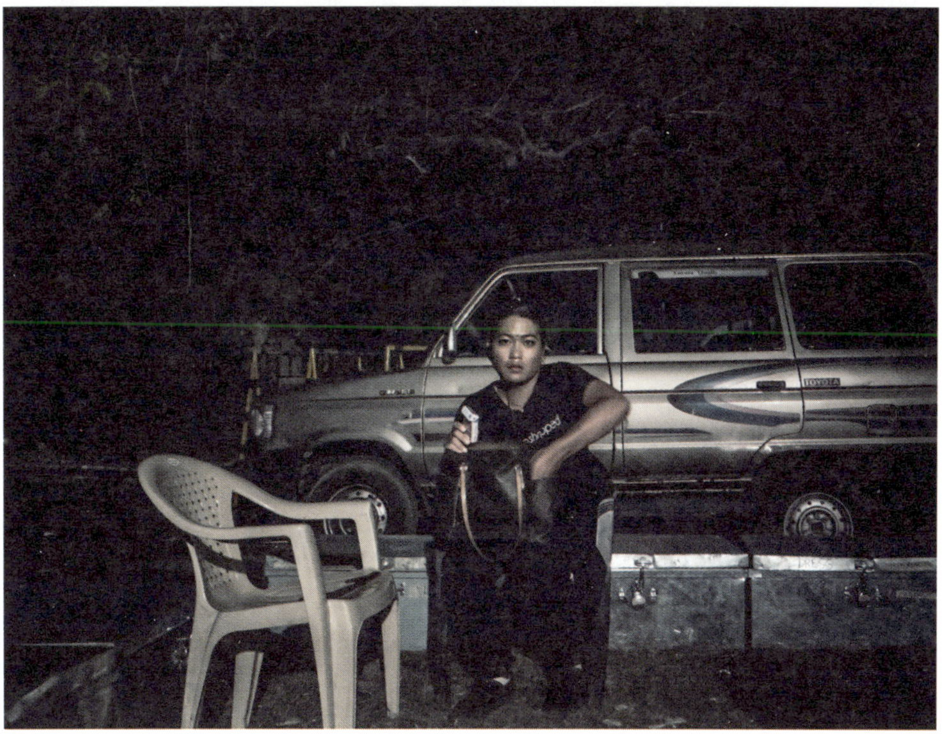
TOYOTA

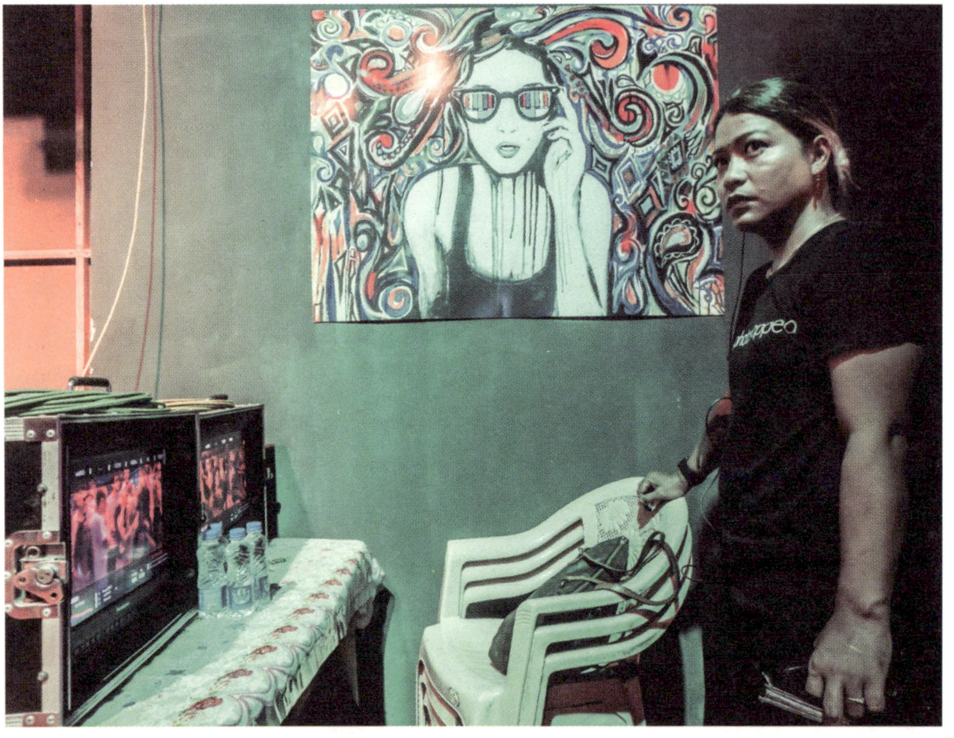

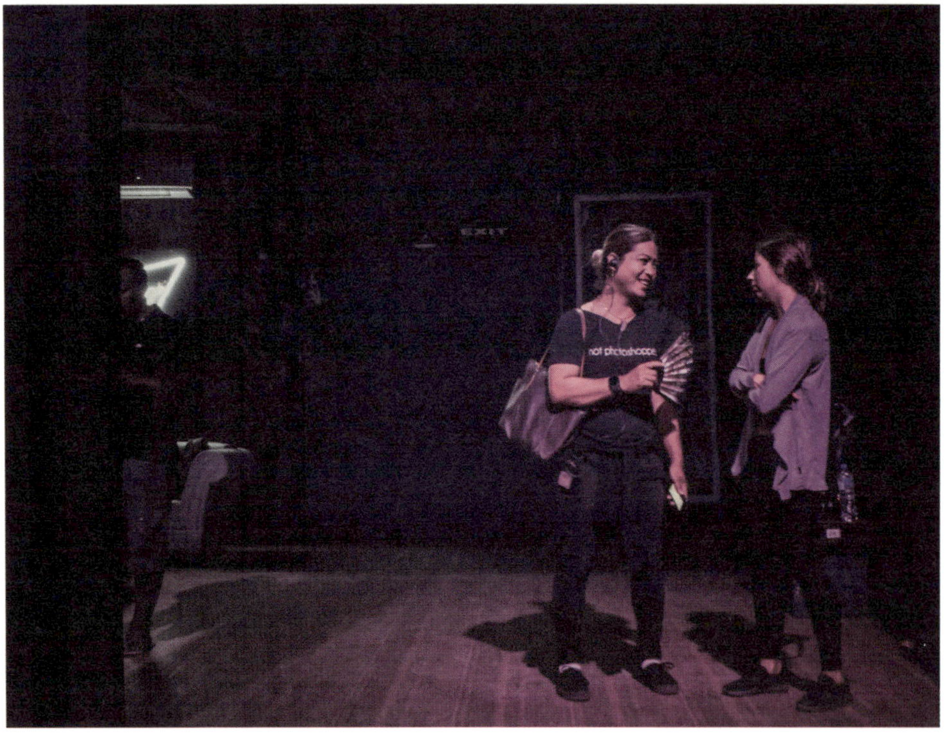

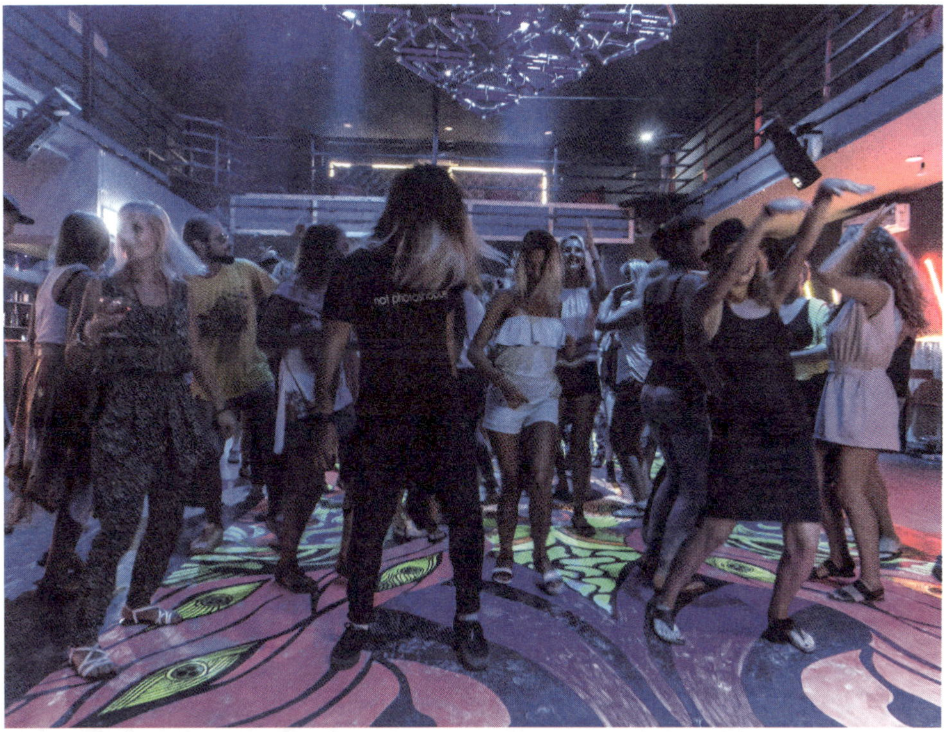

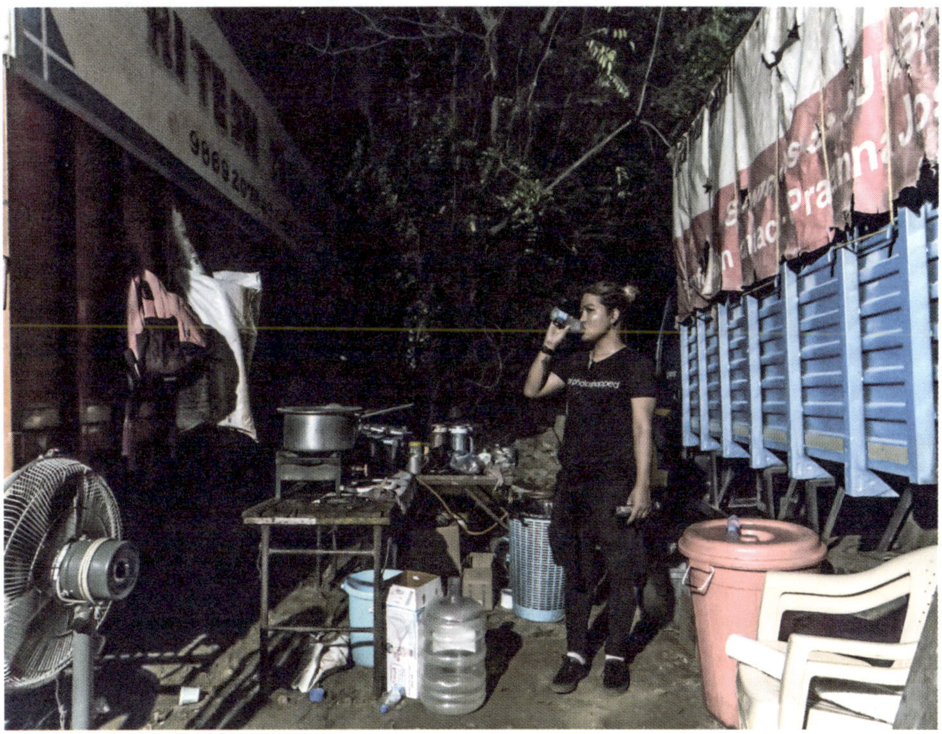

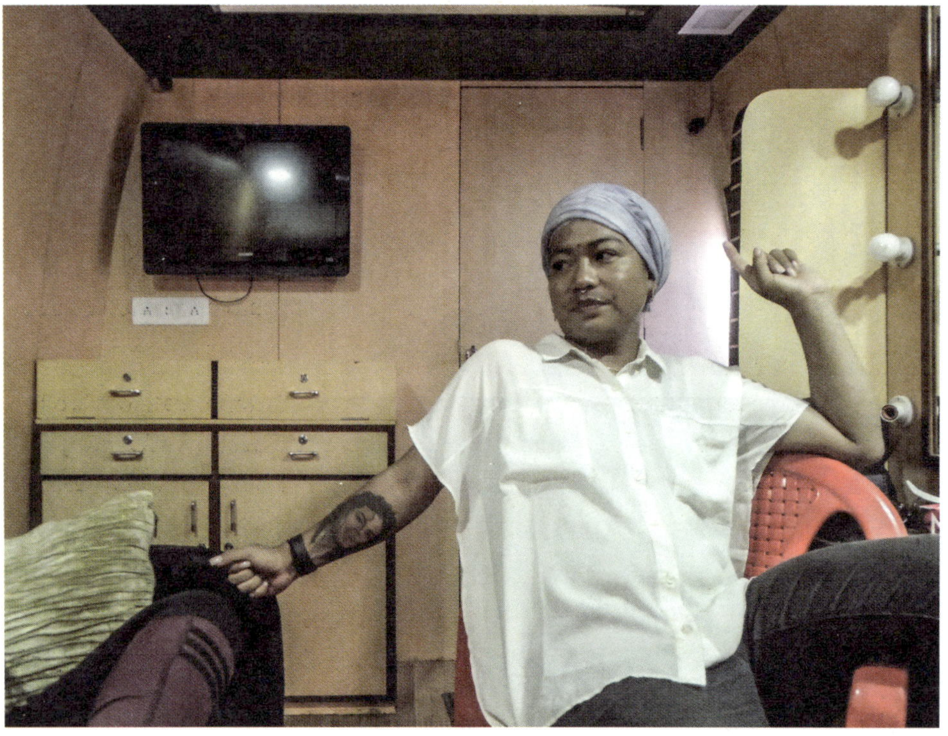

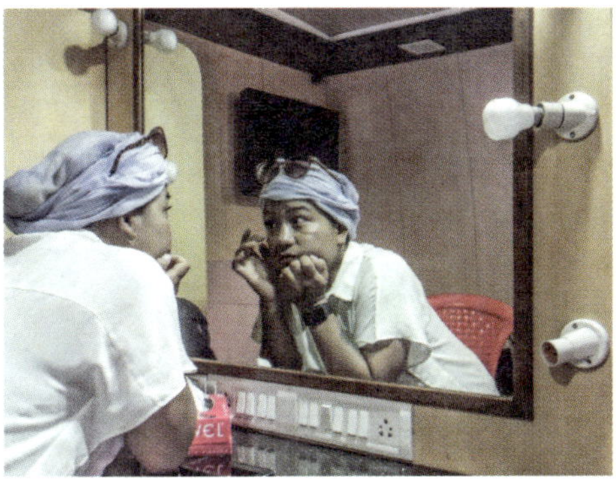

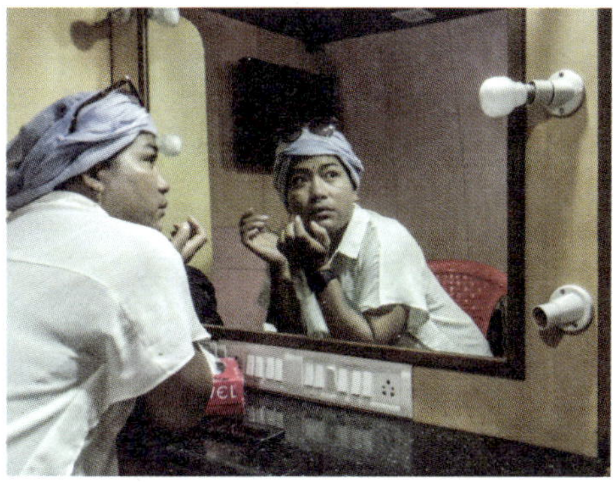

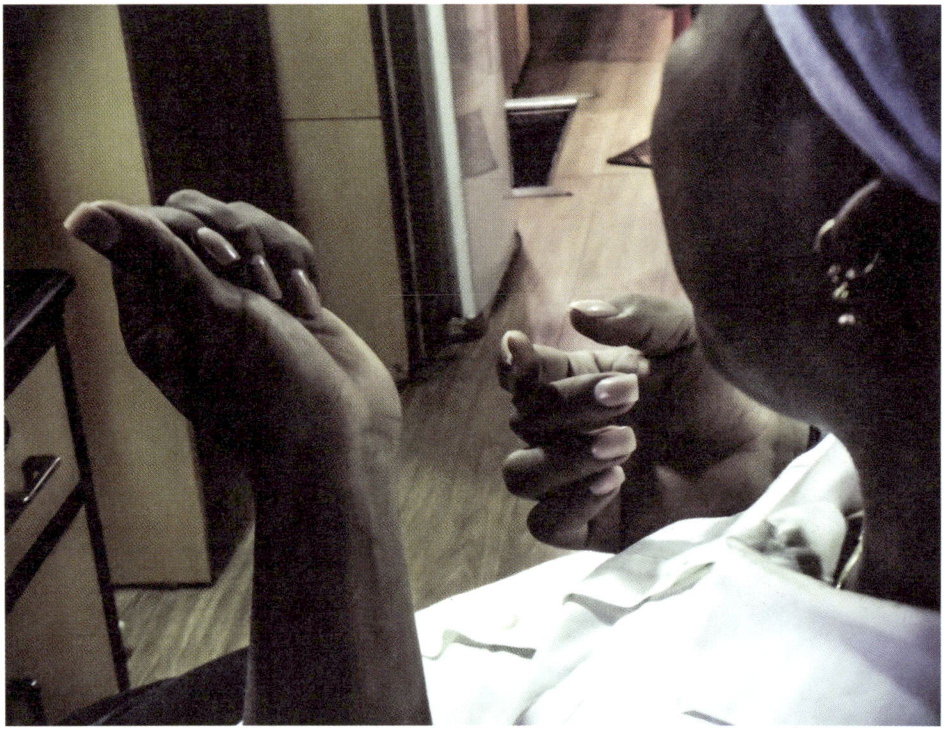

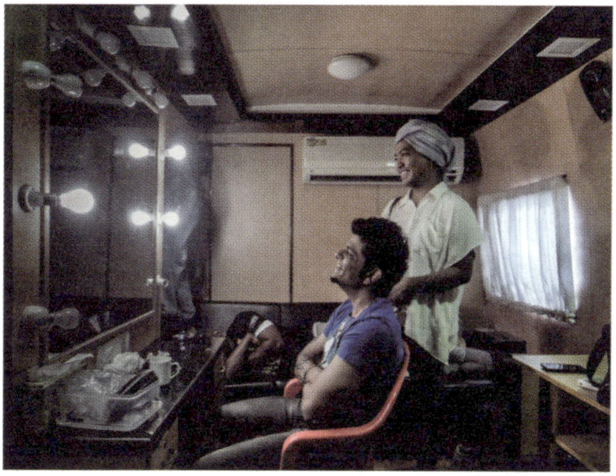

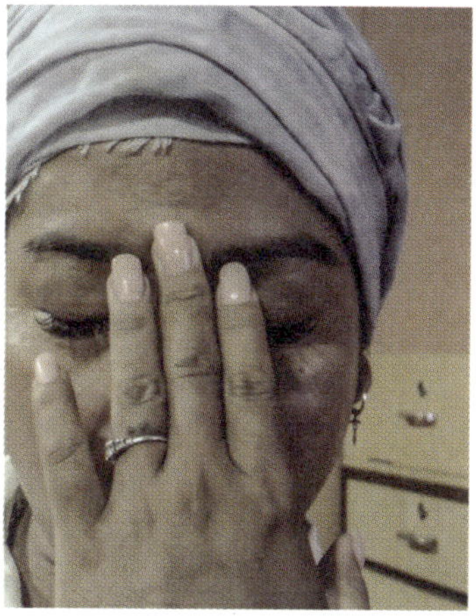

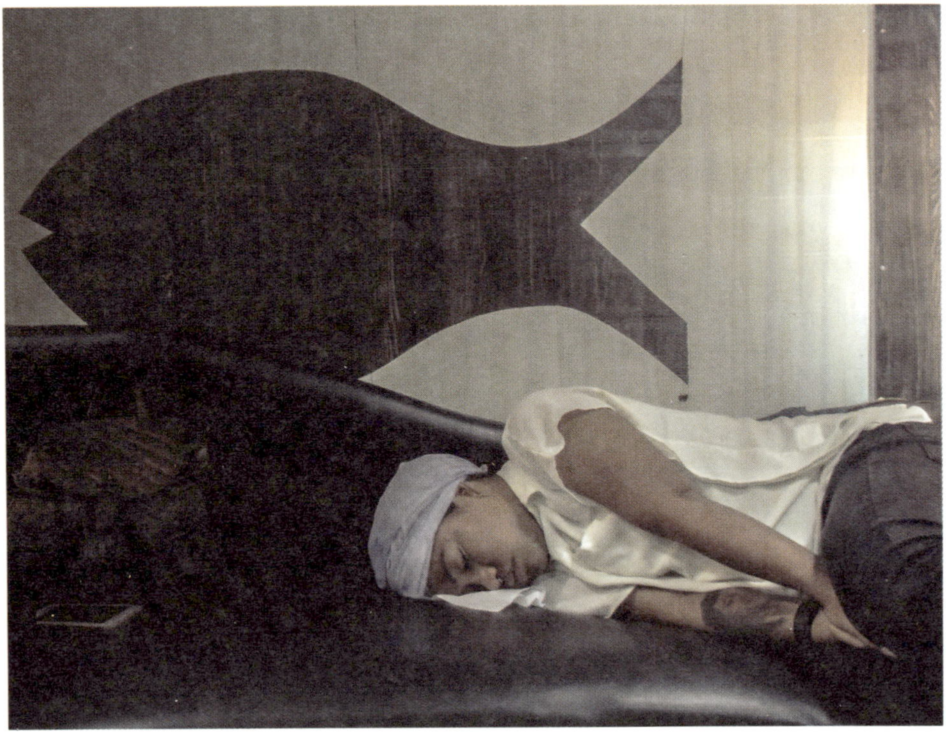

daksare sketches: through the needle and the loom

SHREYA DEBI AND BILSENG R. MARAK
BUMBUM DESIGN STUDIO

We are amazed by the humble tenacious existence of humanity amid hilly landscapes, wild rains, pretty streams, vast open fields, tropical vegetation, palm trees, narrow meandering roads and broken wooden bridges over small ponds and streams, where electricity is so infrequent, and the roads so pitted. It is a time-worn irony indeed that it is under-development that keeps a place serene and beautiful. The exuberance of nature and the simplicity of life here, the lifestyles and livelihoods, inspire us. Joint families live in small houses with slanted roofs. They rear hens, cows, dogs, pigs and goats. Clucking, mooing household animals, the barking of dogs, grunting of pigs, bleating of goats, chirping of birds and buzzing of insects.

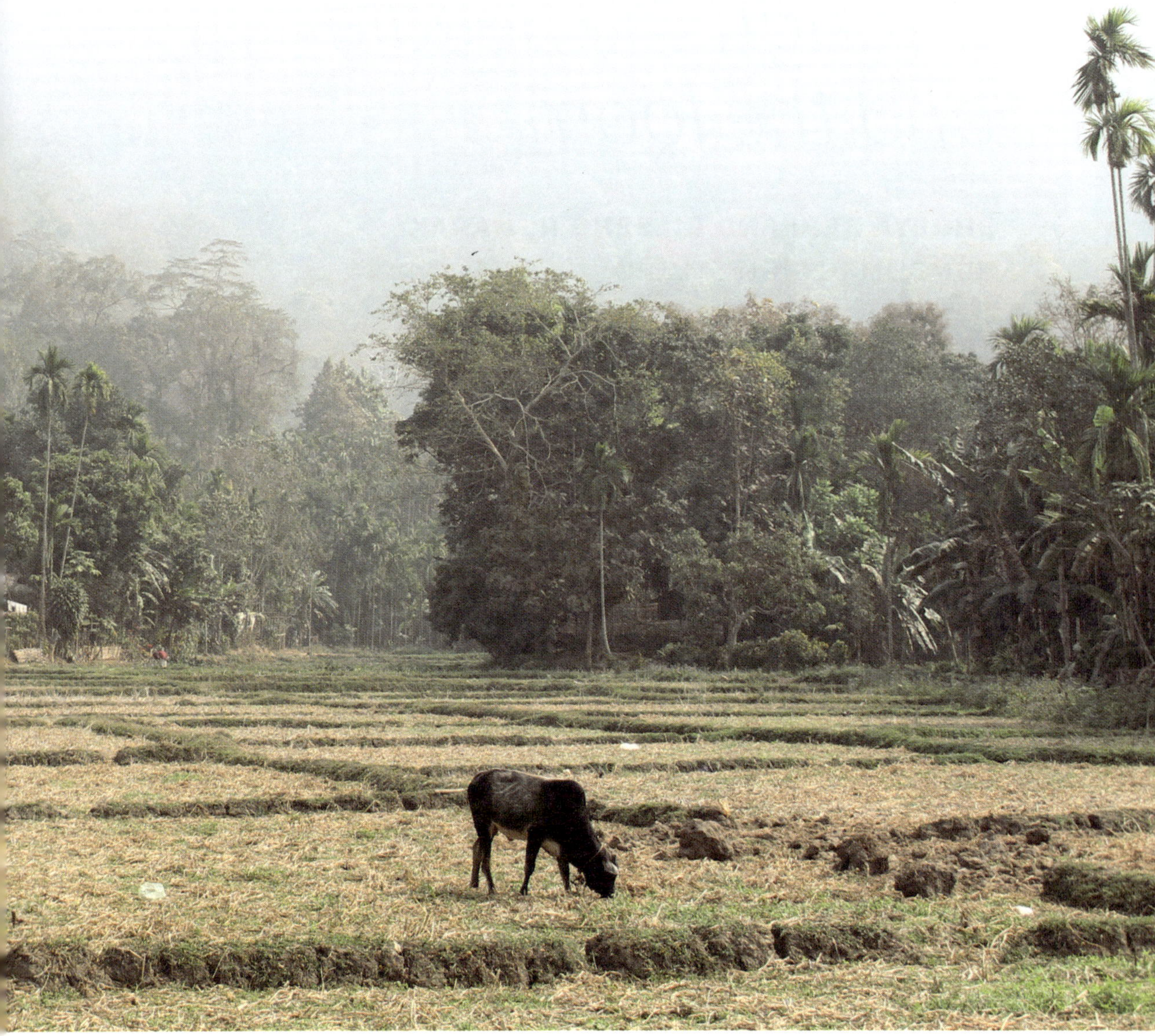

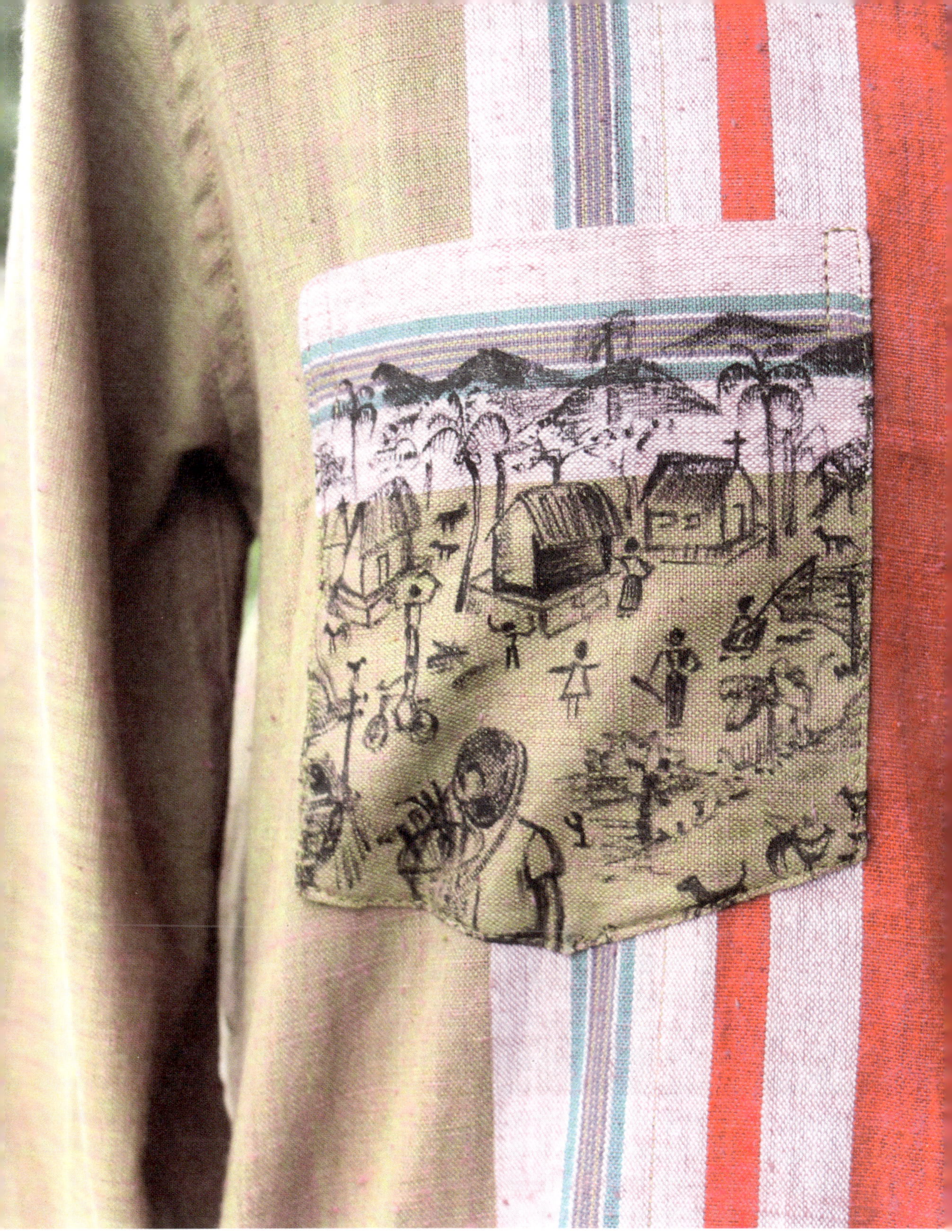

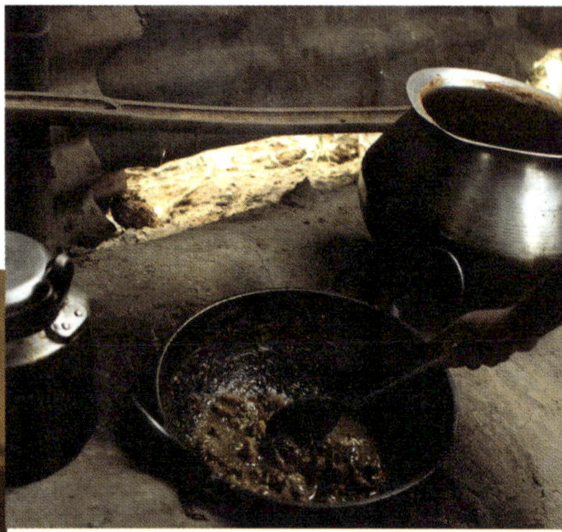

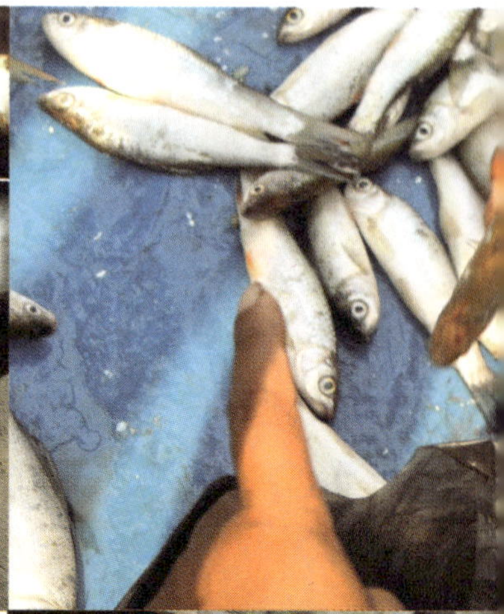

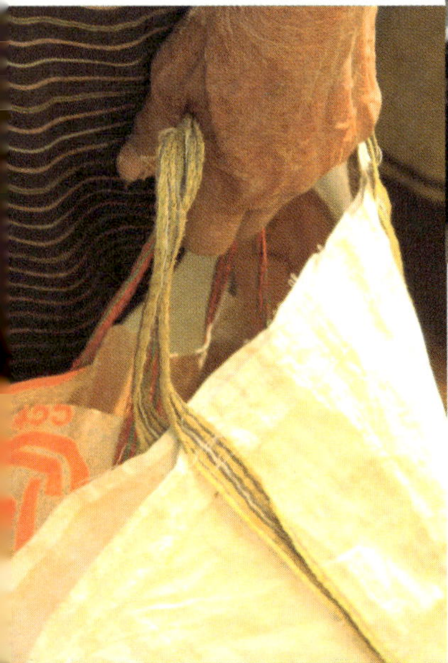

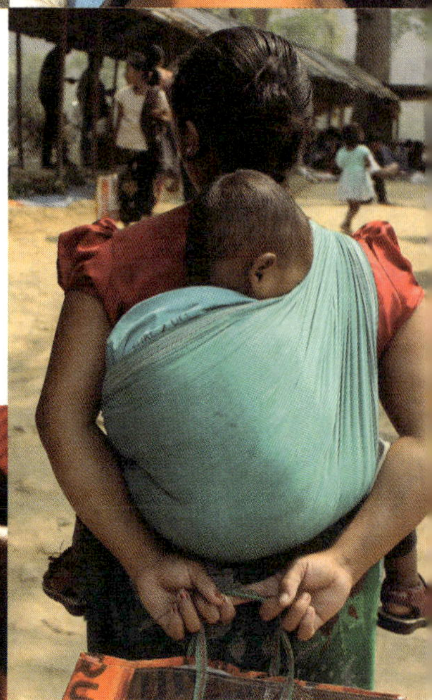

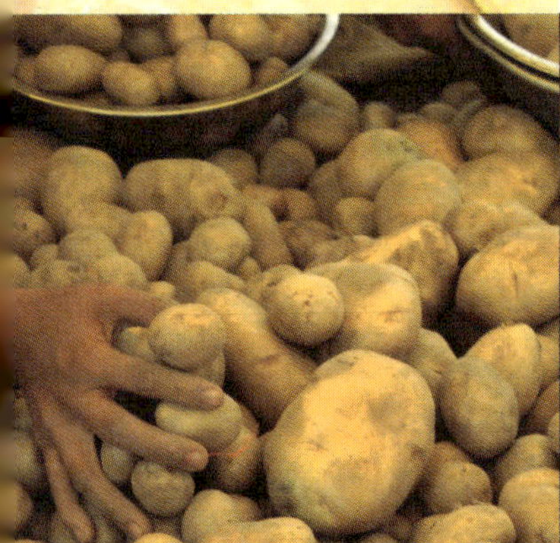

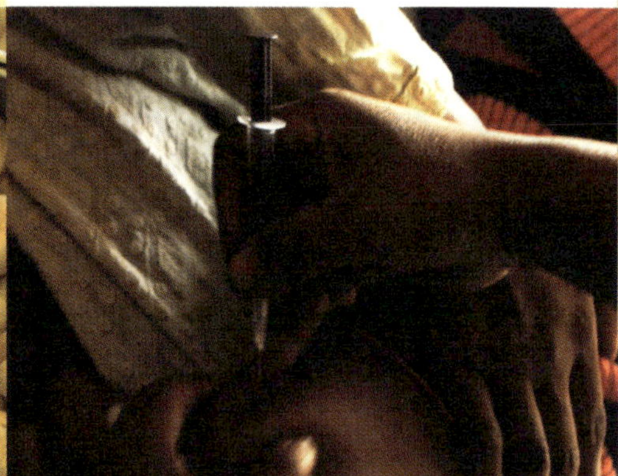

We see women every day. Women walking to the market, girls walking back from school, young women on cycles and scooties, singing and working in the paddy fields, women bending over their toddlers, gossiping and giggling

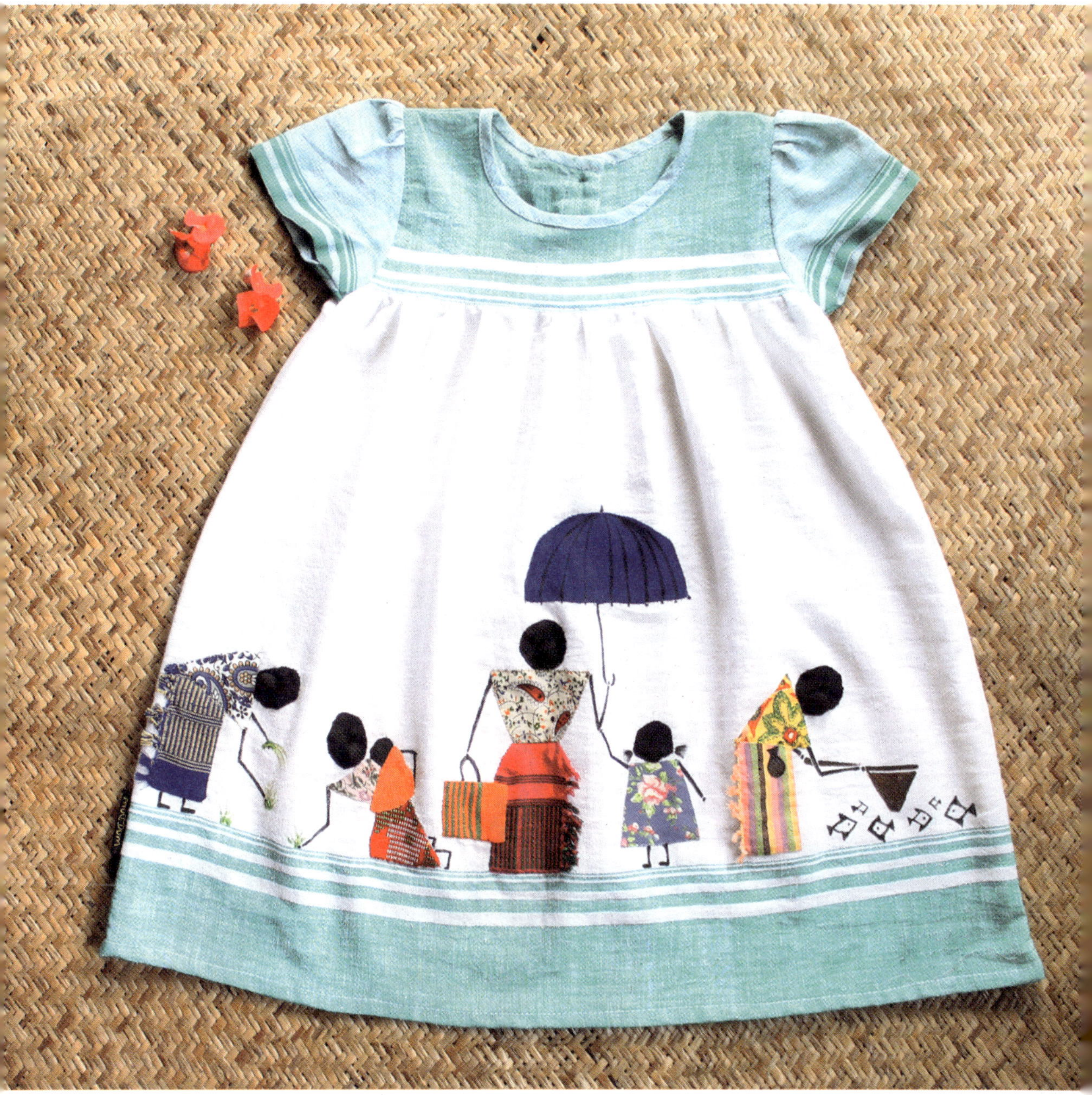

The stories we tell through design, fabrics, textures and colours, are a subtle tribute to Garo hills. Each motif has a hidden motive and each design has a purpose. The humble cotton daksare, also known as ganna, is traditionally worn as a wrap-around by Garo women while doing their daily chores and at informal social gatherings. The more it is worn the softer it becomes, taking on the wearer's body shape and movement. The designs are a mix and match of colours and stripes.

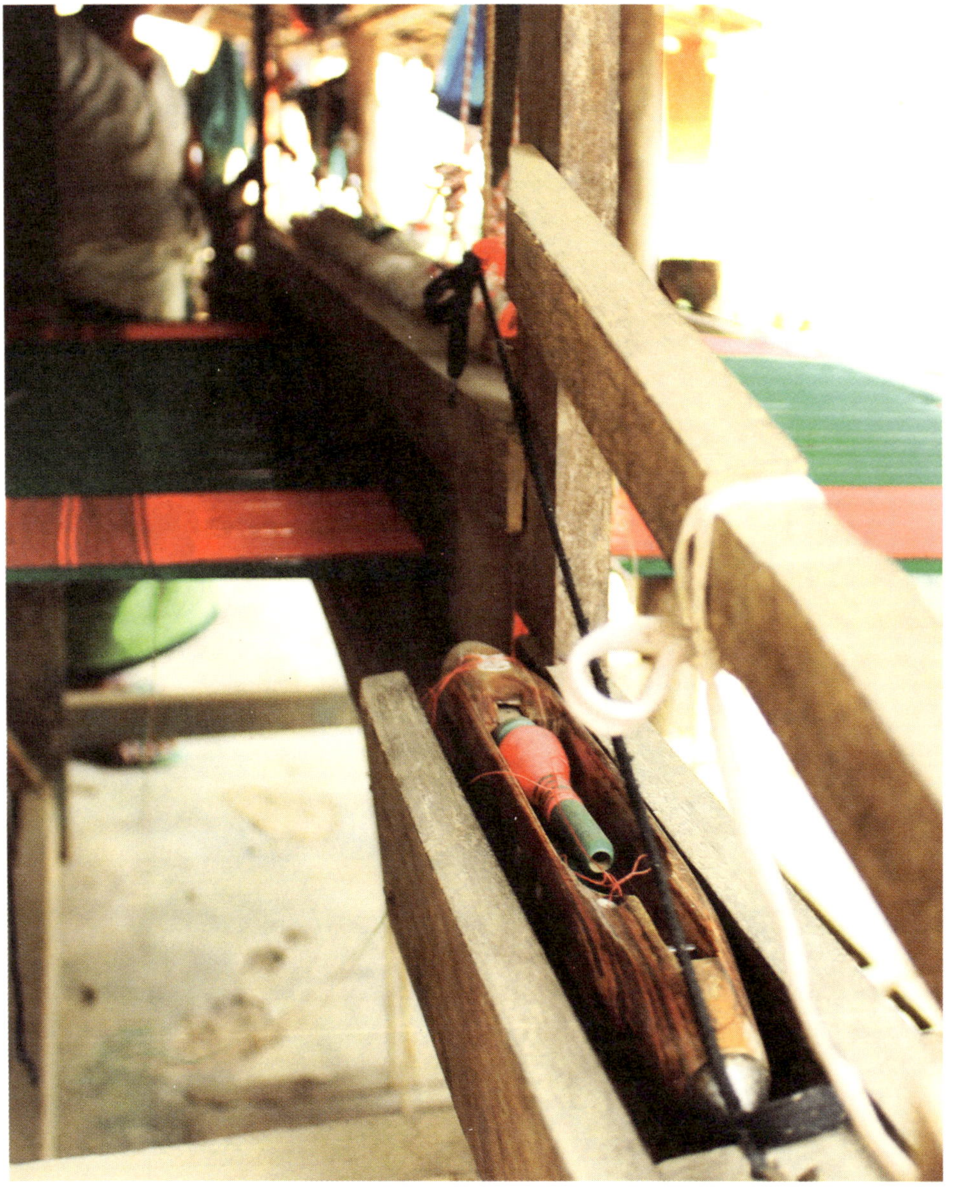

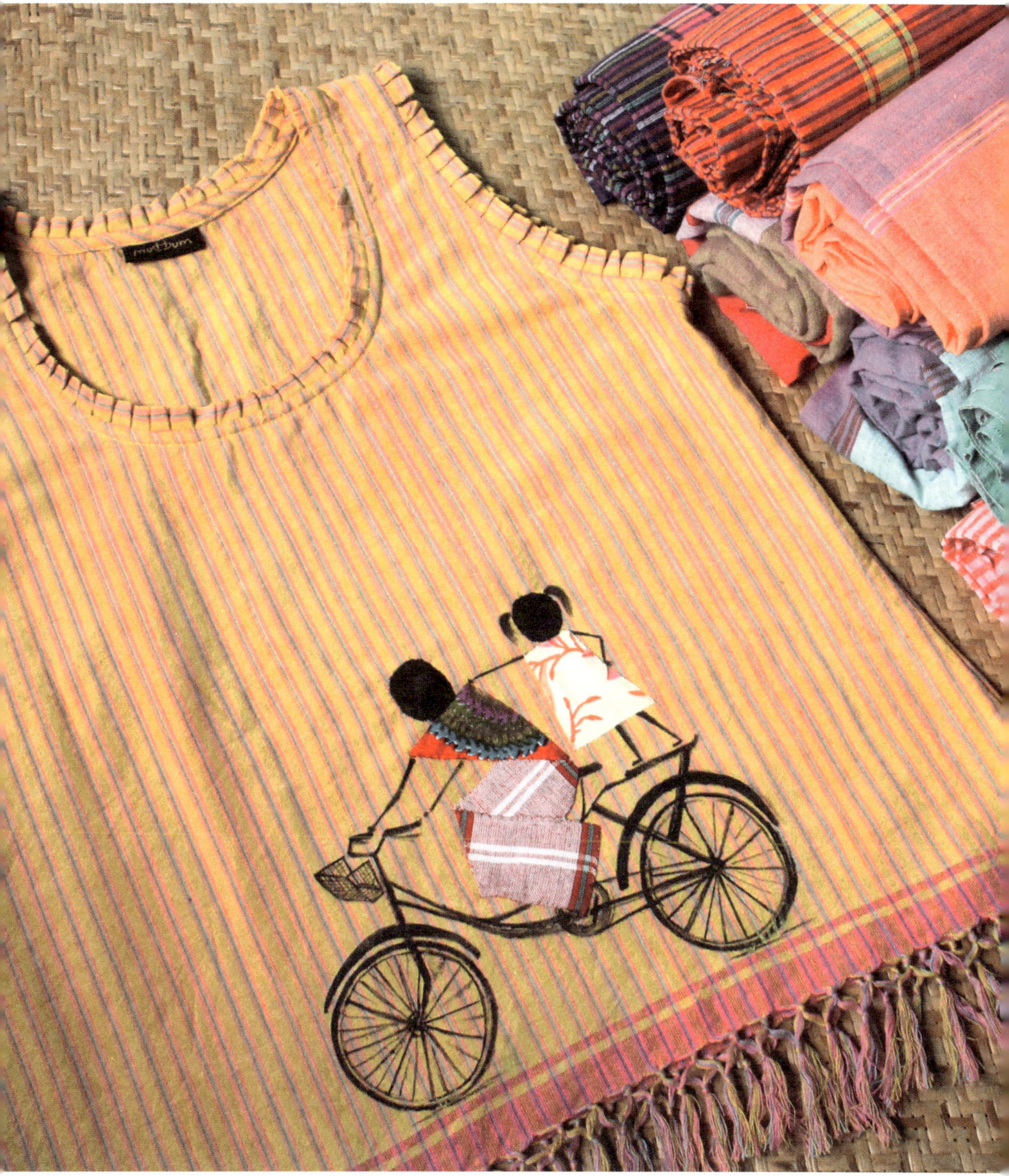

maria and the vixen

MONA ZOTE

At the end of the day, we don't know what we want anymore
Or who we are and who we thought we were meant to be,
Who were our friends and who were the ones who led us away
From the scenes of mourning and the places of contentment.
Since these things are out of our hands,
What we are left with is a mirror showing our movements
Some who are mothers and some who are sailors
Some who stand under street lights displaying their embroidered beauty.
Some who reveal a sense of daring in photographs
With their smiling eyes and their feet braced apart
In a challenge, a question mark thrown at the world
Some who are gnomes and some who, being gnomic,
Understand the complexity of making pies.

Mara or Maria or Mariam
Navigating these pools of clamour, you must be tired
Of holding court each day, wading ponds of duck weed
Sometimes in jeans, sometimes wrapped in splendour.
I'm sure you set aside your face at evening
When you sit at your dressing table to undo
The faces daylight has forced upon you,
Placing them in a drawer, rubbing out their lines,
Lines that flatter you and draw many more eyes.
Your eyes perform a full striptease of me.
And yet in the evening, you put them away
In a drawer packed with myrrh and crumpled tissues
You think your face belongs to the world
If they think it's beautiful, it is for them
If it smiles, it is for them
If your hand reaches out in grace, it is for them.

I agree that beauty is a fine thing to own
If only it were not owned by them
I agree kindness is a good thing to show
It means you have known faithlessness
Tempered by the solicitude of friends.
There isn't much about friendship we know
Except that it happens to all of us
Like birth or death but somehow more prone
To threaten us with prolonged loitering.

Her sister has no face at all
But says she has a gun
Then changes the subject, afraid I might be afraid
Of knowing a woman who has a gun.
She asks how the day has gone
We keep circling certain questions,
Something deeply conventional about pies
Something about good armour and the need for them.
She leans in shadowed doorways, her face quicksilver–
From nowhere I see blurred fur among damp leaves
She's gone deep, she's gone to earth.

Birds on telephone wires
A pigeon with a twisted neck
She looks at me with eyes full of questions,
Her mouth full of warm feathers.

chitro of the dung buckets

NABINA DAS

Chitro has no clue about this thing called "bucket challenge". She can't read or write. No, wait. She can, just a little. Assamese sentences that say: "Polio drops for children this Sunday"; "Construction ahead, drive slow"; "Namghor annual kirtan invites the faithful", "Your daughter is poor in Math, meet class teacher", "A healthy wife makes a happy family", and so on and so forth. Besides, she reads some English words and numerals. That is impressive enough for her 12 years in the city after she left her rackety village in Karbi Anglong without even an alphabet. But she's heard of this bucket challenge because her employers are talking about it. It's on the TV. And also on computer screens, to which Bou's teenage children remain glued when they don't do homework.

What will you do by knowing, oi Chitro, yells one of the kids, Bou's daughter. She's 16 and rowdy, a constant headache to Bou. Chitro has heard Bou complaining to some acquaintances on the phone about her daughter. Junali, fears Bou, has a boyfriend. A boy who's always on that computer screen and writing messages to the young reckless Junali. Bou even complains about her husband who often stays out at night from home.

Come on ma, Junali screams, I'm only Facebooking. Not talking to any boy. And she rolls her eyes at "boy", at which her younger sister Rupali and brother Jitul roll their eyes further, laughing inconsolably.

Bucket challenge is on that thing called Facebook, they tell Chitro. Bou seems perplexed. She looks at Chitro at these moments in discomfort. The children forget that the work-lady is around, listening to them squabble. But Chitro doesn't know Facebook either. Is it a man? Or food?

Those who know Chitro also know that other than working as a maid in the homes of this middle class neighbourhood, she carries buckets full of cow dung she collects from courtyards of homes, street sides, and empty plots. It's her part time job. It's been almost a hobby too with her since long. Cows are aplenty in the streets, let loose by their owners to roam, invade, and chew on practically everything that lies on the ground, grass or paper or plastic. Then poop and litter. But of course most folks know dung cakes are still used by small businesses.

You think you're a heroine, haan, shouts Chitro's husband Okhondo whose name literally means "indivisible". You think carrying three buckets of goo on your head makes you a star?

Chitro wants Okhondo to be aware that the neighbourhood is ever so grateful to his wife for keeping it clean of the cow dung. Chitro calls her husband by name unlike the ladies of the polite neighbourhood. She threatens him when the going gets tough.

I'll make "khondo khondo" of you, so what if you're my husband.

She lives with her two daughters at the fringe of the neighbourhood, right behind the Namghor where the pious come in the mornings and evenings. She also does sundry cleaning of the prayer house's yards – where no cows are allowed to saunter in – and the steps once a week. Okhondo and Chitro's quarrels miff the genteel neighbourhood but for very pertinent reasons they can't turn out the poor family from the area. After all, she helps keep the upper caste houses clean. Picking up dung from the holy cows that no one will shoo or beat off their premises is also a favour she does to the neighbourhood.

They keep saying bucket, bucket, Mahato-kai. Chitro finally confides in the local chaiwalla.

Mahato, an old man from Bihar, has seen a lot in his life down from his hometown to Assam where he spent a good many years of his migrant life.

Bucket, Mahato utters and scratches his crumpled chin.

Yes, bucket, Chitro's feigns annoyance. She knows what bucket means. She knows that much ingraji o. Besides, she herself carries buckets. What they do with a bucket, tell no Mahato-kai? Chitro is indignant.

Pour something from it, naturally, says Mahato. What else one does with a bucket?

O kokai, don't take me to be a fool. Chitro balks.

No, no, Mahato tries assuring her. Wait majoni, he thinks harder. In my village too, we did a bucket challenge.

Really? Chitro settles down on the wooden bench next to the karahi where Mahato's wife fries oily pakodas, sniffing all the hot oil-generated steam.

Uh, let's see. We were kids then. We dared each other to steal plastic buckets from shops in the bazaar. Each one pick one, Mahato says.

Aisaa? Chitro is breathless. She has done wild stuff but not lifted plastic buckets from shops ever. Dhara, Mahato's old wife, smiles at her husband's storytelling and Chitro's expression of intrigue.

Haan, aisaa hee kuchh, Mahato nods. Something like that. We'd take the buckets to an empty plot and beat the shit out of them till they broke.

And then? Chitro can't wait to hear the rest of the bucket challenge.

Then what? The shopkeepers would find us out and chase us down the main street while we taunted them pulling our half pants down. Ten-year-olds are monkeys after all. Mahato now seriously breaks into a guffaw. Imagine a group of adult men running after boys down a dusty road, yelling and swearing! Too funny, he says. Dhara goes hee hee too, for a quiet person that she is.

Hmm. Chitro likes the story but she isn't convinced that's what is meant by bucket challenge. She leaves in a huff.

She can't ask Okhondo because he won't know anyway. Besides, he's a prick. After two daughters when Chitro said no more kids, he still insisted.

Krishna Mahaprabhu will give us a boy this time. Don't you want our home to run better with a boy who goes to school, Chitro?

Chitro somehow couldn't make Okhondo see the point that their two daughters also go to school. So she's with a baby now and impatient and irritable. With her younger daughter's report card in hand showing the math challenge that the child faces, Chitro meets the teacher concerned.

The teacher, a twenty-something woman, is kind. She explains to Chitro how Ronja can practise math better and score better.

Ask her to gather those glass marbles, you know, those little things boys love playing with, the teacher makes a surprising point. Chitro nods at the teacher. How nice of the teacher to already guess that Ronja plays marbles with boys in the street for the most part of her free time. The girl has two large Horlicks bottles full of those pretty glass things.

Anything else you want to ask me, Chitro? The teacher's silk mekhela sador rustles as she rises from the desk.

What is bucket challenge, baideo?

What is what?

Baideo, who is a good five years younger than Chitro to be an elder sister, looks perplexed and amused.

Bucket, baideo. They're saying bucket on TV and computer. Chitro now feels embarrassed. Come on, she wasn't supposed to discuss anything other than Ronja's math problems with the teacher. But now she has said it.

Does Ronja watch all that on TV? Baideo raises her eyebrows.

No, no, she doesn't. We got no TV at home, baideo. Chitro goes red in the face saying that. I work at Bou's and their kids are excited over this bucket thing and all... Chitro knows she's mumbling incoherently under the piercing stare of the usually good natured young teacher.

Ah, okay, okay. No need to stammer. Baideo smiles.

Then baideo does something unthinkable. She sits down again and turns on the computer on her desk. Light comes on to that blue screen. She plays some video showing men and women throwing buckets on each other, shuddering, shivering, screaming, and Krishna Mahaprabhu alone knows what! Chitro's mouth is agape and she even squeals like the pig near the dump yard by Mahato's tea shop.

That's it! Baideo gives a little laugh at the antics on the videos.

But why do they do this? Chitro can't take her eyes off the slow-fading blue screen. The teacher shuts the comp-tutor – that's what Chitro calls it – and picks up her satchel.

Send Ronja in with multiplication table books. I'll show her a fun way to memorize them, especially 13 and 19 tables. The teacher smiles kindly. She tells Chitro that the ice water is supposed to be very very cold. And that to do that one needs very special courage. Also, the people who accept the bucket challenge not only suffer the ice cold shock, but they also donate towards charity.

What is charity, Baideo?

They give money for a good cause. To cure a disease that afflicts many.

Oh yes, Chitro agrees. We have lots of diseases here. Last year, Madhobi, who works in Bora-madam's house, fell ill so badly. She couldn't even speak, her throat was like a banana stem, plus she had fever. I thought she'll die. A good doctor at Gauhati Medical College set her right although Madhobi, the fool that she is, refused medicines in the beginning and would have only Sukreswar Mandir's holy water her sister-in-law got her in a tiny bottle. The cow!

Baideo keeps smiling. Yes, we have many diseases here. But mostly, this challenge was to gather money to cure a disease in another country. And people thought it was fun to do the ice bucket challenge.

Can one not cure the disease just by giving money, baideo?

The teacher tells her of course one can, but this is also about having some fun and not moping about the problems in life. And because India has less water in so many areas which means ice cannot be used freely, we're doing it differently. Someone has already donated a bucket of rice to the needy.

Um, baideo, I don't donate, but sell bucket-load of cow dung to little shops. Chitro immediately realizes she has gone off track saying that.

Yes, I know, baideo smiles angelically. Cow dung is good. Your clients must be making dung cakes.

Oh, she knows! Chitro is excited. That's why she's a teacher.

People laugh at me, baideo. They call me dirty. Chitro anxiously watches the young woman's face as the teacher locks her room, Chitro walking out behind her.

People can be fools. Cow dung is good thing. Eco-friendly, clean fuel. Dung cakes must be encouraged wherever possible. You know what I mean? The teacher looks at her.

Not really, she does not know all of it. Chitro is simply assured that she too is a part of a noble universe.

Fascinated with her experience with meeting the teacher, Chitro trots back, careful to lift her only freshly washed cotton mekhela sador so as not to get its bottom soiled. She somehow feels connected to this bucket thing which makes her happy, her steps springy. If they're curing diseases abroad by pouring ice water on themselves – they must be having extra large refrigerators for so much ice, she convinces herself – here is a 34-year-old Karbi woman in Guwahati doing her bit by gathering cow dung in buckets and selling it to businesses who are also doing a good thing by making dung cakes, as the teacher just pointed out.

With the sun hitting the sky-roof above, Chitro suddenly feels the August warmth bordering on to a heat that dries betel nut slices spread out on sieves placed in verandahs and terraces of homes. At her own home she has already cooked rice and left a few potatoes to steam in the same pot. A sprinkle of mustard oil, a wedge of a sharp onion, and the wild green chilli pepper from the Namghor backyard – lunch will taste so good today.

But at her doorstep she's held back by furious screams. It's Okhondo. Enlightened by the effect of the local brew and the strong afternoon sun, he is raging. The older daughter Kopili's sobs drown in this ruckus.

Your mother thinks I'm a pauper and she's the princess, Okhondo shouts. Which man eats rice and potatoes for the third day in a row now? I asked her to make the dry fish and there she goes, all dressed up in her starched mekhela to chat with the school gentry. The she-devil.

Chitro feels her temper rise too. Rice and potatoes don't suit you, eh? I'm the one who should be eating, o paapi manuh, for the baby you planted in my stomach. Your sins are endless and you want royal treatment? You never come home on so many nights. Shall I tell that to everyone? I'm cooking, cleaning, looking at my child's report card so she learns well, and all you're concerned is about dry fish? You horrible lazy bugger who hasn't earned anything for straight three months and keeps living on my dung money.

Okhondo yells louder. Chitro screams. The howling continues on both sides. The neighbourhood is not used to such afternoon bickering. Past 2 p.m., the genteel households prefer a siesta.

Amid this commotion, Kopili suddenly stops wailing and stares in terror. Ronja comes running in from somewhere and yells in her tiny voice. Chitro sees Okhondo grimace and make a swift move towards the stone pestle kept in the corner of the room they use as a kitchen. The heavy pestle can smash a head easily.

The neighbourhood will talk about this incident for a long time to come. Especially, the ladies will. More so, Bou, the gentle mother of those teenage kids who had excited Chitro about this thing called "ALS Bucket Challenge". Eyewitnesses will say it was a spectacle. Not a scary one, although Chitro was in greater rage than Okhondo was. The amusement factor – it dawned rather late on those present on the scene – was pertinent. Even before Okhondo dragged his alcohol-influenced sluggish body to hit his wife, Chitro recalled the two buckets she had kept in another corner, ready for delivery to her dung clients. The neighbourhood will recount the great bucket drama thereafter. Six months pregnant, Chitro heaved the buckets on to her shoulders in seconds, one by one, and thrashed the contents on Okhondo's head. Krishna Mahaprabhu alone knows the magnificent stink and slush that followed was something the neighbourhood will not easily forget. Stunned completely, Okhondo slumped down on the floor and didn't move for the next hour, said eyewitnesses.

The neighbourhood ladies, initially a little shocked about the way this lowly Karbi woman treated her husband, will also take a lesson from Chitro's "bucket challenge". In fact, they will start joking that this bucket challenge would cure humankind – by which they mainly meant their husbands – of maladies often unnoticed.

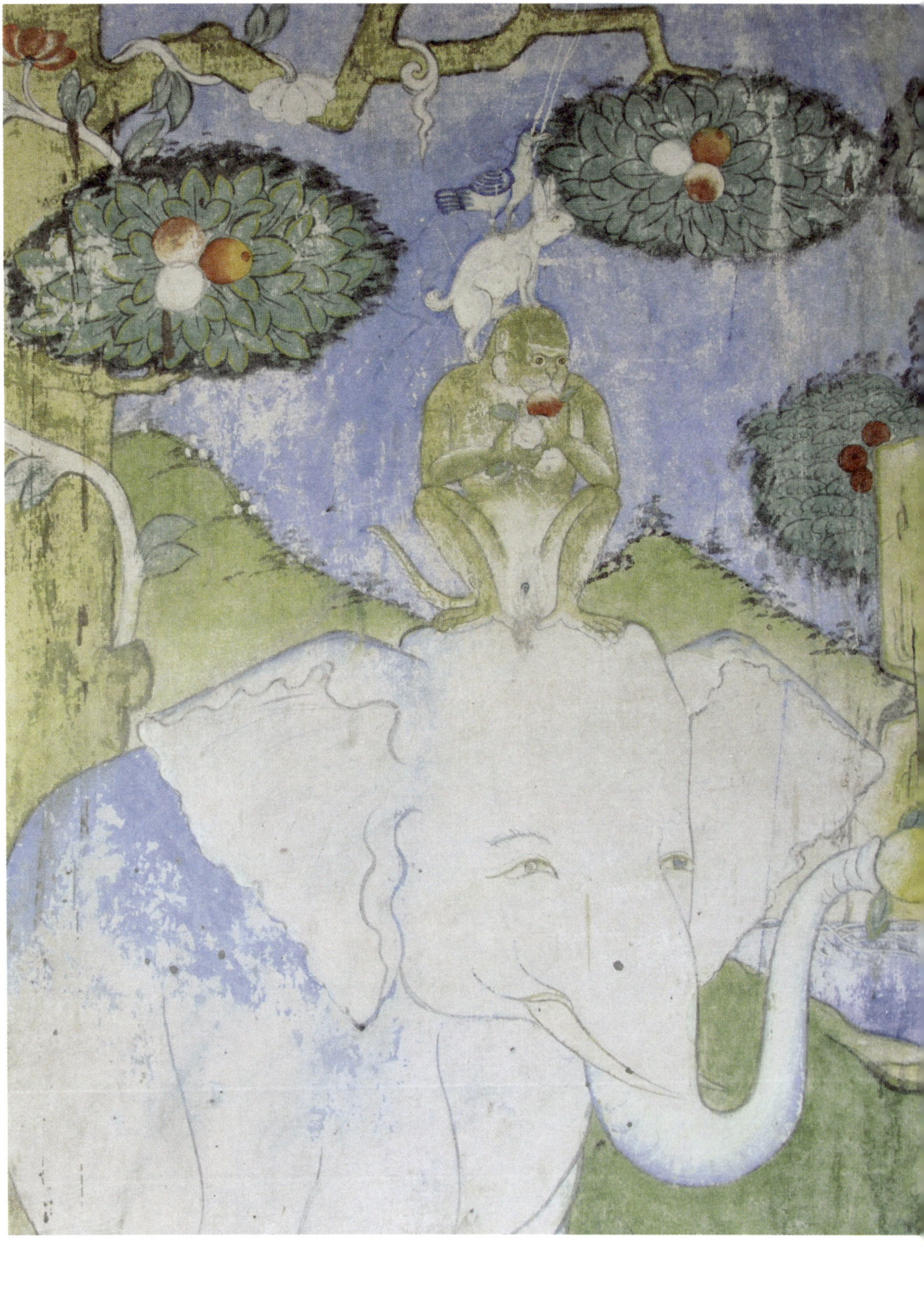

thukje chueling nunnery, tawang

PHOTOGRAPH AND POETRY BY **NITOO DAS**

Every morning I feed you
pieces of my past, O Buddha
Every morning I scatter
my feathers around you, O Buddha
Every morning my fingers
fly over listening wheat, O Buddha

Every morning I dress you
with calloused eyes, O Buddha
Every morning the cold turns
me into firewood, O Buddha
Every morning the mountains
remind me of stains, O Buddha

Every morning the leaf-smoke greys
into lovesong, O Buddha
Every morning the stars seem closer
to your mouth, O Buddha
Every morning my frown
torches the sky, O Buddha

Every morning I fold deeper
into my flesh, O Buddha
Every morning the stones walk
by a fever, O Buddha
Every morning my hunger
edges toward you, O Buddha

the story of tanik – the mythmaker

MAMANG DAI

Today, with new opportunities for employment, many women have branched out into running their own textile units. The weaving centres of yesteryear are quite forgotten, but it was the small centres that kept the art of weaving alive. In traditional society it was the duty of a woman to provide clothing for her household and the implements of weaving for the simple portable loom are an inherited property for women. With the establishment of government weaving centres young women could enrol to train or teach, and they were entitled to accommodation at weaving hostels in the town. In a way these weaving centres offered freedom from the confines of the village and were the first step towards economic independence for women to earn by doing what they were good at. I know romances also bloomed in these places, and many women scraped at their savings to support young men to get a college education. And though some of the attempts at evolving the industry with new techniques and motifs threatened to destroy the original patterns, the early weaving centres alive with the thump of the batten and the lively sound of the new spinning drums and fly shuttle looms achieved the great goal of keeping the traditional cloth of the tribes from disappearing.

The truth about the Daji household was that they had risen from nothing. Sirkung was an old village on the last range of mountains overlooking the river. Everyone here had their fields and their pigs and chickens but only in numbers sufficient for each household. No one had more. The Daji family were no better off, or worse, just the typical villagers in communities that knew no caste or class distinctions, until the night of the storm reversed their fortunes. Suddenly the man and his family began to buy cattle and despite pestilence and harsh weather their mithuns flourished and calved regularly. Their animals grew sleek and big, and their stock multiplied until everyone began to talk about it and traders from far and near began to notice them. In time they became one of the most influential families in an area where the wealth of a man was measured solely by the number of mithuns he possessed.

Tanik grew up in this atmosphere of wealth and benevolence. He was surrounded by uncles and the old parents of his father whom he had never seen. The old man, his grandfather, had cursed when his son left that grey afternoon and not a day passed when he did not utter his son's name with rage to anyone who came to the house, but after many years had passed, he began to mutter to himself and the young Tanik heard the words – "exchange" and "beads" and "the storm". These words imprinted themselves in his mind. He was a quiet child who liked to roam alone, climbing trees and staying out in the forest, and he might have stayed that way like his friends in the village if his mother had not decided to strike out on her own, in search of a better life for her son. She remembered the man who was her husband and father of Tanik, but it was more than a decade that she had seen him. In all this time he had not sent a single word and she could barely recall the tone of his voice. Perhaps he had died somewhere far away. No one spoke about him and she did not seek news of him from anyone. Her old in-laws treated her well and plied her with precious beads and brass ornaments as if to remove the burden of wealth from their house. They sensed she would be leaving them soon. Tanik's mother received the gifts and waited. It was almost a godsend when an outbreak of cholera and strange fevers that rotted away a person's teeth and left the skin raw and blistered crept up the hills and struck their village. It was time to leave.

It was during this time that Gagil had first met Tanik's mother when she arrived one hot afternoon, her face flushed with exertion and her hair soaked with sweat. It was a year before the China war and Gagil herself was a young mother who had moved into the first concrete house of her husband's family in Pigo.

"This is the child," she had said. Gagil saw a fresh faced young boy stepping forward to greet her and it had struck her even then that the boy had a clairvoyant air. His mother had brought him here to introduce him, she said, to families who had travelled to their remote villages as Gagil's brother, the legendary Dinu, had done. Gagil had immediately risen to go into the kitchen to ask the young girls to prepare something for Tanik and his mother who was now speaking in an angry, shaking voice. Everyone knew the boy's father, and everyone knew that he had deserted mother and child. What no one could figure out was why. The man had withstood all the pleas of family and friends and had simply fled as if he could not bear to answer their questions. He was living in a faraway place where, they said, where people were cutting trees and selling them. Other stories reaching them said he had become a soldier and had gone away to live in one of the towns in the plains. No one knew for certain, and as there was no word from the man his relatives ceased to find out anything more about him, saying that for all purposes he was dead to them since he was so adamantly resisting all their efforts to reach him and spurning all their cries of love.

Now he lived solely in Tanik's heart. Tanik never asked his mother anything about him but he kept his ears open and did not miss anything. He heard his mother weeping softly sometimes, but when she looked at him her eyes were bright with a fierce light that halted all the questions churning in his heart. After the visit to the Gagil house Tanik noticed that his mother seemed to take heart. In fact she became determined that he should join college in the town. To achieve this she resorted to an old, forgotten gift that she had. She wove cloth and said that she would sell them to the aying traders who had shops in the market.

"What will we do with this, hah?" The first shopkeeper they went to asked his mother.

"Put it up there," his mother pointed to a corner, and added, "then you will see what happens."

The aying stared at her and, for a long moment, seemed to be trapped in her dark, bitter eyes. Then he laughed and said, "Ok. But I will give you twenty rupees for it, not fifty."

The woman took the notes of money without another word and mother and son left the market. They lived in a shack like a cowshed that Tanik's mother had occupied with the help of a relative. His name was Tasong, but he was an uncle, his mother told him, and Tanik should call him Tasong-Paji. Tasong had left the village a few years before them and he worked in a government office. The man squeezed Tanik's shoulder and promised his mother that he would try to help her earn some money. Now Tanik wondered if the cloth had been sold. When his mother asked him to run down to buy a box of matches he leapt at the chance. A small shop nearby sold matches and bidis and thread, but he sped right past this down to the main market unable to resist the desire to see if his mother's cloth had been sold. He was startled when he saw the corner

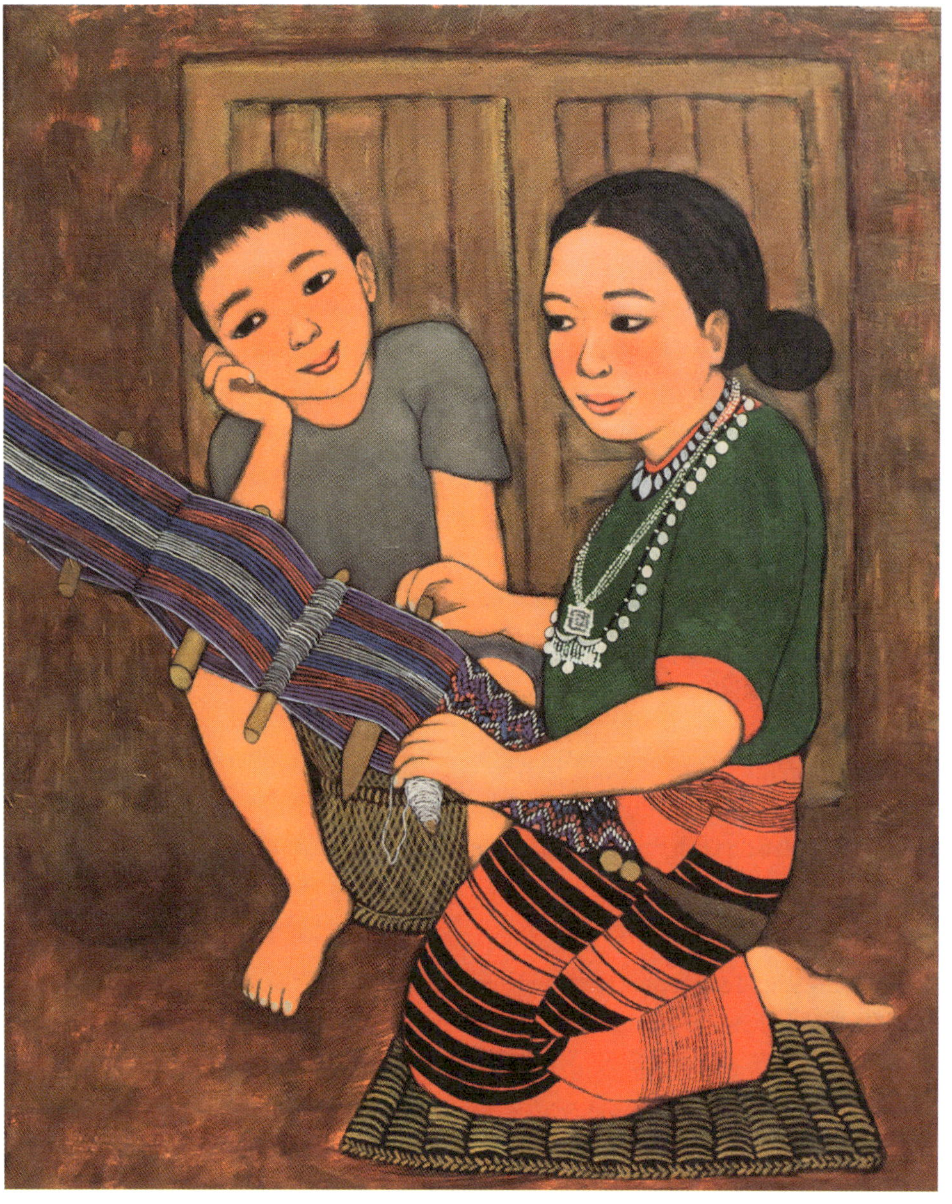

mother and son
MEENA LAISHRAM, ACRYLIC ON CANVAS

empty. It had been sold! Some one had bought it! He ran back and almost choked when his mother said, "Is it sold?"

"Yes! It's gone."

He saw her smiling and his heart filled with joy. His mother was smiling! Later he worried that the cloth might not have been sold after all, but that it had simply been moved to another corner or even put away out of sight, but his doubts were laid to rest when his mother began weaving another piece immediately because the shopkeeper said he wanted more. At this time the government was setting up craft emporiums in the bigger towns and weaving centres were being opened to employ local women to produce cloth for sale to visitors who were beginning to show an interest in the region. This was how Tanik's mother got herself a job as a weaver in the long weaving shed where the first treadle fly-shuttle looms, along with drums of thread, were placed in rows for weaving instructors. The clacking sounds of these looms became the rhythm of their days and nights like the rhythm of the years passing. His mother, however, had no love for these new looms. She worked on them because the weaving centre offered food and shelter, but at night she wove on her back-strap portable loom by lamplight.

The colours of yarn were the bright red of the temen creeper, indigo dye and green from a small rhizome called gamba. Each piece of cloth was unique. From his place near the fire Tanik would watch his mother stooped over the bright pattern. He saw her fingers stretch and curl over a strand of thread as she pulled it through and looped it round again making the dots and small squares that became the "grasshopper's tooth" design. He listened to the soft thump of the batten, the sumpa, as his mother pressed the thread down, and he saw the woven strip expanding inch by inch as the light flickered and his mother still continued with her labour, weaving attentively and lovingly with her legs stretched straight in front of her and the cane belt around her waist holding her up together with the wonderful band of colour. The years passed. His mother acquired a plot of land and opened a small shop of bamboo and thatch with the help of Tasong. Their lives were untroubled and soon Tanik met Kijji Ongo who looked and him and said, "Timber! Timber is the new wealth." Whatever Kijji touched turned to gold. They went into the timber business and Tanik followed Kijji through hot, dusty towns and watched as Kijji stood before timber merchants and stopped in mid-sentence, rolled his eyes and then craned his neck forward to whisper something into their ears. When NEFA became a Union Territory Tanik's career took a turn when he plunged into politics and became a member of the first Provisional Legislative Assembly. Since then he had not looked back. He had enough now to support his mother and make her live like a queen but the woman never gave up her weaving. Tanik did not know it then but in all his life, in all his travels and the long career that was to catapult him to the highest pinnacles of fame and power, he would never again experience that sense of rest and comfort that had filled his heart every night just before he closed his eyes to sleep. His mother spun cotton on a wooden spindle and she was spinning his life, spinning colour and texture, spinning dreams and desire. Each movement of her hand over the shimmering band of cloth — smoothing it, pressing it down, pulling it taut, each thread she lifted, each strand she wove, each beat of the sumpa and each time she leaned back a little and began again was a magical expression of a mother's blessings for her son.

a million stories blew into the sky

MINAM APANG

DETAIL FROM THE SERIES "WAR WITH THE STARS"

COURTESY THE ARTIST AND CHATTERJEE & LAL

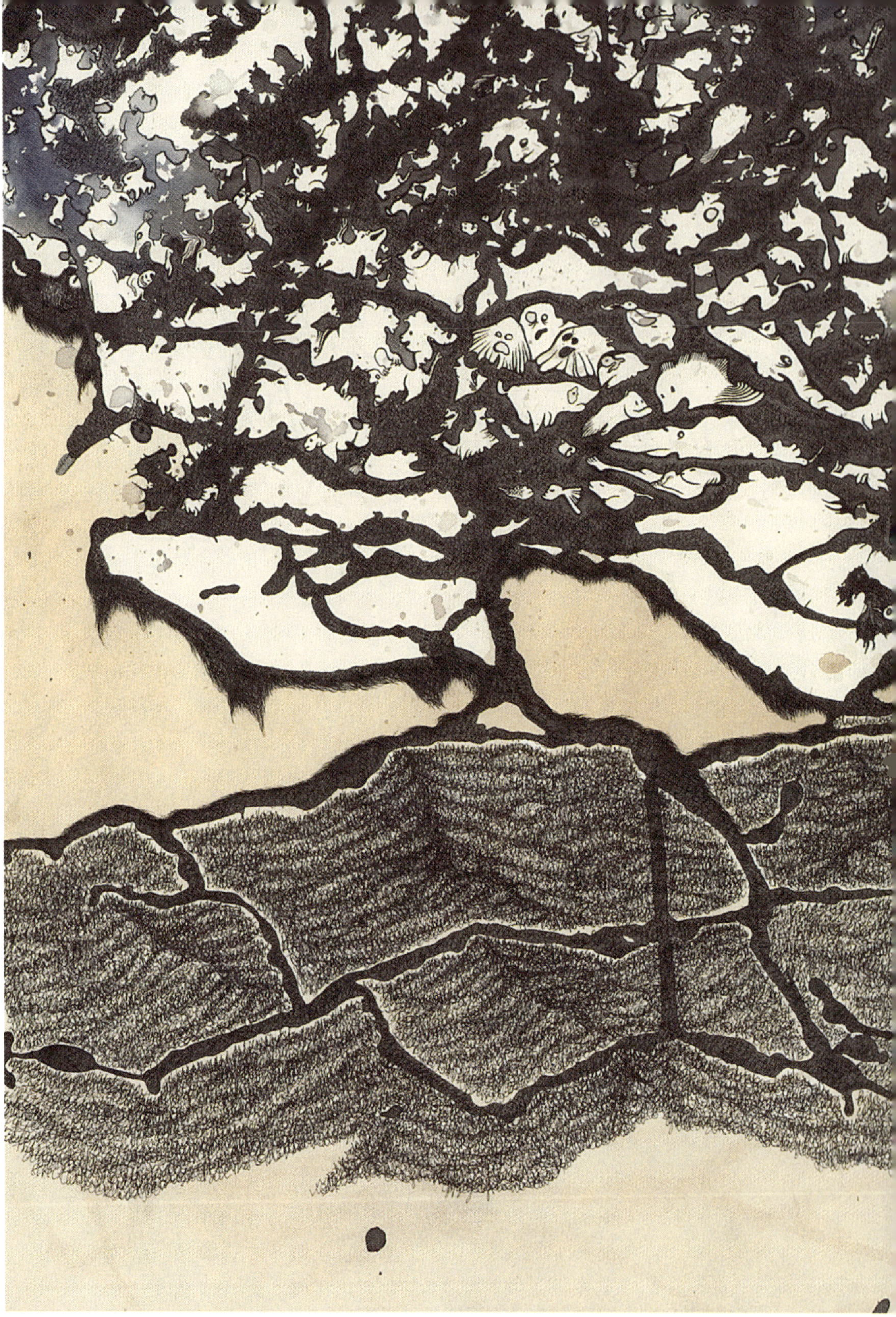

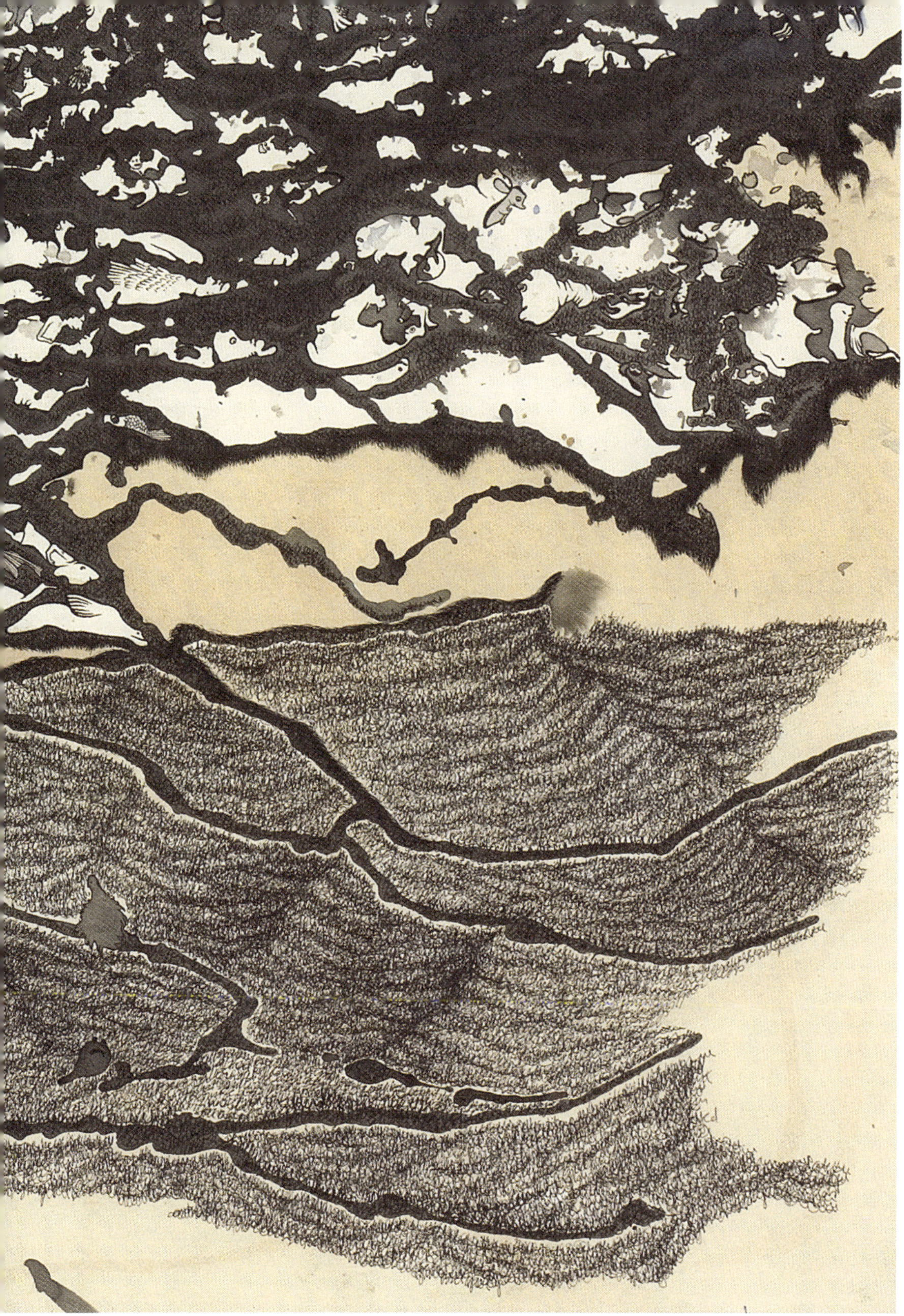

women's literature

SANATOMBI NINGOMBAM
TRANSLATED FROM MANIPURI BY **THINGNAM ANJULIKA SAMOM**

Quite a long time that I haven't held a pen. Don't know what wild literary wind it was that blew from an unknown direction this morning when I was washing clothes, as if aiming to awaken my sleeping pen it softly breathed into my heart a beautiful story of Ta Baikuntho and Inamma Jandhavi at war.

"Ish! What an opportunity." Thinking thus, I hastily half-rinsed the clothes and went into the kitchen.

Didn't look at the vegetables. Started cooking the rice. Wondered what to cook. Let me just boil these potatoes.

The rice came to a boil, the bubbles brimming up vigorously. Meanwhile in my head Ta Baikuntho and Inamma Jandhavi were fiercely battling.

"Hai! What needs of yours have I not fulfilled that you black-market cinema tickets and sell my prestige?"

"Ish! What a joke! This low-rank policeman scattering around wives by the likhai[1] and children by the shangbai wherever posted. Fold your ten fingers and count. Mustn't be enough! While you're running around feeding them, how many months has it been that you haven't put even a red naya paisa into my hands? O, Polygamous Prestigious Thana Babu, since people like us don't even have a salary, we sell our prestige piecemeal to eat."

1. Lihkai and Shangbai are woven bamboo baskets used for measuring paddy. Two Likhai baskets equal one Shangbai basket which measures 25.5 cm height and 48.5 cm diameter at mouth.

This pot too has to spill over at this very instant! Let me just take it down! Took up the pot-holding tongs lying on the gas table.

"Shreng!"

Ish! Hare, hare... I'd thought Inamma Jandhavi was being badly beaten up. Thankfully it was the tongs falling from my hand. My mind settled down a bit.

Lowered the heat on the rice. My mind was unable to stop them from coming to blows. Both Ta Baikuntho's hand and Inamma's mouth were inexhaustible, neither retreated.

The prik-prik sound of the potatoes boiling became the shloka that Inamma ranted before going to her maternal home, "Maha Papi! You Great Sinner! If you want to take ten thousand wives, have them. And then, become infected with AIDS and die, you ..."

I had wanted Inamma's heartbroken rant to become unforgettable words for Ta Baikuntho, but somehow the words could not enter his ears. I tried very hard to erase the bruise from Inamma's face, but failed. A woman myself, I wasn't happy that she should go back to her maternal home badly bruised.

"If food's done, serve it. About to die from hunger."

No sooner said, he quickly washed his hands and sat down. I coaxed Ta Baikuntho and Inamma to silence for some time. Hastily scooping out the rice, I called in the children to eat.

"You also eat, while it's still hot."

Their father said this, while mixing the curry poured onto the rice,.

"I'll be eating. Today I can't linger long in the kitchen."

After serving the others, I also started eating. After three-four handfuls, Inamma Jandhavi's scarred face came up again before my eyes and set off a whirlpool in my mind.

A woman neglected by her husband openly sold cinema tickets in the black market to feed her children, and was punished by her husband who didn't hesitate to stealthily trade in women, to the extent of scarring her face. If it had been me, won't he have known it; I would have died with him!

I finished eating, dream-like, without taste. Cleaning up after the others finished, the image of Ta Baikhuntho, like the hermit cat from the folktales, coming to call back Inamma sprang up before my eyes. Realizing that my mind would not be in peace unless I quickly wrote down the story of this husband-wife, I hurriedly finished all the minor tasks. Tore a couple of pages from my child's school notebook. Took up a pen with mismatched cover and prepared to write.

Started writing the scene when Ta Baikhuntho chanced to see Inamma in front of the cinema hall, selling tickets in the black market.

"Some of your kwa still there? Let me have a piece."

Their father's badly-timed interruption came when Ta Baikuntho stood trance-like, embarrassed before his fellow policemen -- just when my pen was speeding up. Reluctantly I got up, wrapped a piece of arecanut in betel leaf, and handed it to him. Picked up the pen again. For about ten minutes I tried to build up Ta Baikuntho's mortified face again. The pen starts moving a bit.

"Mama, I've got tilaikhombi rash."

My lanky youngest son who loved playing in nooks and crannies tried to break my concentration yet again.

"There's powder in the cupboard, dab on some."

I replied without looking up.

"Powder won't do, give him a bath. Otherwise, he'll be covered in weals by tomorrow."

I had thought I would put in a full-stop at a proper point and then get up. But when my husband looked at me with his end-season-parkia-seeds-like eyes bulging out, a look which I abhorred, I got up without further ado. I ran the soap and wash-cloth cursorily once or twice and ended the bath. Sat down at the table again.

This time round, it took me quite a long time to return to my thoughts. The more I thought, I felt like breaking this small second-hand-like computer in my head supposedly to be used for thinking. At badly timed moments, only while doing the laundry or cooking, it would want to do its work. When I actually want it to do its work, then it won't even power up.

Alright then, let's give a name to the story first. What should I name it? Ta Baikuntho's quite the shameless fellow. Why not name it "Houdong Lamboiba," a hermit cat? Like the one in children's stories who pretended to be pious just to eat fledgling birds. That alcoholic face, all bloated and flushed, did resemble a cat quite a bit.

I titled my short story: "Houdong Lamboiba". This time it will all flow down seamlessly on its own. Built up my thoughts, eyes half-closed.

"Make some spicy mango salad or something, to sharpen up the eyes and ears."

At this point the anger simmering in my mind must have reached about ninety on a scale of hundred. But I still kept it inside. Afraid that it might reach hundred percent and explode.

A woman for a thing within his reach, a woman for the scattered sandals on getting up from bed... the list is endless; no hesitation in ordering around a woman. It is at this, that on days when my anger reach its zenith, I, in my inability to blame this royal-born person who does not want to use his own hands, seethed with frustration and in my pigheadedness, ripped up quite a few of my own sins.

I plucked a couple of mangos from the backyard. Cut them up hastily, mashed them, and served them. Picked up the pen yet again.

Sat for quite a long time and churned my head. No hope. The story of Ta Baikuntho and Inamma Jandhabi's great battle had scattered all over, beyond assemblage. On second thoughts, my fury rose against the one who time and again imposed a blockade on my freely running literary road. At that moment, my husband called out, "Do you hear? A glass of water."

Slashed through the laboriously built up, yet incomplete battle-story twice with the pen, and wildly tore it up. That didn't satisfy me either. Crumpled it up feircely and capped the pen.

"What is it that you are so angrily tearing up?"

Our Saheb-pretender asked, mouth still pursed from the chilli of the mango salad. With resentment, disappointment, anger all gathered together, I replied, "It's women's literature, women's literature."

First published in Manipuri under the title, "Nupigi Sahitya" in the anthology *Naohong*, published by Siroi Publications, Thoubal, Manipur, in April 30, 2006

self portrait, 7th may 2017

KUNDO YUMNAM

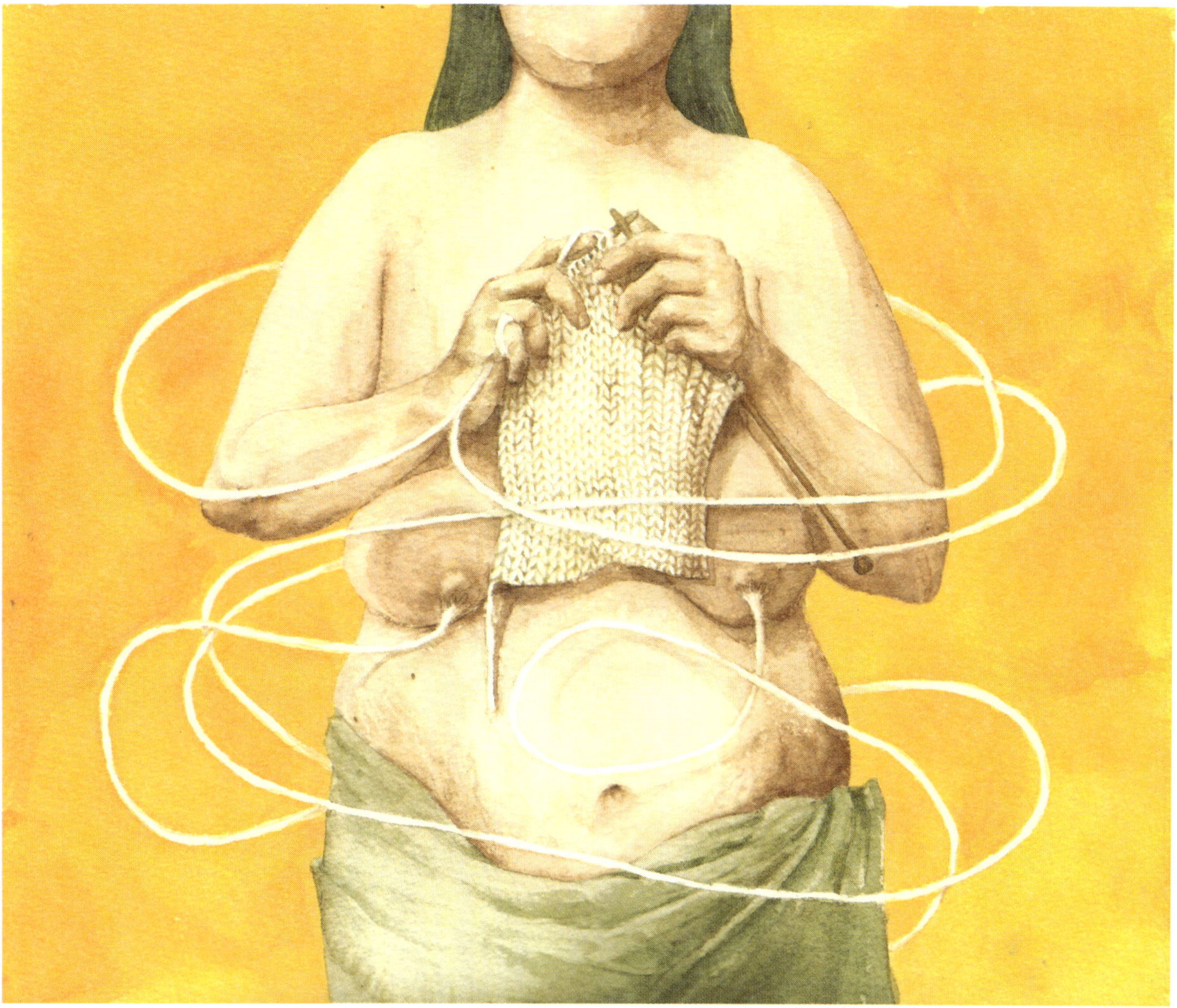

contributors

Aheli Moitra was born in Delhi to grandmothers from the east and west of Bengal. She was raised in Muscat, graduated with a Bachelor's degree in Mass Media (Journalism) from Mumbai, acquired a Master's degree in International Security & Terrorism from Nottingham (UK), worked in Kathmandu (Nepal), and made her way to Nagaland where she lives now. Her work includes news and activism. She is trained in the praxis of Kingian Nonviolence Conflict Reconciliation from the University of Rhode Island (US). She currently works with *The Morung Express* in Nagaland.

Alyen Leeachum Foning is from Kalimpong. She studied Textile and Apparel design at NID, Ahmedabad. She has been working on various projects in the fields of Clothing + Textiles + Printmaking + Accessory Design + Shoe Design + Product Design + Music etc. Her design label ALYEN FONING was founded in Goa but has shifted its base to Kalimpong. It is inspired by Mother Nature and the skills of local artisans in creating contemporary clothing and lifestyle products. It is also the story of likeminded people coming together to collaborate and create, to celebrate, empower and give back to society in small, yet conscious ways. She is currently digging into her ancestral roots, learning farming, gardening and is in the process of starting a women's collective in collaboration with her cousin (sisters) in Kalimpong.

Aungmakhai Chak is an artist from the Chak tribe, one of the 11 indigenous communities of the Chittagong Hill Tracts, Bangladesh. She graduated from Pathshala, South Asian Media Institute and has showcased her work in Chobimela vii (2013) titled "Opportunity Knocks", at the Asiatic Gallery of Fine Arts as well as the Dali Photo Festival (2015) in China jointly organized by the University of Oslo Norway/ Pathshala, and China.

Ayangbe Mannen is a self taught artist, illustrator and graphic designer from Nagaland, currently living in Delhi. She works with a wide variety of mediums, constantly experimenting with her style. Her skill sets include more traditional mediums of art like painting to branding and illustration using digital mediums. Website - *www.ayangbe. com*

Dolly Kikon is a social anthropologist. She teaches Anthropology and Development Studies at the University of Melbourne (Australia). Her monographs include *Life and Dignity: Women's Testimonies of Sexual Violence in Dimapur* (2015) and *Experiences of Naga Women in Armed Conflict: Narratives from a Militarized Society* (2004). Her articles have appeared in *Economic and Political Weekly*, *Inter-Asia Cultural Studies*, *South Asia: Journal of South Asian Studies*, *Open Democracy*, *Seminar*, and *Himal South Asia*. She has contributed chapters to books published by Oxford University Press, Cambridge University Press, Routledge, Zubaan/Chicago University Press, and University of Vienna Press.

Gertrude Lamare is an independent researcher, an activist and a teacher at a Delhi University college. As a member of Thma U Rangli-Juki (TUR), a Meghalaya-based activist collective, she has worked with hawkers in Shillong on various issues confronting them and in organizing the community into an independent hawkers ' association called the Meghalaya and Greater Shillong Progressive Hawkers and Street Vendors Association. Gertrude is also cofounder of and editor at Raiot.in, a webzine functioning from Shillong which has in the past year received significant national and international attention. Raiot.in has been recently recognized as one of the most important alternative media platforms in the country.

Jacqueline Zote is a writer and an ardent fan of folktales from around the world. She began writing short stories at the age of 7 and continues to pursue her passion as a fulltime content writer. She is currently working on a documentation of Mizo myths and legends. She lives in Aizawl with her family and three dogs.

Kundo Yumnam is an artist based in Manipur. She graduated in Fashion Design from National Institute of Fashion Technology, New Delhi; and studied fine arts at Lasalle College of the Arts, Singapore. She works with paintings, drawings, and installations, and is interested in engaging with the overlaps between the personal and the political. Kundo has been a part of many prominent exhibitions and projects. Her works have been exhibited/featured at World of Wearable Art, New Zealand; Exhibit320, New Delhi; and Religare Art, New Delhi. She was resident artist at Peers 2011 organized by KHOJ, Delhi; and TheWhyNotPlace 2011 organized by Religare Arts. Aside from practising art, Kundo is involved in activism for informed choices in healthcare, and human rights in childbirth.

Meena Laishram is an artist trained at the College of Art, Delhi. Her work has been exhibited in several solo and group exhibitions, including the recent Angang Nawa at The Giving Tree, Manipur (2017) and Memories 2 at India Habitat Centre (2016).

Mamang Dai is a poet and novelist from Arunachal Pradesh. A former journalist, Dai's first publication *Arunachal Pradesh- the hidden land,* (2003) documented the culture and customs of her land for which she received the state's Verrier Elwin Award. Her other publications include novels, poetry and children's literature. Dai also worked with World Wide Fund for nature in the Eastern Himalaya Biodiversity Hotspots programme. In 2011 Dai was awarded the Padma Shri (literature and education). Dai lives in Itanagar, Arunachal Pradesh.

Minam Apang is a visual artist from Arunachal Pradesh. Her works have been shown at several international platforms, as well as having four solo shows in Mumbai, where she first began showing her works at a gallery. She lives in Goa and Arunachal Pradesh, spending her time between drawing, farming and making music.

Mona Zote lives in Aizawl, Mizoram. Her poetry has appeared in the *Cordite Poetry Review, Carapace, Poetry International Web, Indian Literature,* as well as in *Dancing Earth: An Anthology of Poetry from North-East India.*

Nabina Das is the author of four books. Her poetry collections *Blue Vessel* and *Into the Migrant City* have been cited as best reads of 2012 and 2014 respectively. The short story collection *The House of Twining Roses: Stories of the Mapped and the Unmapped* (2014) continue to receive critical attention and her novel *Footprints in the Bajra* was longlisted in the 2011 Crossword Vodafone award. Her poetry and prose have been published in *Prairie Schooner, The Yellow Nib: Modern English Poetry by Indians, The Indian Quarterly, The Caravan Magazine, The Missing Slate, Good Housekeeping,* and *The Dhaka Tribune.* Nabina's essays and features have been published in *Prairie Schooner, Economic and Political Weekly, Scroll, BLink,* etc. Winner of several poetry prizes and residencies, Nabina has been a street theater performer, a folk and classical singer for some time, and most recently, co-editor of *40 under 40: an anthology of Post-Globalisation Poetry.*

Nitoo Das is a birder, caricaturist, and poet. Her first collection of poetry, *Boki,* was published in 2008. Das's PhD from Jawaharlal Nehru University dealt with constructions of Assamese Identity under the British. Her poetry has been published in journals like *Poetry International Web, Pratilipi, Muse India, Eclectica, Seven Sisters Post, North East Review, Four Quarters Magazine, Poetry with Prakriti, Vayavya,* etc. Her interests include birding and bird photography, fractals, comic books, horror films, poetry as hypertext, and translation from Assamese to English. Das teaches literature at Indraprastha College for Women, University of Delhi.

Parismita Singh is a writer, graphic novelist and educationist. Her graphic novel *The Hotel at the End of the World* was shortlisted for the Shakti Bhatt First Book Award (2009-10). She helped conceptualise the *Pao Anthology of Comics*. Her publications include graphic novels for children *Mara and the Clay Cows* (2015) and *Crab Chronicles* (2011). She has been working on a primary school education project in Assam with the NGO Pratham since 2009.

Prashansa Gurung is a photographer with five years of experience in telling stories through photography, writing and videography. Born in Darjeeling, she has travelled extensively while growing up. The founder of the photo exhibition, "Pictures against Prejudice", Prashansa has been an advocate of the gender justice movement. She holds a Master's degree in Mass Communications from Xavier's Institute of Communications, Mumbai and a Bachelor's degree in History from St. Stephen's College, Delhi. Her work can be found on Instagram *@prashansagurung* and *www.prashansagurung.blogspot.in*.

Rini Barman is a freelance writer and researcher based out of New Delhi and Guwahati. Her essays have appeared in a host of publications like *Hindu Business Line, Mint Lounge, The Indian Express, The Sunday Guardian* etc. She is currently working on a research project funded by the India Foundation for the Arts.

Sanatombi Ningombam is a writer based in Thoubal, Manipur. Her publications include *Kektus Manbi* (1999), *Naohong* (2011) among others. She has been the recipient of several awards for her writing.

Shreya Debi and **Bilseng R Marak** graduated from National Institute of Fashion Technology (NIFT) in 2008. After graduation, they joined Barefoot College in Tilonia, Rajasthan for a couple of years. The institution instilled in them the need for social entrepreneurship, embracing and respecting rural lifestyles, and using design as a tool for developing vocational skills. Shreya continued to work in Delhi for a few years. In 2011, Bilseng and Shreya were able to finally set up the Bumbum Design Studio in Kharkutta, a small village nestled in the lush North Garo Hills of Meghalaya. It is an employment and creative skill development initiative for rural women. Today Shreya and Bilseng's young design studio is known for ethical ethnic-wear, quality and comfort. Their work is available online at *www.bumbum.studio*.

Soibam Haripriya, Assistant Professor, Tata Institute of Social Sciences, completed her PhD from the Department of Sociology, Delhi School of Economics. Her poems have appeared in anthologies and journals - *Tattooed with Taboos* (2015); *Samyukta: A Journal of Gender and Culture* (2016); *Guftugu* (2016); *Indian Cultural Forum* (2016); and *Muse India* (2016). Most recently her work has appeared in *Indian Literature*.

Thingnam Anjulika Samom is an independent journalist based in Manipur. She writes for various press agencies and publications including *Women's Feature Service, India Together, Inter Press Service* and *Eastern Frontier* and *The Wire*. Her *Better Half* column in a Manipur newspaper, *The Sangai Express* profiles Manipuri women achievers. Thingnam has worked with the National Council of Educational Research and Training, the United News of India and *North East Sun*. She is also an award-winning translator. Her two sons Taibangnganba and Punshiba have contributed the illustrations to her piece.

Zubeni Lotha is a photographer based in Dimapur and Delhi. Her photo exhibition "Portraits of Dimapur" was showcased at the India International centre in 2012. She has also received an IFA grant in 2015 to study and understand the construction of identity and representation of the Konyak Nagas by looking at the photographs taken by the Austrian ethnologist Christoph Von Fuhrer-Haimendorf in 1936.